SCISSORS & TWEED

J. ERIC LAING

For Colm & Quinn

Chapter One

There's this girl I've never really met that I know everything in the world about. Well, most everything. Not the big stuff, I guess. Like what she prayed about when she would cry at her bedside or whether she really believed those prayers might get answered. And I never knew all of the reasons for the crazy things she did. But hey, who really does? I did know other stuff, though. The real for freak shit. Like how she would crack open her father's disposable razors with a pair of pliers she kept stashed behind her dresser and go to town on herself. Sometimes I think she left her window blinds open that way just so somebody, anybody, me--a guy she'd never really met--would know. Not that she was some kind of attention whore. Just about everybody is some kind of attention whore. Not Scissors, though. And I could testify in court to that shit since I'm some kind of authority on the girl.

Yeah, I'm pretty much the only person who even knew for the longest time, so I'm pretty certain it wasn't for attention. And Scissors wasn't her real name. I didn't even know her real name for the longest. That doesn't matter though. Like somebody once said, what's in a name? Okay, it was Shakespeare. So we all did tenth grade. Big whoop. But he made a good point that time. I mean, ninety-nine point nine of all the people in the world go by whatever name they were given when they were born. And ninety-nine point nine of them had that name picked out while their mother was still smuggling a watermelon. So how's that work? What's the chance that anybody's given name has any hope of really pegging them? Who they really are. None, I'd say. No, the spot-on names, the best names, the names that get it right and truly say something about a person, those are the names that come to them over time, from experience, for a reason.

So I called her Scissors. I could have gone with Razor I guess, but that didn't really fit. She was too pretty to be a Razor. Sounded too harsh. And besides, I already knew this dumbass who wanted everybody to call him Razor. Except, he spelled it wrong, with an E. So it was Razer. Told you he was a dumbass.

So I knew this girl. Probably--no, not probably...definitely--better than even her own family. And so what if a lot of it was because I watched her through her window? I'm no perv. At least, no more than the next guy. My name's Tweed. You've seen it around, no doubt.

School hadn't quite let out for the summer yet. At least, not for the chumps. I'd already excused myself early, though. Like the joke goes, my brain was full. Maybe I'd go back next year. Maybe not. The jury was still out on that one.

Razer and Heft, two of the guys I hung out with sometimes, they'd been missing the last days of the school year as well. For them it wasn't the same though. Razer was just plain ditching and Heft, he'd had some kind of incident at the school he went to with Scissors and they let the whole student body off early. Good thing for Heft, because otherwise, he wasn't getting out of nada. His dad's a lawyer. A real stickler. That and Heft's brother had died when they were just kids, so my boy was lucky if he could sneeze or cut one without parental scrutiny. Not to say Heft didn't get away with anything. He did.

That was some other stuff I knew. Scissors had been secretly dating Heft. Screwing him is more like it. But what did I care? I wasn't in love with her or anything. So what if she was hot and all? Lots of girls are. I just liked to keep my eye on her. She was interesting. A lot of people--most people--you could watch all their lives and be just bored out of your brain by them. Not Scissors. She was one of those people who, even if she was just reading a magazine or doing some girlie crap like painting her nails, well, you'd be knocked out by her. She just had this intensity. And it wasn't because she was so hot, like I said. A lot of girls are hot, but not all of them are intense. It's hard to explain.

I wasn't in love. That's what most tools like Razer would think. But then again, most don't. Think, that is. The first thought that worms its way into their tiny little minds is the one they forever assume is right. But it wasn't that way at all. This stuff with Scissors and me was complex. Like frickin' algebra. And trust me, you don't solve for X without the right formula. So that's what I needed, a formula. Then I'd have things figured out. The perfect solution. Although in this particular case, I was going to avoid showing my work, if you know what I mean.

This leads me to another big secret I had on Scissors. The girl was knocked up. Bun in the oven. Pea in the pod. With child. Not any immaculate conception, either. I knew who was to blame for all that. Yeah, you know it. Heft. That little load. This kid who has always had it all, and here he had to come along and screw up Scissors. Literally. What a prick. What a selfish, self-centered, thinking of nobody but himself prick.

That's where things get even more complicated, because Tweed's here to save the day. Even if Scissors doesn't even know it, I'm going to fix Heft but good. I'm going to settle his hash, man. And like the best kind of hero, I'll do it all incognito-like. Behind the scenes. How? I'm not sure yet. Like Hannibal said, either I shall find a way or I will make one. That'd be the general, not the cannibal. And as far as Heft being my best friend and all, I couldn't give a rat's ass. My building's superintendent, David, he likes to say that. 'Rat's ass.' Normally I shake my head to his kind of lowbrow idioms, but here, well, here it seemed to fit. Truly. And girls like Scissors are one in a million. You don't mess around and ruin the one in a million deals. Not and get away with it. Not when I'm on the clock. So I've got a lot of plans to make.

But first I have to say what a beautiful day it was. I don't mean to bore you with the weather; that's my Pops's gig. But, no doubt one for the record books, it was a nice day. Sun and blue sky like something out of the movies. And I felt like a movie star. I was a little polluted. I had some cash. And best of all, I had my freedom. School was out and summer was truly afoot.

I put the window down and told the cabbie to turn up the tunes. He unleashed his mouthful of crooked teeth in a stupid grin to think I was into his Bollywood musical extravaganza. I guess that was a big deal for him--me asking him to turn up his idea of music and all--because the worry lines left his brown face and it was easy enough for me to imagine all his cares drifting off down the FDR behind us. That'll change soon enough, I thought as I considered his immediate future. Off over the Harlem River, Yankee Stadium haunted my thoughts for the briefest.

Pops and I will never do that now.

The giant bat, the parking lot phallus granddaddy of all hulking erections, was in need of a little work. The strip of aluminum sheeting wrapped around the handle--or whatever it was that was supposed to be grip tape--had started to peel away. Even from the distance you could see the top end of it stuck out by several feet and the sun glinted off it as though God was winking to get your attention. Meant for you to notice how it was going bad. Made me think maybe there was something up there, or out there, or somewhere, with plans for everything, for us all. Not comforting. I reached over my shoulder and found the unused seatbelt and strapped it around me. As it clicked into place I shot the driver a look into his rear view.

"Arrive alive," I said, quoting the old Florida license plate slogan. Used to live there.

I don't know if he heard me over the stereo blare, or whether he was just keen on me, but either way I got another toothy grin. We exchanged stupid nods and I went back out the window. Back out into that beautiful day. I was coming home from the library. Not the branch in my 'hood, but the real deal, the cool branch way down at Bryant Park. I go there pretty often just to hang. I'm a bit of a bookworm, I'll admit. Lot of people don't know that about me. Well, Pops does. Or, at least, he used to. I don't know what Pops knows anymore.

Pops. What can I say about old Pops?

When my Pops was my age he used to sand doors. Yeah, doors. How the hell do you get a job sanding doors? I asked him that when I was a little kid once. I did. He acted like it was a stupid question. The guy who sanded doors acted like I was the dumbass in our equation. Sand *a* door, *one* time, fine, but what, people line the block, doors under their arms for you to sand? I sure haven't ever come across any door sanding shops. I'm pretty sure I said as much too.

"You go around," Pops explained with a sigh, like the effort took more work than the door sanding. "Buildings under construction," he'd wheeze. "You'd go there and sand the doors for the guys to paint."

Trust me, I didn't ask for more details. There was something about his door sanding days that made Pops go all misty-eyed and far off. We'd had that same conversation a trillion times and that's as far as it ever got. I never even had to make the effort to change the subject. Those must have been some doors, I tell ya.

Following his exciting door sanding tour, Pops was a mailman. Did that for pretty much the rest of his days I guess. Not like at the post office behind a window, but one of the courier guys who delivers. Outdoors, not too bad a gig. You know, rain, sleet, snow, gloom of night and all that jazz. I'm not a hundred percent on how it goes. It's actually inscribed over the doors of the colossal 34th Street post office if anybody has a real burn to know. Or you could ask my Pops. He knew it by heart, it being the courier's creed and all. But do not, and I mean *do not*, get the old guy talking about the mail. That's one of my cardinal rules. I swear to holy macaroni, I'm a dot on the horizon the very second he starts getting misty-eyed and jabbering on about his mailman days. I don't care what. Because, not only does he go on and on and on, but I don't want to test my theory that the old man has somehow kept up his mailman connections down at the old P.O., or worse, with the door sanders union of America. He hadn't gotten the idea yet, but if he ever did I'd probably find myself harnessed in mail bags like some letter-humping mule or down with door sander's wheeze before I even knew what hit me.

I guess I should be thankful. Pops doesn't talk so much about those mailman days anymore. Or his door sanding days, come to think of it. He stays misty-eyed, sure enough, but he doesn't really talk about much of anything. He's got the dementia. It's not so bad. He doesn't even bitch about stuff so much. Doesn't even change the channel when the commercials come on. It's like he's baked twenty-four seven. I hope I get it so good. Probably won't. Most don't.

I was still thinking about all that when the driver cut the radio. We'd left the river behind, but somehow I felt like I was still drifting over its dapples. The driver shouted something. I wasn't sure what, but I nodded all the same. He likely would have caught on to me if I'd been nervous. I was too stoned to be nervous though. Truthfully, as many times as I'd done what I was about to, I doubt I would've been on edge if he'd been a nun with a gun, as Heft liked to say. What a spud, huh? Heft used to go to a private Catholic school when he was little, that's where he picked up expressions like that gem. He still has nightmares about nuns to this day. Heft. What a kook. I really needed to upgrade my friends.

The cab had just gotten caught at the light at Saint Nicholas, still a dozen blocks from the bogus destination I'd given him, when I threw off the seatbelt, jumped out, leapt over the guard rail, and trotted off like a dog into the day. Behind me I wasn't sure if the driver had cranked the Bollywood back up or if he was cursing me for stiffing the fare. Either way maybe he should quit his day job and get into the Indian entertainment industry, because I couldn't tell the difference.

I had plans to put in motion. I had to settle Heft for what he did to Scissors; that was first on the list. Then I had to figure out what I was going to do about Pops. Maybe nothing, I wasn't sure. I needed time to think things through. It was a bit of a trek, but I hustled it up and over to Fort Tryon Park so I could smoke some more and get my head right.

An uneventful twenty minutes later found me on a bench watching the Hudson do its thing while I did mine.

Money makes the world go around. Root of all evil and all that crap. Ain't it the truth? That's rhetorical. Don't be like Razer and try to answer. I could think of a trillion ways around my problems if only I had a bankroll. I could hire Heft to take care of himself. I could; he's just that stupid. His dad might be crazy smart, but I guess Heft was robbed in the genes department. Got his mother's side instead, you ask me. What was kind of irritating though is that everybody seems to think the opposite. They think he's gifted. Whatever. He's not gifted. He was just gifted enough--lucky, I should say--to have been born into money. Not everybody can be so lucky.

Speaking of.... When my Pops was my age he claims he had a windfall. He didn't win the lottery or anything ginormous like that, but still he'd tell you, he hit something pretty sweet.

As he tells it, he was taking a cab downtown to deliver a package, this cake box, for this guy he worked odd jobs for. I guess that's the kind of thing he did on the side when he wasn't battling the life-threatening elements to deliver grocery store flyers and birthday cards. Pops loved to tell this story, although he never would offer up the guy's name. And that wasn't the dementia talking. This guy Pops worked for must have been the real deal--the mob--because the old man never let on who the guy was. He was always, "This particular gentleman...I can't recall his name." Yeah, right. So this particular gentleman had "instructed" Pops, to use the old man's words, that "under no uncertain terms" could he take the subway. He had to take a cab. And so the particular gentleman had given Pops fifty bucks for the fare. Five tens. Now that was a big deal, because this was back in the forties or something, so that would be like a couple hundred dollars these days, what with inflation.

Pops, he could have still taken the subway and pocketed the money, he'd explain. And explain he would. Every time he told the story, Pops never failed to repeat that part twice, sometimes three times. He could have taken the subway and pocketed the money. And he liked to pantomime sticking the bills in his shirt's front pocket. I guess that's where people stashed their loose bills back in the day.

But he didn't. Pops did as he was instructed. You'd get that part more than once too. So the long and short of it was that Pops found this practically priceless violin in the back of the cab and he took it back to his unnamed employer who gladly paid him "a very tidy sum" for it. Pops said he knew it was worth a helluva lot more than he got, but he didn't think it too wise to "gallivant" around town with such a big target on his back. Probably a good point.

That was his big, "Always do as you're told," story. In his mind it was only because he took the cab like he was told that he had the good fortune to find the violin. How crazy, yeah? Probably saved him from being gunned down after walking into that bar with his special delivery, not to mention making him a very tidy little sum to boot.

Only he didn't collect that tidy sum as he'd claimed. I know this because even before he'd told me that story for the first time, I'd already found his violin case up in the back of his closet. Looking for presents or just snooping, I don't really remember, because that was like ages ago. Thing is, though, it wasn't any violin that Pops was keeping in that case. Far from it. I kept waiting for a follow up story, the truth, to hear Pops explain what he really had hidden there, what had really happened, but he never did. I wanted to ask him about it. Then again, I was smart enough to know it'd be better if he didn't know I was on to what he had hidden back there in his violin case. Still, if the old guy kept up with the way he'd been going, then sure enough I was going to have to do something about all that too. As much as I wanted things not to go sour--for things to just stay the same--my life seemed hell bent on getting crazy.

After clearing my head up at the park I figured I'd best check in with Pops. Besides, I needed my bag with all my stuff in it, so I had to go home. Home wasn't so bad. Fifth floor walk-up, a little tiring sometimes, but that helped keep Pops indoors most days and nights. That's where he was best off anyways. Like I already said, he's got the dementia. It's been with him a few years now since I first noticed. It isn't debilitating or anything like that. He just gets himself in trouble every now and then, getting into things he shouldn't, that kind of jazz. Sort of like having a little kid brother, or a bad dog, or something, I guess.

"I know you," Pops beamed when I came in.

"Hey, Pops."

He smiled even broader. "Yes," he said wagging a finger at me from his recliner by the window. "I know you."

"Of course you do, Pops. I'm Tweed, your grandson."

He smiled with a knowing little nod and then turned back to his television program. I went to the kitchen. I suddenly realized I was fierce hungry.

"I'm going to have a microwave dinner. You want one, Pops?" No answer. "Pops, you hungry? I'm starving." No answer. I picked two frozen dinners from the freezer, same things, turkey with mashed potatoes and gravy. I nuked Pops's first and laid it all out with a half a glass of orange juice like he liked on his TV tray. Myself, I can't drink orange juice at just any hour of the day. But Pops, he'll take juice morning, noon, or night. He should be on the tube. "Orange juice, not just for breakfast no more, Yo." That'd kick.

"Eat up," I said, sliding the TV tray table closer.

He ignored the world. Whatever. I went back in the kitchen and fixed mine. By the time I got back Pops was shoveling mashed potatoes like a madman.

"I know you," he said again between mouthfuls. I didn't say word one.

Pops and I had gone through a few phases in our years together. Ours was one of those, what Heft called a "storied relationship." Heft. Sometimes he talks like one of the old Jewish grandmothers forever hanging around out on the sidewalk. But I guess that was a pretty good description for how things were and had been between me and Pops. Storied.

When I first came to stay with Pops I was eight. I'd come up from Florida with my parents around Christmas. I still remember that first day.

...

I'd never been so far up north before, and since we weren't planning on staying I really didn't have any clothes for the season. Not to sound like a stuck-up fashion diva or nothing. My point being, when they hustled me out the door one morning to give themselves a break from me and my cartoons, I looked like the incredibly shrinking refugee. They'd decked me out in some of my Pops's old stuff. Great old tweed coat, scarf, and hat. That hat. The worst of the lot. One of those flat deals with a button on the front that snaps to the brim. I looked like a demented newsy or some kind of Dickensian poster boy for the Goodwill. Take your pick, go ahead, laugh it up. Others did.

"Go on. Go meet the neighborhood kids. Have some fun for a change," Mom said and pulled the door closed with the brass knob easily slipping through my protesting hands, all bundled up in Pops's oversized wool mittens like they were. Screwed, I tucked the stupid hat in my coat pocket and wandered downstairs.

The freaking Donner party had it better. I'd only made it three feet out of the lobby vestibule before the hat found its way back from my pocket to my head. I hadn't really been outside since arriving and wasn't sure where to go. Not that it mattered. Everything looked the same. Snow. Snow. Snow.

"You goin' out to sled? Where's your sled?"

I'd seen the guy before. Pops had introduced me to him. The building superintendent, or "super," like he'd called him. He had too much of a beer gut to be "super" was what I remembered thinking at the time. I couldn't remember his name.

"You Pops's boy, right? What's your name?" Another set of questions. I hadn't answered the first two. He leaned on his snow shovel and waited for something to come out of me. "Don't worry, I ain't no stranger. I'm David, the super," he said, and took off a glove and offered his hand. "Ain't you got you no sled?"

"No," I said. I'd never met an adult who introduced himself by first name to a kid. It was weird. Also, it seemed he was grammatically-challenged. No wonder they kept him outside.

"Oh man, now that ain't right. C'mon," David said. He stabbed the broad blade of the shovel into the sidewalk drift and took me up by the coat sleeve to follow him back into the building. Back in those days I was a trusting kid. By that I mean, you know, stupid. So I followed him.

We took the stairs to the basement where David used one of the thousands of keys jangling on a chain attached to his belt to open a padlocked door down at the end of the hall. As he did, a suspicious little old woman peeked out from the laundry room like a wrinkled, featherless baby bird straining its head out of the nest in search of a meal. I didn't think the super had seen her, but as he unclasped the padlock and opened the door he called out without even so much as looking back in her direction.

"Hola. Good morning, Mrs. Goldstein."

The old bird didn't answer and ducked back into the laundry room as David disappeared into the dark of the newly discovered room. I stood dumbly in the hall. After a moment there was a double click as a bare bulb above his head came on. From down the hall, Mrs. Goldstein was cautiously peering from her laundry room nest once more.

"Lemme see. Lemme see," the super said, as he rummaged down in the valley between two mountains of sagging cardboard boxes piled in the corner of the small room. He muttered something in Spanish under his breath and I slid in behind him to escape Mrs. Goldstein's curiosity. The room was dusty and dry, but yet somehow still had the smell of wet and rotting cardboard about it. In the corner nearest me, a mummified lump of what was once a mouse lay embedded in a little plastic wading pool of glue. I looked for something to poke the lump of moldy felt with, but there wasn't anything. So while I waited I just batted at the string hanging down from the light bulb fixture instead. I don't know, seemed like the thing to do.

"Ah ha!" David pulled what looked like a giant, red plastic wok from the shadows. "What you think?" he asked, cleaning the dust and spider webs free with the sleeve of his jacket. He was more than a little proud of his discovery.

"I don't know." Well, I didn't.

"Yeah, yeah. Now look here, my man. This one handle, it's bad. No good," he said pulling at the dangling strap that was broken and barely attached. "But this other one, it's still good to go, so you just got to make sure you hold on to it real tight, eh?"

He handed the sled to me and waited like I guess he thought I was supposed to make a speech or something. I'd won the giant plastic red wok award. I just stood there all little kid stupid. I mean, I didn't even know I'd been nominated.

"Hola, Mrs. Goldstein," David the super said as he turned me around by the shoulder while simultaneously pulling the string over our heads to cut the light.

I almost screamed. It was as if we were as trapped as the dead mouse in the corner. There in the doorway, right in front of me, all but right on top of me, the giant, withered, featherless baby bird loomed. From behind, David gave me a little shove. I shielded myself with the giant plastic red wok and somehow made my way out of there.

As I rushed off down the hall, making for the stairwell, I heard David call out after me over the jingle of his thousand keys.

"Whoa! Whoa! You be careful, lil' Pops. Hey, and you're welcome, my man!"

"Who is that boy?" the old bird squawked.

But, man, I was gone.

...

My parents, they split out sometime that April. Notice I said "they," not "we." I wasn't part of their traveling plans anymore. The claim was that they were heading off to set up our new house. I'm not sure where that was ever supposed to have been. I was just supposed to stay on with Pops for a few weeks more, maybe a month or two at the most. That was cool. At first. It was like a vacation. Pops spoiled me and took me everywhere. He seemed to know everybody. He was Pops and the whole city knew it. Or so it seemed. And everything was exciting. One long, boundary-less summer of popcorn, candy bars, late night TV and you name it. I was eight and it was great. We took trips out to the race track a couple of times a week and Coney Island became a regular haunt even if it was a drive. Even took in a few baseball games. Not to Yankee Stadium. For some reason we always put that off. More on that later, maybe. But I swear that first summer was crazy great.

Like just about everything else in life, though, it doesn't matter how good or even great something is, after a while, you just get your fill of it. You're ready to move on, do something else. Sure, you still want that old thing again from time to time. You don't want to leave it behind forever, but you know what I mean. Nobody can eat banana splits and ride roller coasters around the clock forever. Me, I was ready to see my parents again. I missed my mom. I was ready to go home. Wherever that was.

...

"You are home," Pops said.

It wasn't threatening. It wasn't anything. Well, maybe it was a bit more final than I would have liked.

"No I'm not. I don't live here. I want to call Mom and Dad."

"Son--"

"I'm not your son," I said and hurled my comic book at him. The pages fluttered madly like it was some pathetic dying thing as flashes of superheroes and villains flew for real across the room.

Pops threw his hands up in defeat. He didn't bother to stop me or the comic as I ran to the old style rotary phone while the flimsy, colorful pages returned to lifelessness on the floor at his feet. I dialed our old home in Florida madly. Surely they'd gone back there; it was home. The welling of my eyes made the numbers blur. Almost immediately I was rebuffed by the caustic three tones signaling a disconnected line. A recorded woman followed, confirming the same. "The number you have dialed--"

Pops stood a few feet away. He held my discarded comic and said nothing as I hung up before the disembodied voice could continue. I redialed. And then I redialed again, and again, and again.

"That's enough," Pops said. He cut off the call with one hand and tried to gently relieve me of the receiver with the other. I fought him for it briefly only to then shove it to the floor. I ran to my room, slamming the door and collapsing onto the bed. Not *my* room. Not *my* bed. And then I cried. At first I cried as hard as I could. I welcomed it. I relished it. I took to my self-pity, joyfully diving into it over and over like so many waves out at Coney Island. Happy to be so miserable. Just like those days at the beach, even the best of times get to be too much. Eventually I was tired of crying. Tired of fighting. Just tired.

The door swung open announced by a long, slow creak. Pops stood silhouetted in the crack of illumination he'd let in.

"We doing okay in here?"

I didn't answer. I turned my head away. He came in closing the door behind him and crossed the darkened room to sit beside me on the bed. The comic book found its way to the nightstand.

Looking back in the years that followed, I supposed he could have been more tactful. I guess that just wasn't Pops's way.

"My old man ran out on me too. Did you know? Said he was going out to get us all ice cream. I don't know that he got his ice cream. I know I never got mine. He never came back."

I still had nothing to say. Pops gave me a few moments in case I changed my mind. I didn't.

"We got this in the mail, a few months or so after your folks left." He placed a postcard next to my head. I wanted to ignore it. I couldn't. I needed to sit up to read, so I did. Pops leaned over and clicked on the lamp for me.

On the front of the postcard a splashy nighttime shot of the Vegas strip beckoned. Neon explosions of red, blue, and green. On the back were scribbled a few lines from my mom. I recognized her sloppy cursive. Every female I've ever known, with the exception of Mom, has beautiful handwriting, graceful curves, plump and shapely and consistent in spacing and tilt. Not Mom's. Hers was a rushed, scrunched up mess of routed soldiers, forever frustrated in their advance or retreat by the paper's margins, all bunched up to first one side and then the next, doomed crooked letters spilling out and over the trenches of the page lines. Capital *I*'s looked like *L*'s and little lowercase letters like *e*'s, *a*'s, and *u*'s, were one in the same, just ugly, knotted balls of ink. A real mess.

"Pops," it read without skipping a line, "Something's come up. A really great opportunity. We might be a little longer than we talked about. We'll call in a few days. Love ya."

Especially since her message had been all bunched up like it was at the top of the card there was still plenty of room for more. A lot more. But there wasn't. That was it. She didn't even sign her name. Didn't even mention me. And wouldn't you know it, there was no return address. Unless, I guess, you count the picture on the front of the Vegas strip.

I pushed it away and Pops read it over again--because I made him--and then the old man told me what in my heart I'd known from the first.

"I don't think they're coming back," he said. "At least, well, maybe not for a long time." The old guy was really shooting straight with me. "This is home now." I stayed quiet. "And you're right. You're not my son. But I'll always be your Pops, and this will always be home. Now I'm going to go out to the corner store and get some ice cream. Back in a minute. When you feel like it, why don't you come out and join me for a bowl."

And then Pops switched the light back off, leaving me there in the dark to hold the postcard I could no longer make out. Left me be to consider just how fucked up life could be.

…

"I'm gonna go out," I said when I finished my dinner.

Pops had finished long before and had gone back to staring into his television. I took his empty tray and wiped the gravy from his chin and shirt with my napkin. "I'm gonna be late. You need anything?"

"No…," he finally said in the raspy way that I knew meant he wasn't really answering but refusing to answer.

"Okay. Don't stay up all night. Love you, Pops." I kissed his forehead and he smiled and rubbed the spot without otherwise acknowledging. Who knows what was going on in there. Not me. Maybe not even him.

Chapter Two

I know the kid across the way in my building calls himself Tweed. I've never really met him--he goes to public school and I'm lucky enough to go to private--but on the nights when he's home and not sitting in the dark watching me, I can see where he's tagged his bedroom wall. Plus, I kind of go out with his best friend.

He's a real nuisance. Tweed, not my boyfriend. And not for watching me. I don't really care if he watches me. It isn't creepy or anything. He doesn't watch like that's his whole reason for living. He's just sort of in his place and I'm in mine, yanno? Like zoo animals confined in adjacent compounds. Plus, he's cute. Really cute. He could be a model, or a movie star, or something. Maybe he will be someday. I dunno.

He's still a nuisance. He tags everything with whatever he can get his hands on. Spray paint. Magic markers, glass etcher. You can't walk two blocks in the neighborhood without seeing TWEED scrawled all over the side of something. If my dad knew the neighbor kid was Tweed, he'd probably kill him. For reals. Not for spying on me, although that'd piss my dad off majorly too. He'd kill him dead, because, along with everything else, Tweed tagged the hood of our car.

When I saw it and said, "At least he's gotten pretty good. Most the taggers around here are the suck," I thought my dad would go medical. Maybe he'd burst a blood vessel or something. Well, he sort of did. He made me go with him to practically every hardware store in the Heights looking for some magical product to remove Tweed's tag. Worse than that, then I had to spend my entire afternoon fetching him beers between watching him ruin the car hood even worse than it already was. Honestly, SATs couldn't have gotten me out of it. He spent at least two hours huffing and puffing with all these different chemicals and rubbing compounds and buff pad dealios. It was excruciating. But, then again, it was kind of funny, too.

My dad's really tall and skinny and he reminds me of a stork. When I was little, I remember my mom telling me that I came from the stork and I just thought she meant my dad, which, when you think about it makes sense, because it's true.

Watching my dad do anything is always a little comical because he gets real animated and his long arms and legs are always getting in his way. He's forever knocking over the stuff around him when he's trying to do something. He seems to forget where his feet are, maybe because they're so far away. Even when he's completely laid out, like in his chair reading a magazine or playing chess, he still has this thing about him that makes you think that he's going to knock over his coffee or the reading lamp or even his entire little army. That's what he calls his chess pieces, his little army. Yeah, I know.

Maybe if we had bigger furniture. Then he wouldn't look so ridiculous, I mean. If the furniture was bigger than his elbows and knees wouldn't jut out at odd angles in every direction. He'd fit.

My mom and my dad met at a dance. That's another thing that makes me think my dad is kind of comical. It's not just the way he looks and carries himself, but how he talks. Because, if my dad wasn't so funny, he never could've gotten a girl like my mom. Especially at a dance. Not in a million years. But my dad isn't funny in the embarrassing way most fathers are. Not like the ones that always try too hard, especially in front of your friends or whoever. Always cracking themselves up for forever and a day with some dumb joke that they take too far or repeat two or three times as if that'll make it funnier somehow. Personally, I think that's so broke, and even a little creepy.

No, my dad is more like the subtle, sarcastic breed. Best of all, he never repeats his jokes. Ever. Fairly often you'll hear people ask my dad what he just said when you know perfectly well they heard him the first time around. Too bad, so sad, cause he never repeats himself, like I said. So usually those people just get uncomfortable and try to pretend neither one of them said anything to begin with. Real comical.

Don't get me wrong, my dad isn't rude. He never insults people. Just the opposite, he's very polite, actually. He's just sarcastic. And subtle. Very subtle. It's hard to explain. You just have to be around him to see what I mean, I guess. I dunno.

Then there's my mom. But my mom's long gone, of course. Not like I'm sure I could talk to her if she wasn't. So that's not even an option. I suppose I could call her. If I really, really wanted to. Interrupt her oh-so-busy lifestyle. But that would be the weirdness, since I only really call her on the holidays. And then it's just to do the same old, awkward, perfunctory, "I'm fine. Yeah, fine. Fine. No, really, everything's fine. I love you too, goodbye." Yeah, *perfunctory*. The SAT prep is really starting to pay off.

But anywho, don't blame me. It's not like she ever picks up the phone. Except maybe for my birthday. And that's a *maybe*, a big maybe, because she even forgot to do that when I turned the big one three back when. My dad pretty much makes me call her on holidays. Yanno, just so that me and her can go through the whole, how have I been, how are my grades, am I dating any special boys, BS. Can you imagine how *not-boring* those conversations would be if we actually were honest with one another?

"Yeah, Mom, the grades are alright, but the stress is making me cut more, yanno? No, not cut classes. And I'm not really dating, but there's this one boy I have casual sex with every now and then. You know, FWB, friends with benefits. Oh, and by the way, I'm pregnant. So, what's for reals with you?"

That'd be vicious.

Who knows? Maybe if she'd stuck around instead of abandoning me, us, her and I would really have that kind of relationship. Maybe. It's not like she ever bothered to give us the chance. She split out and left me with my dad years and years ago. Not that that really bothered me either. Lots of kids with divorced parents have a hard time with blaming themselves. Not me. But lots of kids, they're all, like, maybe it was something they did to split their parents up. Yanno? But that's not me.

I have this photographic memory. So I can pretty much keep straight all the stuff that went down back when I was little. All the fights and usual family drama. Yanno, familrama. For a fact I know that pretty much none of that stuff was my fault. Actually, I don't know any of it that was. It was always just them two going at each other. More I think about it, it was mostly just my mom going after my dad. That's one of the reasons I decided to stay with him after the big split. Yeah, my mom was forever riding poor Danny boy.

Sitting on my open window sill watching Tweed's darkened window and my little mind is like one of those View Masters you played with when you were a kid. You drop the little paper wheel of slides into the slot on the top and click the button on the side to pan through them. Big fun. So I sit flipping through the snapshots of this time I came home from school one day--fourth grade--and there was my dad, up to his usual.

Clickity-click.

...

"What are you doing?" I asked my dad.

I plop down my backpack on the floor, far away from the mess at the table where I usually left it. I'd wanted a Care Bears backpack, but my mom said it wasn't practical because it was too small to carry all my things. Instead she got me like a teenager's backpack. Ugly green to boot. The thing's as big as me and some of the girls at school call me GI Jane now. Thanks, Mom. I dump it to the floor every first chance I get.

My dad sits at the dining room table. All spread out in front of him is this explosion of yet another of his strange projects. My mom doesn't like for him to practice his music at home, so I guess he has a lot of pent up artistic energy.

Newspaper has been laid out over the table, the floor, even his shirt has a bib fashioned from *The New York Times*. And that's a good thing. For reals. Egg mess is everywhere. Goop on the table, the floor, his newspaper bib. Broken eggshells on the table, the floor, his newspaper bib. Paints--watercolors, I hope for his sake--on the table, thankfully not the floor, but on his newspaper bib. Even a couple finger smudges of red down his cheek. My father looks like a deranged Indian. Chief Soontobeinbigtrouble.

"I'm making a tree lamp," my dad explains, all happy to see me. "Wanna help?"

Wise for my years, I shook my head. "Mom is going to kill you."

"No she isn't."

"Ya-huh. Scalp you."

I turn off my dad's turntable without asking and oh-so-carefully lift the needle from the record. I can only take so much of his prized jazz collection. Thankfully, he doesn't get onto me for breaking his big turntable-touching rule. He's pretty distracted, and besides, I handle the record by the edges as I put it back in the proper sleeve and reshelf it. Vinyl is never to be left out. That's another big no-no. I go to the couch and turn on my afternoon talk shows. I don't really watch them. I watch my dad instead. He can be much more entertaining than any old talk show.

Clickity-click. A new photo slides into view.

My dad accidentally breaks another egg as his face goes pink trying to blow the yolk out of a hole he's poked in the bottom. Sploosh! Goop goes everywhere. The newspaper isn't going to save anything I realize. Too bad he doesn't. I don't know what he's thinking.

"What are you doing?" I ask again.

"It's going to be great. Wait and see."

He's so excited. I really am sorry for him.

Clickity-click.

The potted ficus tree my mom loves has become part of my dad's design. An accomplice too rooted to get away. He's finally finished with the eggs. He has two or three dozen hollowed and drying in the oven on really low heat. He's decided not to paint them after all. He says they'll be "more pleasing" all white. And, besides, he wants to be finished by the time Mom gets home. He's going to be finished all right.

My dad has moved on to stringing the ficus with a strand of little white Christmas tree lights.

"The eggs will fit over the lights, see? It's going to look keen, don't you think?"

"Keen?"

While he weaves the lights among the branches and then begins gingerly capping each light with an eggshell cover, the mess in the dining room is drying. Drying and sticking the way only egg goop can stick. I stick to the couch.

"I hope this dries quick," my dad says, referring to the glue he's using to attach his egg-shades.

Clickity-click.

My dad stands proudly behind his creation--now just waiting to be lit up--prepared to surprise my mom as she walks in. Around my dad and his tree lamp is the kind of mess only a troop of rum-drunk monkeys could have made. Mom isn't so much surprised as she is furious. Hey, what does she want from me? I warned him. Still, I'm immediately sent to my room--go figure--like the whole thing's my fault, and like I can't hear her screaming through my bedroom door for the rest of the hour.

"You're like living with a troop of monkeys, Daniel. Like goddamned monkeys."

Jinx. I called it.

"Lucky monkeys," my dad says.

"What?"

"I'll just clean up then, shall I?"

"Oh, yes, please. Shall you, Daniel," my mom seethes.

I poke my head out. Clickity-click.

It must be sometime around two in the morning. I've been in my room all night. Ate my dinner there. Didn't want to come out. But, like, nature calls, yanno?

Things have been quiet for a long time now thankfully. As I make for the bathroom, I notice the glow of light from the living room. Sneaky as I'll ever be, and trust me, in the Tobin household I'm going to get pretty good, I tiptoe to the corner and peak around. Suddenly I feel young again. Like real-little, little-kid young. Because there, at the living room window, is a tree. A tree, something like a Christmas tree. It's like I'm just a little girl again, sneaking out on Christmas Eve to spy Santa.

But this tree is different. It's nothing like a spruce or one of the other normal Christmas trees. It's smaller, and more like a miniature apple or pear tree. But it's lit up there in the dark. But not with the regular kind of Christmas lights. No, more like with fruit of glowing orbs...eggs. Magical eggs. White, maybe even golden a bit, glowing magical eggs hanging here and there all along the branches. It's beautiful. More beautiful than any Christmas tree. Much.

Then I notice my dad. He's asleep on the couch. At least, I think he's asleep. From the corner I can't see his face. He's at the bottom of a bucket of dark. I guess I stand there for a little while, wishing I could sneak closer to the tree. But for so many reasons I don't.

A little while later, back in my room again, I decide that I want to ask my dad if I can keep his tree. I'll put it in my room and maybe from time to time I'll pretend I'm a little, little girl once more. It's definitely the kind of tree a princess would have. And I'm proud of Dad for making it. Now I wish I had helped. Maybe next time I will. Not maybe. Definitely.

Clickity-click.

Morning. I come down the hall to the living room and my dad's no longer on the couch. The blankets are folded neatly on the pillows. The tree is gone. I never see it again.

...

Tweed, the kid across the way, he's friends with Heft. Heft's the guy I see. Heft's real name is Chad, but God forbid you call him that. Heft's another one who thinks everybody wants to see his tag all over everything. Heft isn't as cute as Tweed. I hate to admit that. I don't mean it in a bad way. I mean, he *is* cute--real cute--just not *as* cute. He has this cleft in his chin. Sometimes I can't decide if I like that or not. He goes to school with me and he's crazy smart. His dad's a lawyer, and his mom is a doctor. Practically the Huxtable family incarnate. Yanno, like the TV show. That's what Heft says. He's got two older sisters. But they're already off in college, so I'm not sure what their story is. Heft doesn't really like to talk about them. He's had a lot of family tragedy. His brother died when they were both just little boys. Leukemia, I think.

Anywho, Heft's the one that got me pregnant. That's my big, ginormous secret. Nobody knows. Not even Heft. But it's no big deal. I just figured it out myself not too long ago.

Now that I think about it, Tweed might know. He was sitting across the way smoking a joint in the dark watching me the other night when I did the pregnancy test thing. I hadn't noticed him at first, and let's just say that when I got the results I didn't do a very good job of hiding how I felt about it. So yeah, Tweed probably knows. And that means Heft might know. And knowing Heft, he probably blabbed to Tweed about us doing it. Okay, yeah, I guess Tweed might know that Heft is my baby daddy, like the skank girls say. I dunno. If Heft is in the know, I wonder if he's talked to his mom, the good doctor, about it. They're one of those *close* families. Now that I think about it, I'm surprised the whole neighborhood hasn't come beating down my door with pitch forks and torches to drag me to the clinic for an abortion this very second. Fascists.

What else? I dunno. There's only one really big other thing. My other big secret, I guess. But it's nothing that spectacular; it's just this thing I do, so it's not that big of a deal. I first started doing it when I was thirteen. It was one of those long, boring Saturday nights in July. I know this for a fact not because I keep a diary or anything girlie, but because, like I said before, I have a photographic memory. Not for everything. It's more of a selective photographic memory, but in a good way. I can choose whether I want to remember all the details of something that way. It's kind of like I decide if I want my brain to push the little mental button that will take the snapshot or not. Of course, a few things scattered here and there over the course of my short life have pushed that button whether I wanted them to or not, so maybe my fancy brain camera is already broken.

The first time I started doing this stuff to myself on purpose all sounds kind of silly now. Then again, a lot of life's really important stuff gets sillier with the passage of time.

Like, I thought it was the end of the world when my parents got divorced. I cried and cried for days on end. I refused to go to school, and I even did some things to my mom just to hurt her feelings. Real mean stuff that really did hurt her at the time. Childish, I know. But, I dunno, I was just thinking, she probably doesn't even remember any of that stuff now. It's like the parent-set like to say, water over the dam or under the bridge or spilt milk or whatever. And me neither, I don't really remember it all. These days, I don't even think about the divorce. So they're divorced? Real big deal. Lots of kids' parents are divorced. These days, I don't even know why it bothered me in the first place. Passage of time, sister.

But, about my big secret, the first time I did it to myself I thought it was like this real big deal. Ginormous. Actually, it was sort of an accident. Not really, but sort of. It was right after I'd come home from two weeks of summer camp and I thought we were having a big family dinner at the dinner table and everything all special just to celebrate me being back home. I couldn't have been more off base.

...

They're still arguing at the dinner table. I'm not even sure that they noticed I left. I know they didn't notice when I came back. I go into the living room and get all three family photo albums from off the shelf. They're still arguing. I'm gone again.

Great way to come home from summer camp. Hi, Chloe. Welcome home. I'm leaving you and Dad and going as far away as I can possibly go. Love, Mom.

Back in my room I go to work. It's a project. My dad would be proud; he loves projects. I'd ask him if he wanted to join in but he's got his hands full with my mom. Working as fast as I can, I take all the photos out and carefully snip, snip, snip, and start to reorganize them neatly back into the albums. Two for me and my dad, one especially just for my mom. When I'm nearly done, as I'm trimming one of the photos to make it look nicer, I accidently cut myself. A little in a rush to be finished, I suppose. My brain camera snaps a picture of the neat slice that starts at the first knuckle of my index finger and only stops where my fingernail got in the way.

Clickity-click.

I get a lot of blood everywhere. More brain pictures.

Clickity-click. Clickity-click. Clickity-click.

I take the albums back. They're still arguing. Now they've moved into the kitchen, breaking things to make their points to one another. I put the albums for me and my dad back on the shelf where they belong. I take the special album for my mom and put it on her side of their bed so she can pack it in her suitcase and fly away like she wants to.

Eventually the apartment goes quiet. The boy across the way is home in his room. He doesn't have an air conditioner in his window, so he leaves it open and hangs out in nothing but a pair of shorts. He goes to public school, so although we're about the same age I don't really know him. His mother left him too. Even his dad left him. That's why he lives here. He lives with the old man everyone calls Pops. That's his grandfather.

I can't sleep. Now the quiet seems worse than the yelling. Soon enough my mom will be gone and then this quiet will be how it always is. How depressing is that?

In the bathroom I wash my finger so that it starts bleeding again. The cold water makes it sting, but that's okay. It's like the sting of my finger is the only part of me that has any sensation. The rest of me, a big yuck-ball of cold putty. Inside and out. I'm just numb. My heart, my lungs, my brain, my feet, everything about me is just a lump of nothing.

Searching for the band-aids in the medicine cabinet, I find something else; a little box of razors. I've never seen my dad use them; he uses the disposable kind, so I guess they're real old. He'd probably never miss them.

As the boy across the way gnaws on his protruding tongue while building a model airplane at his desk, I take one of the razors and make a thin little cut just under my left armpit. It isn't bad, but it bleeds like crazy and I can feel my blood, me, trickling down, warmly tickling my own ribs as I curl up to go to sleep.

"Chloe Tobin!"

My mom is standing in my bedroom door. In her hands is the photo album I made for her.

Clickity-click.

"Do you want to explain this?" she practically shrieks.

My eyes are crusty with sleep and my throat is dry and froggy. It must be the crack of dawn.

"I made it for you," I croak.

"You *made* it for me? Chloe…," she says, opening the album to me, all at a loss and as if I wasn't aware of its contents. She flips through page after page of little cut-outs of herself.

"I cut you out of all the family photo albums so you could have all the pictures of yourself for your next family or whoever," I explain. "Do you like it?"

She starts to cry. I can tell it's both from anger and hurt. Good. I wouldn't want her to know what it feels like to be all numb inside.

Clickity-click.

…

I'm going to hell. Not for the cutting. Although I'm sure that's not winning me any saintly points either. No, I'm going to hell because girls who have abortions go to hell. I can't have a baby. I'm too young, and besides, it'd be a bastard. Girls who have abortions go to hell. That's my new nightly mantra. I quit praying. I have a mantra now. Praying is stupid. If God really wanted to help me out, He wouldn't have done this to me in the first place. Yeah, I'm going to hell. Most definitely.

I can't help but laugh at myself. Not because of all that--that stuff isn't funny--but because as I cut into my belly with the razor, I'm careful not to slice my fingers. Crazy, huh? So anyway, I do a pretty good job of making more of a mess than I wanted. The cut isn't like, deep or anything, and it's only a few inches long, starting just right below my bellybutton and going down, but it bleeds like crazy. Whatever. I pinch my belly to stop it, but it keeps talking. Like some kind of little mouth saying I told you so. Gush, gush, gush. Yeah, now I've got my period. The red tide, the girls at school call it. My Aunt Flo has come to visit. I wish. Maybe I want to cry a little. But I won't. Instead, I ease the razor back into the little I-told-you-so mouth and make it just a little bigger. Maybe someday I can say the scar is my caesarean.

And I guess it's not God's fault. I got myself into this mess, I accept that. One thing's for sure…now I'll be keeping my pants on. How else am I going to keep this nasty little cut a secret? Heft would kill me if he saw it.

And it is. Secret, I mean. Not even Tweed knows about this one. His light is off. It's been off. And he's not smoking in the dark, either. His window is so close I'd know if he was. He's been kind of absent for a while now. Like a few days. Maybe he has problems too. But nothing worse than me, I'll bet.

It's not like I'm the first girl in history to go and get herself pregnant. There's this girl, Lindsey Becker, she was in my honors chemistry class, third period last year. She got pregnant. She tried to hide it for the longest. She thought she was so smart. Like being pregnant is a temporary thing. Like, it'll just go away. Well, I mean, yeah, it is temporary. Until the baby comes. Duh. Anywho, little Miss Becker got herself knocked up by guess who? The captain of the debate team, Paul Michaels. Na-huh. Yeah-huh. Mr. Smarty Pants couldn't debate his way out of that one because everybody knew they were the steady item. He denied it was him, of course.

I don't know what happened to Lindsey. I'm not even exactly sure how everybody found out. But, after they did, Poof! She was gone. Outta there. Oh, Mr. Debate Team stuck around. Yeah, the boys always get to stick around, don't they? He's going to Rutgers in the fall. His life wasn't ruined. His life wasn't even put on hold.

About a million times a day I want to talk to somebody about my own little dilemma. But there isn't anybody. I can't tell Heft. I dunno, I've thought about it, but he'll just freak out and say what any guy his age--actually any guy, any age--would. First, it'd be, "Are you sure?" Yes. Then it'd be, "How do you know it's mine?" Duh. Like now I'm some sort of skank slut all of a sudden. Then it'd be, "I'll stick by whatever you decide to do. So what day do you want to go to the clinic for the abortion?" How noble, yanno?

I mean, yeah, I probably will have an abortion, I guess. I dunno. I haven't thought about it all the way through yet. But I'm not having that conversation now. If that's what I decide to do, then yeah, I'll tell Heft. Probably. But, until then....

And I don't really have any girlfriends to tell. I have a few friends, I guess. Nobody close. Not "I'm pregnant" close. But that's okay by me. For reals. The more I think about it, it was probably one of Lindsey Becker's girlfriends that told the whole school on her, yanno?

I've thought about telling my dad. Really, I have. Because my dad and me, we have a pretty tight relationship. But that'd just be more of the same. More problem than solution, I mean. Maybe I wouldn't be the first girl in history to get pregnant, but I'd still be "his daughter." No matter what all the other girls did, I wouldn't be following them in some jump off of the GWB. That's the good old George Washington Bridge, for those who don't know. Not that my dad has ever used any expressions as tired as that old, "If your friends jumped off a bridge," thing. Like I've said before, my dad's kind of different. But he's still a dad.

Which just brings me back to Heft. I've got to tell him. I know I do. It's partly his decision too, after all. So I just need to find the time. The way. The nerve.

Chapter Three

My brain camera goes into overdrive. Clickity-click. Clickity-click. Clickity-click. Clickity-click.

A tater-tot lands on the green linoleum of the cafeteria floor, bounces twice or maybe three times and then rolls away like a greasy little tumbleweed. Tater-weed. Utensils follow. Just a knife, fork, spoon. The fork chasing off between my feet to catch up with the tater-weed. When the lunch tray hits the ground, it and everything on it dances. Dances, then falls down. This creates enough racket that all the other kids finally become aware. One girl screams and then everybody is screaming. Lemmings. An explosion of panic.

This isn't supposed to happen here. We're a private school. These are privileged kids. We don't have drug dogs scratching up our lockers, no metal detectors to herd through. We worry about college prep, extracurricular clubs, grade point averages.

Then again, I never fit in and so what do I know. After it was over they brought in counselors, held assemblies, and conducted "Friendship Jams" along with "Awareness Squads." I attended in body only. They sent us home early.

Clickity-click.

Now I have this great brain photo of milk commingling with blood on green tile. Looks like some poor kid dropped her strawberry sundae.

...

I knew Scissors better than she knew herself. I know that kind of sounds cliché. I guess not *sounds*, but *is*. Even maybe a bit something like Pops would say. Just the same, it was the truth. That's how I knew as I watched her from my window while she just kind of goofed off doing much of nothing that it was going to be one of those nights. One of those bad ones where the pliers and razor blades made an appearance.

I'd heard what happened at her school. Everybody had heard. It was the neighborhood gossip de jour. Some girl had gone off at their school. I'd heard several different versions of what went down so I wasn't a hundred percent on the facts, just that Scissors had been the other girl involved.

As I watched Scissors illuminated by the glow of her aquarium I was blown away by the irony of it being Scissors who'd dealt with the psycho. Talk about the whack. I didn't get too far thinking about all that though. Just as I'd expected the pliers and disposable razor blades came out. That was it. When they made their appearance I made my disappearance. I just wasn't in the mood to see it. Not down with it in the slightest.

I grabbed my bag and hit the streets.

I hadn't planned on going into the tunnel. The only reason I was even in the subway was just to tag "TWEED" on a few movie posters and whatnot. Which is why, after the train came in, it left without me. With the train departing, a bit of cooler air pulled into the station to trail it as it rumbled off into the black.

I found myself wandering over to the end of the platform to watch it go. Probably wouldn't be another for at least a few minutes, I reasoned. And before I knew it, I was walking down the narrow steps that led onto the tracks. Even crazier, I pulled my light from my backpack and started down the tunnel.

If I'd been following my nose I would've been screwed. It was all too clear that certain assholes had no problem with taking a leak, or even worse, down in the tunnel. It smelled so bad--beyond description really--that I was more worried about stepping in a pile of some hobo's latest dump than I was about anything else. Well, rats did come to mind. And once they did I forgot to worry about hobo shit anymore.

Almost immediately I was surprised to discover another set of steps that let you get back up to a ledge, or catwalk--I suppose you'd call it--on the far side of the tracks. Go figure. That was on the other side of the electrified third rail, some little wary voice in the back of my mind noted. I know you had to touch it for it to be dangerous, but still, that was like a frickin' lightning bolt of juice. Electric chair wattage. The Colonel Sanders' treatment.

The catwalk dealie ran along the far wall down into the tunnel for as far as I could make out. I didn't want to turn myself into a char burger crossing over the third rail, but getting up off the tracks was certainly the path of the prudent. Not wanting to risk coming near that electrified rail in any way, shape, or form--as Pops liked to say--I hopped over it as high as I could, landing almost on the catwalk itself. I was off.

I wasn't too far in when I did a double check behind me to be sure about the lack of any oncoming trains. I was off the tracks, so I wasn't going to be mowed down, but I didn't need any conductor calling John Law down on me. Especially when I was lugging my stuff like I was. Satisfied, I screwed up my nerve and started into what was almost a little trot. Don't ask me why. Nervous ènergy I guess. I don't know.

As I went along I kept my flashlight busy illuminating the graffiti even though there were bare bulbs illuminating the way every so often. And the graffiti, some was actually pretty good. Go figure. And I recognized a good bit of it. Among the fat lettered slang and tags there was this wicked looking bee that I'd seen before over on the east side of Broadway. And then there was the guy who did the Superman S thing. His tag was Sandman, but with the S from Superman. Book freak, I guess. I think his name was Rollo or maybe Rolfo. I wasn't sure. I'd never met him; just word of mouth and all. But his S wasn't all that hot. Especially not when you considered how ubiquitous that gnat was.

"Practice apparently makes squat in your case, Sandman," I said to his crappy Superman S.

The rails, polished like they were from the crush of the trains, caught what little yellow light there was. Twin golden snakes gliding down the tunnel towards two faraway colorful lights, set close to one another and different from the pale yellow bulbs that led the way to them. One of the two distant lights was green, the other blue. I don't know what the blue signified, but the green made me think of Jay Gatsby. You know, *The Great Gatsby*, spending his nights standing out at the end of his dock staring out across the dark water to the green light of Daisy Buchanan's. Real lonely shit.

But still a good read, by the way. It was one of the first we'd had in English Lit this past year. I'd even read it over again later after we'd moved on. It was that good. Funny thing though, my Lit teacher got it all wrong. She liked to blab on and on about how Fitzgerald was defining the American dream. Streets of gold. How people can invent themselves. The usual crap. How Gatsby embodied all that by rising up from obscurity to become "The Great" and all. But that's not the way I read it. The way I saw it was that Fitzgerald was saying the American dream is a sham. Sure Gatsby gets rich and all, but that doesn't get him what he really wants--the only thing he wants--the love of Daisy.

Do you think they'd keep Gatsby on the curriculum if they realized the real message? Don't bother studying. Screw working hard, making something of yourself. Because, hey, loser, none of that can buy you happiness, and odds are your life is going to be suckage and then you die anyway.

And while I'm on the subject, the other funny thing about the past year's Lit class was that some pissed off parents had that book *Lord of the Flies* pulled from the reading list. Something about 'homoerotic perversion' and all. You know, from when these kids all lost alone on a desert island sodomize another kid by ramming a stick up his ass. Yeah, I read it. And so did everybody else, to include the spuds and dipshits that probably wouldn't have bothered except for all the bitching and moaning from the PTA about it in the first place. No such thing as bad press, huh?

Here's the other funny thing about that. That book is all about conformity. It's just what *they*--the teachers, the principal, the book burning parents--are always so desperate to instill in America's youth. Conformity violently forced onto the few kids who want to be apart from the groupthink of all the bullies and cliques. And then, in the end, the acceptance of conformity by the whole tribe of kids when they get rescued back into the adult's world. How the lot of them are on the verge of killing one another until the grownups miraculously show up just in time to save the day and restore the little lost savages to civilization. So the message then? Don't knock society, kid. Without it, you're screwed. Pun intended. So sit down, shut up, play by the rules, and be thankful you're not living in anarchy with a stick up your ass.

Banned books or not, nobody ever gets the message though. Walking along the tunnel, thinking about Gatsby, and Piggy, and all that, I was surprised to see how many people had trespassed there before me. What a dump. Beer bottles, batteries, an old ironing board, newspapers, candy wrappers, drug baggies, condom wrappers--and worse, their spent former contents--and all kinds of other refuse. You name it. There was even one of those dorm room refrigerators crammed back into an alcove. It was missing its door, but, still, there it was. So I guess I'm just saying it was a little surprising. An eye opener. I mean, I knew people other than the metro transit authority went into the tunnels. And not just the homeless. You could always catch the gang tags from the subway window. But being right there, taking my time, you know, well, I don't know, it made it all the more apparent that this was some whole other world--microcosm--if you know what I mean. And then I saw it. "RAZER."

You believe that shit? In the same big, red sloppy, lopsided cursive bullshit as always, “RAZER.” The R’s capped off with little crowns like I guess he thinks he’s king of something. I could have stepped in hobo shit, fallen backwards onto a giant rat, and been run over by the A train all at the same time, and I wouldn’t have been more surprised.

“Since when?” I said out loud. Meaning, you know, since when did that lump come down into the tunnels? He’d never said a word about going into the tunnels to me and Heft.

It didn’t take hardly a minute, but I was still surprised the train hadn’t come along by the time I’d finished spraying “SUX” after Razer’s tag. I was considering adding something even worse when another tag caught my eye.

“CC181,” it read in bold black letters outlined in white. The outline wasn’t around each letter, but just one thick line going around the lot, like a corral holding them in. I’d seen this before too. I’d seen it before and it was just what I’d been looking for. I got my red out and sprayed right over it. “HEFT.”

“See what you get, chump?”

It was sloppy and only took a second. Hell, I wanted it to be sloppy. Even so, as I finished, there wasn’t any time to admire it. Way off down the tunnel, the first inkling of train lights glistened. I whooped once or twice, you know, victorious like, as I ran along to make the platform of the stop just ahead.

You need to know that CC181 was a gang. Real criminal element as far as I knew. And now, as far as they knew, Heft had dogged their tag. It was what he deserved for doing what he did to Scissors. But I wasn’t done. It still wasn’t too late and now that I’d found what I wanted to do, I needed to find a few more of the CC181 boys’ marks to dog out. You know, on young master Heft’s behalf. He was going to learn. Another book came to mind as I made the platform. Emerging from the dank reek of the tunnel, I felt like Edmond Dantes. You know, *The Count of Monte Cristo*.

...

Me, Heft, and Razer were just sort of hanging out a few nights after Heft’s school had finished early, after their big incident and all, when Heft almost let slip that he’d done it with Scissors. Razer wasn’t swift enough to catch it, and me, I let it go. I wanted to see if Heft was going to brag about that shit.

Far out and below us, from where we loafed around on high from the walls of the Tryon, dimly lit barges churned the Hudson. Long and low freighters slowly slipping under or peeking out from the George Washington Bridge, the GWB, but otherwise crawling along so slow they seemed motionless. Razer lit another firecracker and held it as the madly hissing fuse illuminated his imp grin. An acrid whiff of burning gunpowder overtook the exhaust from the cars zipping along the highway, snaking along the river's edge beneath us. When it looked as though he was out of time, Razer chucked the firecracker and bit his lip in anticipation while Heft and I plugged our ears. Razer's expression suddenly went sour and we all relaxed. Just another dud.

"Shit, man. I'm goin' to go get my money back. This be the bullshit," he said, letting his frustration make him sound too much like all the other English-challenged, or at least English-lazy, speaking Dominicans, the ones I refused to associate with for mostly just that reason.

Neither Heft nor I paid him any mind. We both knew he wasn't going to do a damned thing.

"They look like toppled skyscrapers sort of, don't they?" I said to Heft.

But it was Razer that responded, "Who?"

"The barges," I said.

"No, no," Razer argued like some kind of petulant little child.

I ignored him. "It's like they're taking the city away, piece by piece. Am I right?" I put to Heft.

"Maybe they're bringing it in, putting it together," Razer said, still trying to dig at me. I refused to play his game and we went quiet. Then we all three laughed, suddenly surprised when one of Razer's duds finally exploded with a weak "pop" down someplace among the brush and trees below.

"Slooow burn," Heft said.

"Bronstein delay," Razer said.

"What?" Heft and I both asked.

Razer shook his head. "Nothing. I still want my money back," he complained.

We laughed some more and that's when Heft said, "Query."

Heft was forever saying shit like '*query*,' and then postulating some crazy-assed thing he thought was the end-all-be-all of profound crap.

"If you could go back in time," he said, "to any day, your choice, and live all the days since then over again, but have no memory of what's to come, the future, your future, would you?"

"I--" Razer started, but Heft interrupted him.

"Wait. Or, if not, if you could pick one hour, just one hour of any hour from your past and live it over again, and like, know that you were, you know, re-living it, and what was going to happen, would you do that? And if you did, what would that hour be?"

"I--" Razer tried again.

"*And.* And if you did, would you change anything, or just live it over like it was the first time around?"

"You said, query." Razer finally got in.

"What?"

"You said query. Singular. That was *queries*, homes," Razer said.

Heft only shrugged and pulled out his cigarettes to light a smoke as though he was really satisfied with himself. Job well done and all that crap. After he took his first drag, he stared at us, raising an eyebrow and exhaling over his shoulder, pretty boy-like, waiting for one of us to enlighten him with our no-doubt stupid answers.

"Is this one of your practice essays?" Razer pressed, referring to the endless studying Heft did for his SATs. By his tone it was clear Razer wanted nothing to do with any of Heft's test prep.

"Nope. Just a question."

"I'd need more than an hour. I'd need a day," I said.

Heft pulled at his cigarette then said, "That's why it's a tough call."

So I threw it back at him. "Which would you choose?"

Razer jumped in even though I was putting it to Heft. "I'd take the hour. I'd retake my Algebra final."

"That's why I didn't ask you," I said. "And besides, you should take the hour before the test to study or make a cheat sheet or something, dumb ass. If you just take the hour of the test over you'd only fail it again." I turned back to Heft. "And so?"

"Well," Heft said, taking a pause and really milking it, "If you'd asked me a while back, I would have said neither."

"Neither? Then why you asking us?" Razer said.

Heft ignored him. "Who needs the past? I mean, that's what I would have said. But lately I've been thinking about this girl I hooked up with...." Heft said, and then he turned his attention back out over the water as if he had stepped back in time just as he'd put it to us.

"I change my answer," Razer blurted out, changing the subject from Heft's hook up with Scissors like a dolt. "I'd do everything all over again from the day I was born."

It was too much for me to let go. "That's so broke," I said. "What, do you think you're that bad off?"

"Don't knock 'em," Heft said in Razer's defense.

But I did. "If you can't remember shit, then you're just doomed to repeat the same shit as the first time around. Then what? You want to redo and rewind, redo and rewind, over and over again? Broke. And plus, like he said, you wouldn't even remember that you're doing it over. Ultra-broke."

Razer stared at me and then looked off when he answered. "Yeah, I know. I wouldn't know." And to me I thought maybe he looked like he was going to start crying. "But *He* would know," Razer said.

"He who?" Heft asked.

"God."

I couldn't believe my ears. "God?" I said.

"Maybe if He saw how bad I wanted things to be different...that I was willing to start all over again, then maybe, you know, maybe He'd feel bad. Take pity on me or something," Razer said.

Even though I was sure he was about to bawl, I couldn't help but say, "Pity? That's pathetic."

Heft, sporting his oh-so-philosophical voice, chimed in. "No. I don't think so. I mean, what else is God good for if it isn't to pity us? I think it's noble," he said. "Maybe that's why she did it."

Somehow I knew Heft was going to go there. Him and his school's big incident. People always have to make things about themselves, don't they?

I guess Heft and Razer got themselves all moved or whatever with all their talk, since they shut up then and just leaned against the wall. Like I told you, pathetic.

"Give me a fire cracker, ya lump," I said.

Chapter Four

It wasn't a spectacular day in any kind of way in the old book of Tweed. It wasn't a crappy day in any kind of way. Yeah, if not for the garbage that went down, it for sure would've just been another one of those days adding up along with so many others, accumulating all but unnoticed like loose change in the jar on the hall table next to where you toss the house keys, drop the book bag, kick off the sneakers. A day you wouldn't need to pray you could forget. Praying to rewind the clock, to flip back in the calendar, it just doesn't work. If I didn't know it for sure before that day, I sure knew it after. It was the day when all the serious shit got started.

I was hanging out with my boys Heft and Razer--told you it wasn't anything too spectacular--and we were kicking around the idea of going out bombing that night. Spread a little spray paint noise around the Heights. Razer was dying to tag a billboard, something he'd yet to do and just lately come to see as the end all-be all of tagging.

At first I didn't see the point, but Razer persisted, and after he pleaded his case I had to admit he was on to something. I came around to see things his way. Let's face it, billboards are an eyesore. It's bad enough that you can't turn around good in this world without some bastard forever trying to shove whatever it is they're selling down your throat. So why not turn the tables on those pricks and let them be your canvas? Those were Razer's words. And I liked it when Razer actually used the word canvas. It spoke to the aspiring artist in me. I guess there were a few reasons why he was my friend after all.

"I'm in," I said. And that, as they say in the funny papers, was that.

That's why we decided to wander up to Inwood--the other park just north of the Tryon--to look for some suitable targets, something for later that night. That, and to scope on girls. You know, just something to do. Things did not go as planned.

"The CC181 is a bad gang, homes. The baddest. You better best be leaving them boys alone," Razer said.

Razer was referring to a tag we'd come across. A splotchy spray paint piece of shit all scrunched up on the rail of a park bench of all places. It was so crap that I didn't even recognize it as a CC181 tag until Razer started going off on Heft about it.

"Do what now?" Heft asked.

I had to fight to keep a straight face.

"You diss the wrong people is all I'm saying," Razer said. "Going to get you messed up."

"Fuck you talkin' about, Willis?"

"Talking about you. The fuck you think I'm talking about?" Razer said. His voice pitched up a bit like it always did when he got too excited.

"Dissing? Who'd I diss?"

"The CC181. That's who."

"CC181?" Heft said looking to me with an expression of utter confusion.

I shrugged. "Don't ask me," I said. "You huffing again, Pedro?"

Razer particularly hated when I called him Pedro. We'd actually had a fistfight a couple years back over it. He might have won--and that's a matter of opinion, mind you--but I still called him Pedro right on whenever the mood struck me.

"Aw, man, you know what, to hell with the both you fools," Razer said, flipping a pair of birds at us. "Don't say I ain't warned you." He turned away leaving us there, one a good deal more perplexed than the other.

Heft shook his head. "What the…?"

I shrugged again. And maybe I smiled a bit.

"You know what, screw this," Heft said.

And the next thing I knew he was gone too.

I called after him a few times, but all I got was a dismissive wave and a good look at his back.

"Oh, no. No you don't," I said all sotto voce even though he was mad out of earshot.

I let him round a bend in the path along the way we'd come and then I fell in behind him. Don't really know why. Guess I just wanted to see where he thought he was going.

Where he ended up was the subway. And obviously the call he made on the way was to Scissors, because there she was waiting for him. After they kissed and played grab-ass for a minute, they went down the stairs. I gave them a head start and for whatever reason I kept up my surveillance.

Below where I stood behind an iron column on the platform, down between the muck of the subway tracks, there's a discarded umbrella. A twisted steam punk looking dystopian octopus. It billowed and shuddered with the passing of a train blowing past in the opposite direction. Heft plugged his ears and grinned to my girl as the conductor blasted the horn to say the train wouldn't be stopping.

Scissors looked good. All frail and strong both at the same time. Funny how some girls pull that off. I couldn't hear what they were saying to one another, but it didn't really matter. Actions, like the cliché goes, they speak louder. With one hand Scissors kept Heft at bay, all while with the other she pulled him close, never letting him go. Under the sleeve of her shirt on the arm that kept him, I knew there were fresh cuts. Heft didn't know. He should have, but he didn't. She wasn't his girl.

Unseen by the two of them, I tucked myself into my nook on the platform bench between a dusty and beat down construction worker and some pious Hasidic guy thumbing a book of prayer. The platform was crowded as hell. There must have been a game and all, because the idiots had their jerseys and big foam # 1 hands and crap. Lots of drunk bastards too. Lots of laughing and high fives, war whoops, and just run of the mill stupid.

It was there that I started to feel as alone, forgotten, and as strange as that dropped umbrella. "DissedToPeon Tweed," I'd later tag. It was a new phrase and I ran with it for a few weeks following that day. I tweaked the spelling and lettering as the mood and inspiration struck me, and sometimes--I have to brag--I thought it wasn't half bad. Eventually I got tired of it though, it being just another passing Tweed fad and so I moved on. I'd imagine you can probably still see one of them here or there if you kept your eyes peeled.

...

The stop was mad crazy. Heft was being sweet, nuzzling his little cleft into my neck as we walked through the crowded platform. It was a game day. Almost all of the people decked out in the blue and white and having fun. Off to the side, Latino boys--our age, I'd guess--were among those who were 'sauced on suds' as my dad would say. You could smell the beer sweat on them, like they were homeless or something, I swear.

"Number one, yo! Number one!" they chanted repeatedly to no one in particular.

"What's your name, yo? You look so fine, yo!" The bravest loudmouth boy called out to another pair of girls. Real classy.

One girl blushed and the other pretended not to hear them although she threw her hair extensions around and stuck out her boobs, proving otherwise. Skank.

"Aw, c'mon, now, don't be playin' me, sweets. What's your name?" he continued hopelessly. His friends taunted his failure.

"You ain't got no play, fool!"

"Ah ha, she don't even want to be hearin' you, homes!"

We'd stopped walking and I noticed that Heft kept his eyes on the tracks, kind of like in deep thought or something.

A small stream trickled between the first two rails where the muddy earth was shallow. It was disgusting. Batteries and bottle tops and the detached head of a plastic baby doll. Creepers for reals. Blonde hair sprouted from the doll's pink scalp in a formation of sprigs like those gross guys with hair transplants. The doll's face was streaked in places with mud. I wondered if the little girl who'd lost her doll knew that the head was stuck down there on the rails. I wondered if she had to come down here day after day on her way to wherever and see her sweet little dolly looking like something out of a horror movie. The unlucky blonde cast member. Sad, yanno?

The drunk boys still harassed Miss Skank and her friend.

"Yo, you gonna wish you didn't disrespect me when I'm gone, yo!"

The baby doll head was creeping me out even more when I noticed Heft was staring down into its empty blue eyes.

I pulled him back from the edge and pressed him up against the side of the iron column--one of those girders--that had a meaningless "WET PAINT" sign taped to it. Cutting through the cacophony, an overhead PA announcement warned everyone: "Keep an eye on your personal belongings. Beware of pickpockets." But the message's advice came out garbled and a mess of static. Not that it mattered. Nobody paid it any attention.

"I need to tell you something," I said.

Heft turned his attention from the doll's head to me, a bit groggy-like, like I'd shaken him from a stoner nap, and his little devil grin made me feel guilty. I'm not really sure why. Just did.

Two lights flickered in the distance of the tunnel. The crowd sensed the approaching train and began to shift to the platform edge in anticipation.

"What's up?" asked Heft.

Poor Heft. I think he thought I was going to tell him I loved him. Behind us in the crowd a man yelled, "Hey, hold up a minute! Kyle! Caitlyn!"

I looked over Heft's shoulder to see who'd shouted. I was chickening out a bit from what I'd wanted to say and was glad for an excuse to be distracted.

A typical fanny pack, pudgy dad-type, with a slobbering toddler in one arm and a folded umbrella stroller in the other, was having way too much trouble getting down the stairs to the platform. I guess, between his toddler, his potbelly, and his clogged arteries, old dad just couldn't keep up. If he could have, I'm sure he would've saved himself the sweat of a few flights of stairs by driving them all down to the platform in the family SUV.

Typical dad yelled again to his two young children, typical boy and typical girl. "Kyle!" Caitlyn!" Big influence that had. The two typicals ignored him. Instead, they screamed and laughed and darted as loud and as fast and as obnoxiously as they wanted. Like anybody really expects a girl named Caitlyn to do anything other than what she wants? Yeah, right.

A bushel of bland, mealy apples from the same orchard, as my Dad, liked to say. Meaning that, the family was nothing but cookie cutter. Boring.

All four of them, to include the toddler, were wearing stupid yuppie name brand labels that were still crud mall clothes maybe one J. Crew step up from the Gap. And they all four had Mets baseball caps on. Yanno, to prove they were one with the rest of the yahoos going to the game.

Typical girl was probably a year younger than typical boy, who looked, I dunno, maybe six. Still, typical girl had taken the lead in their footrace, zipping ahead through the crowd leaving typical boy to deal with her wake of rudeness.

Typical dad eased down a few more steps and then paused to yell at his typical kids some more. But the brats just pummeled on, yanno, like kids do, bolting like nut-jobs along the platform, closing in on the edge near where me and Heft stood, typical little girl a full arm's length in the lead.

"Yo, you goin' to the game?" I heard one of the drunk Latino boys yell from somewhere in the throng of people. I started taking little pictures in my mind and the world sort of slowed down.

Typical little girl pumped her arms furiously. Clickity-click.

She wore her hair in a ponytail that ran through the hole at the back of her adjustable baseball cap, and her brother strained to snatch it to keep her from beating him. Clickity-click.

Typical boy clearly had his old man's nonathletic genes. He wasn't going to outrun his little sister or catch her by the hair. With arms raised in victory, little typical Caitlyn came to a hopping stop just ahead of us in the stripe of yellow caution paint. Clickity-click.

Heft gave her a big smile. Clickity-click.

Typical boy's eyes went wide and a hint of a squeak escaped his lips when he suddenly tripped on his untied shoelace. Clickity-click.

He stumbled forward, hands outstretched and desperate fingers splayed looking for anything to catch himself. Nothing but empty space to claw. But his fall was stopped as his hands accidentally pummeled his typical sister right between her shoulder blades. He caught her right where her angel or fairy wings might have been. Like a page of littered newspaper caught on an updraft, the girl sort of billowed as she lifted lazily into the air off the platform, drifting out over the rails. Clickity-click.

Typical girl was in midair, a clumsy little flying trapeze artist, terror-stricken without a net, just another little girl in trouble because of another little boy. Clickity-click.

A woman with an oversized handbag shrieked so loud I thought it was the train. I could still smell the stale beer reeking from the crowd, from the Latino boys nearby. Maybe it was the scream and smell that glued the world together and we were all caught in that strange amber. Clickity-click.

In the next frame of my memory, like something out of a movie, like some guy with secret superpowers, Heft lunged out as far as he could and pulled off what typical little brother had not. Heft snatched typical girl by the ponytail and yanked her back from her fall. Clickity-click.

People were frozen in confusion, everything seemed crazy quiet. My mind stopped taking photos.

"Jesus, Heft!" I screamed.

Typical girl would be crying in a half a second--bawling hysterically, actually--but for now she looked at the two of us in shock. The next few moments were a blur of pats from strangers on Heft's back and even a hug from typical dad to the both of us. I think we were still, like, a little dazed, and both typical girl and her typical brother had decided that now it was time to cry. That got typical toddler in typical dad's arms going too. I kept patting Heft's shoulders and neck and cheeks to give my shaking hands something to do. He was a hero.

"Yo, homes, you Heft?"

I heard the voice before I saw the face, since he came up from behind. I recognized it either way. It was the drunk Latino boy who'd been hitting on skank girl. I was turning around, and I guess Heft already knew there was trouble because he pushed me off and away from him.

"She called you Heft, yeah, homes?" Latino boy said pressing in and coming on hard. I guess he wasn't really a boy. Messy tattoos scribbled up his forearms to his muscled biceps. They were those poorly drawn, done out on the back stoop by some glassy-eyed friend at two or three in the morning, tattoos. The kind that let you know he wasn't a trendy kid throwing away mommy and daddy's money in some oh-so-hip parlor down in the Village. I could see in his eyes, this wasn't going to go down with a bunch of trash talk. This was going to get ugly. Bad ugly.

There was unmistakable menace in his voice, and the little you could see of his eyes, from between the slits of the lids, were glazed and bloodshot.

"Yeah, what of it?" Heft said.

I was going to step in. I was going to say let's go. I was going to get Heft out of this. I was going to, I dunno....

"Yeah, I'll tell you what of it. You don't fuck with the CC181, that's what of it, bitch!"

Heft had been quick to save typical girl, but he wasn't so quick to save himself. He got clobbered right on his cleft before he knew it. And it was a hard punch too. It sounded like a mallet smacking meat and knocked him right off the platform. Flying. Right off the platform and into the path of an A train screaming into the station.

Dozens and dozens of people and still there wasn't anybody around to save the hero.

Chapter Five

I'd known Heft for the longest. As far back as I'd known Razer, and that was going back several years to when I'd first come to visit Pops with my mom and dad. Back when she dumped me on Pops. Which, at the time, hurt a bit. I mean, what the hell, we're talking my mom and dad here. Or, that's what they were supposed to be. But now, it's all good. Fine by me.

Truthfully, I was none too surprised that they'd split out the way they did. Wasn't like somebody capable of doing something like that sinks so low without any warning. Just the opposite, as I'd imagine you'd suspect. It's kind of like, face it, at no point during *Moby Dick* do you anticipate Captain Ahab saying, "You know, boys, this thing with the whale has gotten outta hand. Whatdaya say we make for port and put this nasty business behind us?" No way. That crazy, crippled bastard is going to chase after that big ass white whale until his peg leg rots off. I know it, you know it. No surprises there. I guess that book's a classic for the same reason people crane their neck to gawk at a car wreck. Kind of pathetic when you really stop to consider it. At least I can say *I* know how to look away. No, really. I can prove it. Never even finished *Moby Dick*. Didn't feel the need to see how far old Ahab would sink. I mean, I'm sure I will one day. You know, when I'm older and given to moping over maudlin garbage just like all the old dudes past their prime. There's always tomorrow to look forward to, eh?

Since I'd known Heft for so long he was something of a brother to me. Razer, not so much. I mean, sure, Razer was a good friend too. My other "best" bud. But, Heft, even for being such a dumbass like he could be, well, he still was like I said, a brother.

...

A few seconds before he'd been in my arms and kissing me, and now Heft was face down, sprawled between the tracks as the A train was plowing into the station to mince him up. I couldn't even think. I might have screamed. I'm not really sure. Maybe it was my voice, or maybe it was the whole of the crowd roaring around me. Maybe I just stood slack-jawed, my camera's shutter stuck open, my brain overexposed; a waste of film burned black.

I didn't recognize Tweed when he leapt down off the platform. I mean, I did and I didn't. He hit the ground right next to Heft, landing like Spiderman. Yanno, on all fours. Then he stood and it was the craziest thing. Even with the train barreling down on him he looked up at me. Right into me. I knew it was Tweed, this kid I knew but never knew, but still, all I ever remember thinking in that moment was, who is this guy?

I suppose there is something to all those stories you hear about mothers lifting cars off of their babies with some kind of superhuman strength, because Tweed scooped up Heft like he was made of air and feathers. They can't make it, I thought. They wouldn't make it, I knew. I was going to watch them die. I wasn't going to look away. I was going to watch. If I didn't know any better I would've said it was right then that Tweed pulled off yet another super-stunt. It was as though he stepped right into the concrete platform beneath me. Maybe the two of them had already turned into specters. Maybe I could visit this place from now on and be haunted by their ghosts.

...

When they pulled me and my boy Heft alive and well out from under the platform, the dude looked horrible. I mean, nowhere near as horrible as I'd expected. I expected mangled limbs or him coming out two or three pieces at a time. I thought we'd both look like we'd gotten the blender treatment courtesy of the MTA. I'd find out later he did break his arm, but other than that and a cracked skull, Heft was none the worse.

I heard guys on the news before, the ones people call heroes. How many times they said something along the lines of, 'I just did what had to be done.' I know it's the truth now. They also say he who hesitates is lost. That's true enough too. Although, if I had paused, screwed around and stayed up on that platform, it would have been Heft that would've gone the way of the dodo, not yours truly. But I didn't. Hesitate, that is. And I didn't do anything amazing. I just did what had to be done.

I hadn't considered it when I jumped down. I really hadn't considered anything. But as it turned out there was plenty of space underneath the platform to get away from the train. So that's what I did. It was close. That's for damned sure. As I kind of half-jumped and half-duck-walked the two us into our little haven, I felt the train rip at the back of my shirt. And I mean just as. If I had lingered just one heartbeat more to look up at Scissors.... I can't even think about it.

Heft looked something like a drowned rat. Make that a drowned rat with a shit-eating grin. Talk about luck. We'd gotten all nasty from the little rivulet of water between the tracks and it took a few additional bruises to avoid all those tons of steel when they came ripping into the station. I cracked my head on a pipe something good. Weird thing was I never even felt it. So we were the both of us a little roughed up, but alive. Alive, can you believe it? Yeah, and the worst of the bruises Heft got was from the face whack courtesy of that crazy CC181 thug. What a pack of mouth-breathing animals those goons turned out to be. They were all long gone of course.

The crowd on the platform started whooping it up as the emergency workers slid Heft out from the front of the train on a gurney. It'd taken a while to back the train out and by then my boy had come around. Heft hammed it up, doing this cheesy thumbs-up thing like he was some kind of splashdown astronaut back home to Mother Earth from the Moon or Mars or someplace. In the hand he kept clutched to his chest he held something round and pink. That freaked me out because I couldn't tell right off what it was. For half a second I had to check myself for hands and feet. The paramedic and a firefighter attending to me must have thought I was flipping out or some shit. Once I was all accounted for I relaxed.

I was getting the same gurney treatment and was due to come out next. As they pulled Heft over the ledge of the platform one of the paramedic guys took the mystery object out of his hand and dropped it back down beside us on the tracks. Turned out it was this head off of a girl's baby doll. Just the head. Apparently Heft had asked them to give it to him, and, not thinking much of it, one of them had. A little souvenir of what we might have been, I guess.

Everybody was all excited and shit. High-fiving, carrying on like it was a street fair. Plenty of snapping pictures and repeating to one another what they had or hadn't seen. Stories that got exaggerated and blown out in every direction before they were even finished being told. What a load of bullshit. That lasted for all of a few minutes. As I was being hauled up the stairs somebody in the crowd screamed for them to get the train running again, they were missing the game. That realization ended the party quick like.

Welcome to the city. You got run over by a train? Thank God you're alive. Lucky you're in one piece. Now get the hell outta my way. I'm running late here.

Chapter Six

I'd lost track of Pops.

Yeah, I'd been keeping some odd hours. There'd been all the hoopla following our brush with the CC181 and I'd even done the news interview thing right there on the platform. Not that the CC181 was mentioned, because I didn't tell the police shit about them. Heft was smart enough to know that it'd be best for him to do the same. The cops, they might get that one CC boy, but they couldn't get the whole crew. And even nabbing the one was a mighty big "might." On top of everything else, now everybody knew who we were, but who the hell knew who the CC181 were. Am I right? So like I said, we kept stupid. Stupid smart.

I hadn't been hanging out with Razer, and Heft was on lockdown. Even if he hadn't, I probably would've been avoiding him. It's hard to explain. Still, I'd been out and about, gallivanting, as the old guys like my Pops liked to say. Or, I should say, might say, if he was anywhere to be found. And that's more what I meant when I said I'd lost track of him. I'd drug home one night--one morning--still a little scatter-brained, dope-upped, blitzed, shit-faced, however you wanna call it, and Pops, he wasn't there. He wasn't there and somewhere between the yuking and the microwaving of the ceremonial mac-n-cheese, I figured that out. Halfway through my meal I recovered enough for it to hit me that I couldn't even say when the last time it was that I'd seen him. Tuesday? Wednesday? Was today Thursday? Yeah, had been. It was Friday morning.

I thought about going to bed. Thought about yuking some more. So I did the latter and wished I hadn't wolfed down so much, so fast, and prayed to the porcelain gods to have mercy on me. I guess they must have since I slept on the bathroom floor like a real hero and woke up feeling like a newspaper that'd been left in the rain and dried in the sun. Back on the couch, and wishing Pops would bring me a bowl of corn flakes like he'd usually do, I managed to remember again that I'd lost track of the old man.

So I thought about going to bed again. My real bed this time, not the tile of the bathroom. Guilt over losing track of Pops tried to get the better of me--as it should have--but I let the hangover beat it down. I went to my room and slept most of the day.

I woke up in the clothes I'd never bothered to take off. That wouldn't have sucked so much but for the yuke on my shirt. For the third or fourth time I bumbled around my haze and almost lost my shit again--my mental shit, not my cookies--until everything found its place and settled back down like fish at the bottom of a bucket. No sense getting all bent out of shape if there were only circles to run in. Figuring that much out, I poked around the apartment, playing some half-assed detective that really needed his whole ass if he was going to crack the case of the disappearing grandfather. Pretty much as could be expected, that got me nowhere.

I was flipping through a pile of mail, mostly bills, and trying not to think about my rumbling gut, when panic took hold. What set me off was this past due electric bill I came across amongst the assorted junk. It wasn't the fact that I'd found an electric bill, or even that it said we were lucky the juice was still on. No, what really flipped me out was the realization of how out of whack Pops must be.

Pops's daily routine had become pretty much one of the few things I could count on over the years. The old guy would go down and wait on the mail every day. Sure as the sun shines he'd go down and stick around and chat up every poor son of a bitch who had to traverse the lobby during those magical two hours after lunch. And then he might put in another half hour to hour after the mail had arrived, you know, just so he could torture a few more residents with his small talk and rambling stories. But then, once he got back upstairs, the mail was dealt with. Bills were paid and those envelopes didn't have to wait for tomorrow's lobby watch. No sir. Nope. Not a chance. Pops had those fuckers in the mail drop right off. At least that's the way it had been for as long as I could remember. But now here was Con Ed telling me that the old man was off his game. Pops was past due.

They didn't know the half of it.

Another funny thing--not that I ever said any of this garbage was funny, but you know what I mean--as I'd been flipping through the mail, I'd entertained this really naive notion that maybe there'd be a letter from Mom. Mom, the woman who'd left me like so much luggage. No, that wasn't true. People care about their luggage. People go out of their way to claim their luggage. They bitch when they can't find their luggage. They make a stink about it. They keep little tickets in places where they can find them and check on them over and over to be sure they haven't misplaced them and then they elbow one another to be the first to get their luggage and they go to lost and found desks and scream at vacant-eyed clerks when their luggage doesn't turn up at the carousel waiting for them like they expected. Luggage was a big deal.

No, I was gum. Old, spent, chewed up, no-fun-no-more gum. And that's how they'd left me. Like some wad of gum that'd lost its flavor. For whatever reason it hurt most that Mom had done me that way. I guess because sometimes dads, they bail. But moms, they're supposed to always be there. Not my mom. She'd plucked me out and stuck me up underneath Pops to make sure I wouldn't get globbed up to the sole of her shoe and somehow manage to tag along. I'd been too little to keep up with my parents and now I was getting too big to keep up with my Pops. How fucked up was that?

Not knowing what else to do, I put my tweed coat back on--even though it was hot as hell out--crammed the past due electric bill into my pocket along with the check to cover it, grabbed a wake-up and start your day beer from the fridge--since nobody was there to stop me--and stumbled downstairs to see what I could get myself into. Ruffle some feathers. Pay the juice bill. Find the old man.

Even in my piss poor condition it didn't take long. There was a pub just around the corner from the post office where Pops liked to hang, and sure enough, there he was. When I opened the door it was like casting out a coven of vampires. Four or five losers propped up at the bar threw hands over their eye slits and moaned and hissed their displeasure at the shaft of midday light that announced me.

"Kid, what have I told ya? You know you ain't allowed in here," this guy behind the bar yelled at me. I didn't know his name. Pops called him the Bourbon Monkey.

"Like I'd want to hang in this hole, ya Bourbon Monkey," I said.

That should have been it except for one of the losers came to my rescue. "Hey, hey, you know who this is? That's the kid, the subway hero."

There was a hesitation of drunkenness before a few others came around and then they were all cheering and clapping. I'm not sure Pops followed any of it. Actually, by the time they'd finished, I wasn't sure that some of them even remembered what they'd gotten so excited about. Turned out they weren't vampires. That was too good. Blurry-eyed, slurred-tongued, brain dead zombies, the lot of them. I guess it was pretty cool and all to be recognized though.

Bourbon Monkey was pissed. Still, I was a local hero. He waved me off with an angry scowl and a, "You got two minutes, A train."

Yeah, whatever. Big whoop.

Pops was sitting at the bar with this skanky barfly, probably paying for her drinks, and he smiled as I came over. "Hey, Pops, you gotta come home, man," I said, putting a hand on his shoulder.

"That's my grandson," he told her.

"Hola. Hey there, baby Papi! The A train hero!" she squealed.

She leaned in and laced her hands around my arm, her fingernails long and painted white with some fancy little designs like flowers on them. Even over the musty air of the place she smelled of cocoa butter, her only redeeming quality. That was before I caught a whiff of her breath. It was kickin'.

"Yeah, hey, how you doin'," I said just to be polite and all. "Come on, Pops, you coming home or what?"

"A lie is like a shoe," Pops explained to the woman, like he hadn't even heard me.

"A lie?" she asked all perplexed like. She was drinking her bottle of beer through a straw, leaving even more of her bright red lipstick there as she puckered her lips to finish it off.

"Ah yes," Pops explained. "At first, a lie is uncomfortable. It hurts a little to tell it, like new shoes that cramp your feet."

The barfly smiled a knowing smile. I'm not sure if it's because she understood lies, shoes, or both.

"But, just like shoes, after a while, after you have told it for so long, the lie, it becomes comfortable."

"Like the shoes broken in," she said, rubbing my arm to include me and ridiculously proud of herself for figuring such a simple thing out. "Oh, Papi, so true. So true!" She laughed louder than she should and it really didn't do my hangover a bit of good. And neither did the bar, all reeking of smoke butts, spilt drinks, and piss. All that and two blaring televisions at either end on competing channels. Talk about your sensory overload.

"C'mon, Pops," I pleaded.

The bartender came over. "Okay, Pops, you can stay, but get your boy outta here."

I never liked the guy, but really he was doing me a favor. A few minutes later and I got Pops out on the street and we were heading home.

"Have I ever told you about Tony Two Diapers?" Pops said as we walked.

"No."

"*No?*" Pops pushed for reassurance.

I may tune the old guy out a pretty good deal, but c'mon, there was no way I'd forgotten any story about a guy named Tony Two Diapers.

"Most definitely not," I said.

"Oh, well, well, well, then," Pops said, and rapped his cane on the sidewalk. "Tony Two Diapers was a cardsharp," Pops began. "Actually, he was what the fellows called a chip. This was short for blue chip, which back in the day was a way of saying that he was a fix. Rigged card games, you see. Poker. They'd bring old Tony Two Diapers in when they had a mark in town. Usually one of the whales from back out West who didn't know no better. And of course Tony, his name was always something or the other, not Tony. And for damned sure not Two Diapers. Which was a name he got because of the bowel obstruction that came from eating cashews while he played. He refused to leave the table once the cards came out. So after years of holding out during card games, and eating God only knows how many thousands of pounds of cashews, the doctors, they had to cut him open and give him one of those colostomy bags. Live and learn, I say.

"Hated to leave the table and relieve himself like he should. That's how he got the nickname Two Diapers. At first, the fellows called him Tony Diapers, because, like I said, he hated to leave the table. So they'd tease. 'You must be wearing a diaper,' they'd tease. But he didn't. But then later, after he got cut open and they put that bag on him, well then, I don't know, somebody or the other said Two Diapers one night and that stuck.

"Now Tony, he was alright, just the same. Nothing rattled him. He was the best. A real cardsharp. So they'd bring him on the fix. Milked a lot of knuckleheads that way. A fool and his money. You know the saying."

I nodded. I'd seen Pops like this before. This was the old Pops. The Pops I used to know. The twinkle-in-the-eyes Pops. The charmer. He was having one of his moments of clarity, I guess they called it. I was pretty happy to see it. Moments like this were coming fewer and farther in-between these days. When one did come, it always had something to do with something that had happened decades ago. As he was fading into the future my old Pops was fixed on the past.

"Right. Now one night some years back, when I worked for this particular fellow who may have ran these card games, Tony Two Diapers was there, so I knew the fix was in. I didn't play, you see. I had better sense than that. I had started by bringing the drinks and what have you. They tipped me. I brought the drinks, sat in the corner, kept my mouth shut, that sort of thing. Later, which was around this time, I had moved up in the world, because I knew how to behave, and so I was dealing the cards. It was a good skill to have. Used to be I had dreams that maybe someday I could deal cards in a real casino, Atlantic City, or maybe Vegas. But then, as you know, dreams they do not very often come true.

"Now this night in particular, there was this fat bastard who thought he was the real business. Asshole from Detroit. Have you ever met anybody from Detroit who wasn't?"

I shrugged. "I never been to Detroit."

"Me neither. So this fat bastard was losing. This was to be expected. The fix was in, right? Tony Two Diapers and all, like I said. And this fat bastard, he isn't none too happy about getting back on the plane for Detroit with a light wallet. So whatdaya know but he starts accusing me of cheating the game. 'The kid's givin' signals. He's floatin' cards,' Mr. Bigshot Detroit starts whining.

"Waa, waa, waa. Givin' signals. Waa, waa, waa, floatin' cards. This and that. But nobody's really paying the fat bastard much mind. And it is kind of funny, because the game *is* fixed, but thing is, me, I got nothing to do with it. It's all Tony Two Diapers, like I been telling you. Right? So the fat bastard's going on and on, 'Waa, waa, waa,' and the next thing I know, as I'm laying out a new round--he's heads up with Two Diapers, who don't drink, by the way, because then he'd have to leave the table to piss--and whatdaya know but this fat bastard from Detroit snatches me by the neck and starts poking a pistol in my face. Can you imagine?"

As he was speaking, Pops stopped and took up my nape with one hand and brought his hand, cane and all, up to my face to shake his index finger pistol at the tip of my nose.

The old woman who lived across the hall from us, Mrs. Goldstein, she was on the corner making not the least bit of effort to hide that she was very concerned with what looked to be the scolding of a lifetime. Probably thought Pops was really putting it to me.

When Pops noticed her he got kind of irate. For some reason she bugged the old guy. Actually, I guess I know the reason. The woman was a snoop. Pops waved her off.

"That woman," he said to me. "Go home, old woman, quit pestering!" he called out to her. She acted as though she didn't hear him. As though she hadn't been watching us in the first place. Horrible actress.

"Women," Pops said. "That woman," He said, raising his voice, "Heartache, that's all they're good for. Meh!"

I was worried Pops had forgotten why he'd been pinching my neck. The story, it's been going pretty good. "Yeah, but c'mon," I said. "I mean, wow. So…what'd you do?"

"Do about what?"

"The gun in your face. What did ya do?"

"Oh, yes, that. *Me*?" Pops chuckled. "*I* didn't do diddly."

Pops released me finally and patted my shoulder as if to say I was going to be okay. This was a huge disappointment for old lady Goldstein. She shook her head and went back to poking her nose in other people's business.

"Let me tell you, when you fix your eyes down the barrel of a pistol kissing your snoot, well, mister, you tend to seize up in the old thinking department, if you follow my drift."

"I imagine."

"But old Tony Two Diapers, always real calm and collected like a cucumber, a real customer, see. He leans across the table and just as politely as you please he wraps a hand right around the muzzle of that heater and eases it outta my face. Right around it. Can you imagine? Like there's nothing to it," Pops says, holding out a shaky hand to illustrate his story.

"You don't sa--"

"Bam!" Pops yelled and smacked his hands together as he did. He was rather pleased to startle me but good. "The fat bastard pulls the trigger."

"Pulls the trigger?"

“Pulls-the-trigger,” Pops said.

“He shot…”

“Tony Two Diapers is now Tony Eight Fingers. That’s right. Can you imagine?”

“He killed him?”

“Who? Tony? No. But the fat bastard blew two of Tony’s fingers clean off. Pow! Just like that.”

“So what happened?”

“What happened? Tony Two Diapers never did the fix again. That’s what happened,” Pops said with a wink.

“Because, what, he didn’t have the fingers to cheat cards anymore?”

“Nah, nah,” Pops waved me off as if to say I was coming out of left field. “No, because after Mr. Fat Bastard Detroit went back home, and after Tony Two Diapers got out of the hospital, Tony flew himself to Michigan to pay Fat Bastard a visit. Walked right into Sunday Mass, right up behind him and splattered his brains all over his communion wafer. Accidentally clipped the priest in the kneecap.”

“Jesus.”

“Exactly. And then, old Tony Two Diapers, he went over and shut himself in the confessional. Was still there just waiting for the police when they finally hustled in. Went as quiet as you please. Not a peep. Traded that confessional box for a slightly larger one.”

“That’s some story, Pops.”

“Not a story. The truth!”

“No. Yeah, for reals,” I agreed.

“And do you see this here?” Pops said pointing to his pinky ring, a silver band set with a fair-sized stone that I guess might be an emerald. He’d had it forever. Wore it every day. “This belonged to Tony Two Diapers. I found it in my shirt pocket when I got home that night,” Pops said with a pat over his heart.

“You found Tony’s ring in your pocket?”

Pops wagged his cane and held up his other hand to silence me as we reached our building. “The whole finger.”

Chapter Seven

"What's the sudden fascination with Tweed, Chloe? You sweet on him?" Heft scoffed at me.

"No." I took the cigarette from his fingers where it sprouted out from his cast. We sat close, nearly on top of one another. He was resting his broken arm on my thigh and in the dark the cast looked like one of those ghosts made out of a bed sheet. "I'm just curious, okay? He is your best friend. And he did save your life and all."

"Yeah, yeah."

"Yeah. So, honestly…what's his story?"

"Honestly? He's a spud," Heft said.

"Real mature."

I decided against taking a drag. Instead I tossed the freshly lit cigarette over the rail of the fire escape, off into the dark and down onto the sidewalk six floors beneath us.

"Hey," Heft complained and chased after it with a desperate hand. But it was long gone. "What's your problem, Chloe?" he moaned as he watched the cherry stick flip end over end until it splattered on the concrete sending little orange flecks off to die on their own. "Man," Heft continued to mope, leaning over to press his face between the rails. He was seriously an addict.

"Jeez, Heft, you're as bad as my little sister…if I had one."

"You owe me a smoke," he said.

"Don't be such a little bitch, Heft. I told you I didn't like you smoking anyhow. And we aren't even supposed to be on the fire escape either. What if the neighbors tell your parents?"

"You shouldn't curse, Chloe."

"Why? Because I'm a girl?"

"No. Because it's immature. And what's with the tough girl ghetto talk? Please, you're too smart for that."

He was right. I shrugged indifference. That was one of the things I liked about Heft. I knew he was good for me. He stood and turned back from the rail. I liked the way his face looked in the shadows. His chin with its little cleft. Everything chiseled. A little dangerous looking.

"The neighbors are in Italy until the end of the month," he said.

"Italy? Must be nice. So?" I asked again, both to get his mind off of the cigarette I'd wasted and because I really wanted to know.

"So, what?"

I just stared him down.

He sighed. "Well, for starters, there's that fucking coat he wears...."

"Language," I reprimanded.

"Yeah, for reals."

"Hypocrite."

"He was wearing that exact same coat back when I first met him."

I crinkled my nose in disgust. No really. I mean, like that coat must be....

"Must be twenty years old," Heft said, finishing my thought. "It was a hand-me-down from his Pops for chrissake. I mean, jeez. At least it fits now. When I met him we were eight. Eight years old. Thing was down to his knees. Looked like, I don't know what."

"Like a spud?" I offered.

"Yeah. Precisely. Thank you. Idaho gold."

"And you decided the spud would make a good friend?" I said, reaching in with a short tickle.

"A king must embrace his subjects."

I also liked Heft's confidence.

"King? Yeah, right."

"So, yeah," Heft continued, "he was a weird kid. Kept to himself. Ran around up in the park doing God knows what. Normally I'd never have much to do with such an introvert...but, whatever, I guess we got off on a good foot."

"Yeah?"

"I was with Razer over in the park...."

"Razer? That Latino boy he hangs out with?"

"Dominican."

"Whatever."

Heft continued, "Yeah, so me and Razer…."

"How'd he get the name Razer?" I interrupted again.

"That's his name," Heft said.

"No it's not, *Chad*."

"It's what we call him, okay? I don't know. And don't call me Chad." Heft paused to slap down my argument or apology.

It was clear he wasn't going to continue until he got one or the other. With a bit of dramatic flair I said, "My apologies, oh great torch of knowledge, Heft."

He smirked. "That's more like it. So, as I was saying, before being so rudely interrupted, *Razer* and I were over in the park one day, like in the winter, and it's all snowing and stuff, and we see these other kids."

"Who?"

"I'm getting to that. So these kids, like four of 'em, are throwing snowballs and sticks and shit at this squirrel up in a tree, right?"

"Language."

He waved me off. "But it turns out it's not a squirrel. We snuck up closer, right, and turns out it was a kitten."

"Aww…little cretins."

"I know. But that sort of made sense, because I was wondering why a squirrel would sit there and take their abuse, right?"

"I'm promoting them from cretins. What a bunch of little assholes," I said, and then made a big deal of covering my mouth with my hand for the curse.

"No. Sometimes language is appropriate. They were little assholes. Some Dominican kids that Razer knew."

"So…you stopped them, I hope."

"Well, we were going to…."

"Yeah, right. Big hero," I said, punching Heft in his bicep.

"We were just kids, Chloe."

"So what? So were they."

"There were four of them," Heft quibbled. "Plus, like I told you, Razer knew who they were and he said they were real trouble. Delinquents."

"Oh yeah, eight-year-old trouble." I faked a shiver, teasing him some more.

...

The day I first met Razer and Heft I was mad. I was wild mad, actually. Mad with Pops and my mom and dad for putting me out on the tundra like they did. Freezing my keister off, trudging along like Nanook of the North. I had my big red plastic wok of a sled, and I'd found my way into the park and it was a great day to be a kid under those conditions, yeah, true, but, I don't know, maybe I somehow sensed all the bullshit that must have been going down back at Pops. Whatever. So there you have it.

I heard these kids whooping it up before I saw them. I guess I headed their way to see what all the hoopla was about. When I got over the hill between us and first saw them I didn't know what they were doing other than acting like a bunch of idiots, throwing crap up into this tree. Not knowing what else to do I wandered down the hill.

"Hey, wassup?" I said as I got close. You know, classic kid greeting.

One nodded, the rest ignored me and continued harassing the tree.

"What're ya doing?" I asked, but as soon as I did, I saw.

Up in the tree was this kitten, nothing much more than a ball of mewing fuzz. One side of its head was caked in snow where one of the kids had already smacked it good with a snowball. This didn't sit well with me. It was quite fucked up, to be honest. Then, as if that wasn't enough, one of the punks pulled a stick out of the snow and gave that a chuck at the damned thing. That settled it.

It took me a minute to find just the right dead branch in the snow. Oh, about three feet long and just the right thickness; something very baseball bat-like. The sun was almost through with its morning rise and so, kind of like the Arthurian knight Sir Gawain, one of my heroes at the time, I thought my strength was really peaking.

As I charged, I roared something real heroic--I don't recall what precisely--probably like, "Naives and cowards, I smite thee." Yeah, that'd be it.

...

"He said *smite*?"

Heft laughed. "Yeah, see? I told you. A real russet."

"So, like, what happened?"

Heft got his cigarettes out and lit another smoke. I could tell he was taking his time enjoying the limelight, making a fuss over dealing with his broken arm. What an attention whore. I let him take a couple of drags. Along the back of my arm I ran my hand over the cuts hidden under my shirt. Across the street some salsa music began to blare from an apartment. But it wasn't a good time. It was camouflage for an argument between what looked to be a gay couple.

"You know how a cardinal stands out against the snow?" Heft said, offering his cigarette and pulling me back. I waved the cigarette off.

"Do what?"

Across the way, the smaller of the two men smacked the other one's face and it looked like maybe they both started to cry. I wondered why. Not why they fought. Or even why they hit each other and why they cried. I mean, I wondered, why bother? What could be worth so much drama? I dunno.

"Blood red," Heft went on.

"What?"

"Cardinals. Blood red. It looked like a flock of cardinals by the time me and Razer ran down there. Boom, boom, boom!"

"Tweed, he used this snow saucer like a shield, see?" Heft held his cast out to demonstrate. "And he just started wailing on 'em with this stick. It was awesome. A couple of the guys tried to fight back, but they couldn't do shit. He was all shield and sword, shield and sword," Heft said, mimicking Tweed's sword with his cigarette.

"For reals? They were bleeding?" I took the smoke away from him.

"Before they ran away bawling. Yeah. You know it. Copiously."

The music blasted on, but the gay couple disappeared from view when one came to the window and drew the blinds. A few seconds later the lights went out.

"And that's how we got Gawain," Heft said, tapping the glass of the closed window where his cat sat pretending to be disinterested with us. He took back his cigarette--which I hadn't even bothered to have--and we both just laughed.

"Vicious," I said.

...

After I ran those clowns off, that's when I met Heft and Razer. They came running over like a pair of wild-eyed mad men and so I almost started wailing on them too, but

Heft threw up his arms and said something I don't really remember. Something like, "We come in peace," or some stupid shit. I mean, c'mon, who says stupid shit like that anyways? Am I right? We come in peace. Dork.

Chapter Eight

"Scissors is pregnant," I said.

Heft took another bite of pizza and ran his god-awful greasy hand, the good one, through his hair.

I guess I stared at him like he was a nut job. We were sitting in the living room of me and Pops's place. Only, Pops wasn't there. Again. Off tomcatting, I guess. But me and Heft, we'd been hanging and getting shitfaced. Something to do.

"What?" Heft snorted, not to acknowledge my world-shattering proclamation, but in defense of his disgusting table manners. "Nothing drives the babes crazy like a guy who smells like pizza." He winked. Yeah, winked.

"You gotta quit doing that shit," I said. I was referring to the winking, of course. Heft probably thought I meant the greasy hair act. Whatever. He ignored me on both counts.

"You hear me?" I said. "Scissors. Is. Pregnant."

"Who the hell is Scissors?" Heft asked. I'd gotten his attention despite his bullshit front of indifference.

"Don't pretend you're a moron. I mean, any more than you already are."

"What? You talking about Chloe? Chloe's pregnant?" he asked, going for his Academy Award.

"Yeah. You got it. Congratulations. Chloe. Your girlfriend. She's with child," I said.

"How do you know?"

"I saw the test."

"You saw…? Dude, you've never even met the girl," Heft said.

"So." I didn't want to let him in on the truth there.

Heft put his pizza slice down on the lid of the box and sat back. "*So*? So she knows you're a little peeping Tom. How's that for *so*?" he said.

"I ain't no…shut the fuck up."

"Yes you are. But, whatever. What are you talking about, 'you saw the test'?"

"Don't get your greasy paws on the sofa cushions," I said.

"What test?" Heft demanded.

"I told you. Pregnancy test. She's pregnant."

"C'mere," Heft said, grabbing me by the shirt with a glistening hand.

"What--" I protested without really protesting, if you know what I mean, as I followed his lead of Moe-handling me like a stooge down the hallway to my bedroom. He crossed us over to the window and we looked out to Scissors's place.

You could see it in his face that he meant to prove me a liar. There was no way I could have seen something like a pregnancy test from my bedroom's vantage on Scissors. But his defiance deflated quick as some spacey nithead's whippet balloon when he realized that if I'd ever wanted to, I could've whispered sweet nothings to our girl from my window sill.

Across the way, the glow of a twenty gallon fish tank illuminated the dark. No fish were there, but shimmering silvery bubbles came up from a little flying saucer that'd crash-landed into the aquarium's pink and blue gravel bottom. On the wall above the tank was that famous X Files poster. *I Want to Believe* captioned under a grainy photo of a similar, but less cheesy-looking flying disc hovering against the background of this densely wooded hillside. Like what they have out in Pennsylvania or someplace. Chloe was a bit more elusive. She was nowhere to be seen.

"That's Chloe's room?" Heft asked.

"Yeppers."

"But she told me she's never even talked to you. Why would she lie about that? Why would she tell you she's…?"

My boy was so out of sorts he couldn't even bring himself to say it.

Being the humanitarian I am, I set him straight. "We haven't talked. And so she hasn't lied. Man, you are not listening. I already told you. I saw one night--by accident--just a little while back, when she did the test. And, I can testify like in court, there is no mistaking a chick's reaction to those kind of results." Heft was still clutching my shirt with his good hand. I slapped his hand, hard. "Now get the fuck off me. *Dad.* Gonna have two broken wings, you ain't careful."

He let go and wandered out of my room and back to the living room couch, a feeble zombie with too much on his feeble brain. Jeesh, a guy could almost feel sorry for him.

I followed--in my own time--and sat back down in the recliner across from him. I motioned to the pizza box. "You wanna move that?" I said, referring to his abandoned slice. I wanted to get into the box.

Heft lifted the slice off the lid and just plopped it down on his blue jeans. No napkin, nothing.

"Man," I laughed. "You got it bad. Sucks to be you."

"Tweed, I'm impressed," Heft said.

"Yeah?"

"Sure. If you think my life sucks so bad, then that means you actually stopped to think about somebody other than yourself for a nanosecond," he said.

"Not really. But what's the name for half a nanosecond?"

Heft ignored me. He was getting better at that these days. Preparing for his solo flight to college, no doubt.

I got my slice--the last one--even though I didn't need it. My stomach was beyond full and the grease ball between my ribs was clearing the buzz drunk from between my ears. And, truth be told, that was probably a good thing. Of late I hadn't been sure that I even wanted this conversation with Heft. So much for that. My own beer-loose tongue had gotten away from me and taken us there before I even knew better. Maybe Heft was as confused as me and he'd let it all go. Such was my short-lived hope as I munched on crust.

"What would you do, Tweed?"

Talk about your unexpected.

"Do what now?" It was my turn to play dumb.

"If you got your girlfriend…if you had a girlfriend…if you got her pregnant. What would you do?"

"Shit, mang, I ain't nothin' 'bout getting no little chick-ittas preggers." I thought my glib ghetto boy act would get him irked. You know, pissed enough to let it go. Usually worked. This time it didn't.

"But if you did?" he asked again, his voice cracking right in the middle.

I made the mistake of looking Heft in the eyes. That turned out to be like the old rule about going to the grocery store when you're hungry. Which I did quite regularly, since I was the one that handled that kind of stuff for me and Pops, and I was forever putting it off until there was nothing but maybe ketchup and lima beans in the cupboard. Or maybe a better example would be like going to the animal shelter to get a puppy. Only you foul it all up by being stupid and looking into the eyes of one of those older dogs. You know, some desperate animal wise enough to know the score. A scared one. A mutt who somehow knows that it's you who could be his best friend and save him, or, if not--and this was much more likely--it was the end of the line for Old Yeller. But, anyways, I'd never done that animal shelter thing, so....

"Listen, Heft," I said. "Scissors--Chloe--she'll be cool. She'll take care of things. All you got to do is pay for the abortion." As soon as the words came out of my mouth I felt like a real Grade A asshole. I wasn't going to be a best friend and save him. It made me more than a little sick with myself. I didn't want to be this prick. How was it that I painted myself into these corners?

"Thanks, Tweed. You're a saint, dude. I guess you are my freaking hero. Really takes a load off."

"I'm just trying to be realistic here," I said.

"I got enough realism for right now. Thanks just the same."

"Okay."

"I think I love Chloe," Heft said. The words kind of blundered their way out of his mouth like he was realizing it for the first time. Maybe he was. How was I to know for sure?

It wasn't something I was ready to hear, or probably ever wanted to hear. Don't ask me why.

"Yeah?" I said, sounding more than a bit simple if I had to say so myself.

"I'm supposed to leave for college soon," Heft said. "You know how hard that was already going to be? I love her." This time he said it like an affirmation. "I love her, and now this. She hasn't even told me. Why do you think? She's got my baby and she doesn't even tell me...."

And then, great gobbly-gook, Heft started to bawl. Not like hysterics or nothing, but fat face-puffing, snot-inducing tears and that was something else I really wasn't ready for. I mean, where the hell was all this coming from all the sudden?

It struck me then--quite unexpected, and don't ask me why--that I didn't remember the last time I'd seen Heft cry. I'd known him for years and years. And, yeah, I was still good and sloppy even after all that pizza, and being liquored up didn't help the old recall synapses. But I knew that of all people, I should know. So I had to think about things for a second or two. And when it came to me--when I'd last seen Heft cry--my guts just went all cat's cradle on me. Just twisted up inside.

As soon as I remembered the last time I'd seen him that way, I realized how far we'd come, how much had changed.

It went something like this. Back when we were kids, me and Heft liked to play a game we called romper. I'm not sure where that name came from, so I'd have to assume it was something my boy, Heft, originated. Razer, being a prick like he could be, hated to play, so I'm pretty sure it wasn't him. Anyhow, we played romper, and it was this game that was cool because other than using a racquetball or handball--or actually, just whatever was on hand--everything else about the game changed every time we played it.

There was no set place for play; there wasn't any court, no hoop, no goal, no boundaries, and no rules other than the one rule that every time you scored a point you got to make a new rule. Games would start all out of nowhere with maybe one of us throwing a ball in the air and screaming, "ROMPER!" And then, if the victim didn't catch it, the other guy, the one who initiated the game, well, he got a point and got to make a rule. Or, if the guy that was challenged did snag it, then the honor was his. Real simple garbage like say, "left hand." Which obviously meant you could only use your left hand from there on out. Just that simple. But you had to be fair. You couldn't just chuck the ball off into the wild blue and holler Romper. Except for a laugh, of course. We did have a sense of fair play that was, like, the unwritten rule. But other than that, it was romper.

Being kids and all, games of romper rapidly progressed into the realm of crazy and then bounded off the map of good sense with a quickness, getting lost someplace in the hinterlands of stupid. Yeah, in a matter of seconds me and my boy Heft would be hopping around on one leg like idiots, right hand stuck in a back pants pocket and screeching, "WONDER BRA!" All this while trying to catch a handball with our baseball caps after two--and only two--bounces. As could be imagined, romper did not endear us to the other ninety-nine point nine not in on the game. Especially adults. God, how I loved that game.

One afternoon we were screwing around at Heft's, doing I honestly don't remember what. We were the only ones there--I know that--and not so surprisingly, a game of romper broke out. Not only was this an indoor game, but, none-too-wisely, it just so happened to involve a basketball. Into the land of stupid, oh yes, we went there. One thing led to another, as romper would, and, long story short, we accidently broke this vase. We broke this vase and Heft started crying. I couldn't believe it. I mean, Heft's parents were strict, yeah. But it wasn't like he was going to get a beating over it or anything. But still, he started crying and I think we even got into an argument over the whole stupid thing so I left. I don't even know what went down over the stupid broken vase. Probably nothing.

Thinking back on that day and the kind of stupid shit we used to cry over when we were kids and didn't know any better, and seeing him now, all torn up over something really being worth torn up over, what can I say? That got the better of me. I screwed up the courage and walked out of my painted corner. Heft's sarcasm be damned. Maybe I could be a saint. Or, if not a saint, at least a friend. Dissed-to-Peon pity party throwing asshole or not, I'm no bad guy. Honest.

"Hey, man," I said, "all this BS…everything…it's going to be all right. Seriously. People go through this all the time. All-the-time. You guys ain't nothing new. Hey, how ya think I got here? Am I right? You just need to talk to Chloe. It's all you got to do. You love her. Love conquers all."

He stared at me like I'd grown an extra head. Kind of felt like it, too. I mean, the way I was thinking. And then I said--get this--"Maybe you'll keep it. You know, the baby. That wouldn't be so bad. Might even be great. Probably even bring you guys closer together."

"Who are you? What have you done with Tweed?"

"Aw, c'mon."

"No, you come on," Heft said, "What gives? What's all this one hundred eighty turn? Why the sudden…?" Heft said, and finished his thought with a vague, rolling gesture of his hands before turning them to dry his cheeks. By the time he was done he looked like a pizza-greased, blubbery-eyed mess.

Being on a roll and all, I kept at it. "You're my friend. You're my best friend, Heft. Besides Pops, you, and Razer, who else do I got?" My head went all bobble-doll. "So maybe I am just thinking of myself again." And there, with that admission, I realized I wasn't just slinging shit for a change. This stuff that I was saying now, it wasn't just another smart-assed speech. It was the truth. And just like they say, it hurt. But it was a good hurt. That's what they don't tell you. Maybe if I'd known that little redeeming detail before, it wouldn't have taken me so long to get around to it.

"Romper!" I shouted, tossing the last bite of my pizza crust high up into the air between us to where it all but touched the ceiling.

It'd been years. Heft was grinning like a madman before it'd even begun to come back down. And me, I felt pretty damned good too.

Chapter Nine

"It's Little Round Top," my dad explained as if no explanation was really necessary. "I'd give you a hug, but..." he said, gesturing with his one free hand to the battlefield he'd recreated atop his head.

I was back from my third failed attempt to screw up my nerve and actually walk into the Planned Parenthood clinic. This time I'd made real progress. I'd gotten as far as the corner across the street. By the time my water was breaking maybe I'd manage to get close enough to tell you the business hours on their door, or maybe even step foot inside to the...gasp...reception. As I booked it away from the place I tried to reassure myself and actually muttered "baby steps" before even thinking about it. I had to laugh at myself.

Home again, I put my bag down and snapped a mental photo for the ages. Clickity-click.

Dad was on all fours in the middle of the living room, supplicating himself to his 35mm tripod mounted camera. On the backside of his head he wore what was once a cardboard chessboard. He'd carved out a circle into the middle and now his bald spot rose from it like a tanned, fleshy hill of no man's land. Except, that is, for the four hand-painted miniatures currently glued there. They were soldiers from the Civil War. Three in tattered grays and one lone figure, prominently at the crest of my dad's pate, dressed in blue. Pate was my SAT vocab of the day. On the board that surrounded my dad's Little Round Top, a dozen more of each army was arrayed with the little gray soldiers clearly forcing the blue into retreat. One unfortunate blue boy even hung, dangling from the board edge, as if Columbus had been wrong all along.

"So what's his story?" I asked as I took turns pushing my sneakers off with my feet. My dad knew I was referring to the central figure glued atop his head, the prominent, lone blue soldier that was soon to have his fancy uniform ruined by several bayonets.

"That," my dad said with a click of the camera remote in his hand, snapping a photo of his little diorama, "is Colonel Joshua Lawrence Chamberlain, my dear."

"More like Colonel dead meat."

"Hardly. You are sorely lacking in your history lessons," my dad assured me. "Do your old man a favor. Any hair sticking out?" he awkwardly gestured, referring to the long salt and pepper curly locks that hung like a horseshoe around his bald spot.

"Nary," I said, leaning in for a better look. "You want some?"

"What, and ruin everything?"

He snapped off three more quick shots with ever so slight tilts of his head between each and then removed his headpiece and came to his feet.

"Shouldn't you be at rehearsal?" I asked.

"Cancelled. The new conductor, Gunter, went and broke his collarbone rollerblading in the park. Trying to keep up with his nearly prepubescent girlfriend, I'd wager."

"Smooth move, Gunter," I said.

"Who are you? What are you doing in my house, stranger?"

"Nut," I said and hugged him.

Not that I wasn't close to my Dad, but the hug was kind of out of the blue. Probably my hormones screwing with my emotional balance or something. I could tell he knew something was up. Poor guy probably was settling for it being drugs. I was saved by the bell. Literally.

Heft had never been to our apartment. So I was really surprised when I heard him on the intercom.

"It's me. Come down," he said.

I would have, but my dad gave me The Look.

"No, you come up," I said. I buzzed the lobby door before he could argue. I kept the button down to make sure the noise would drive him in.

My dad was still laying down the stink eye.

"It's just my friend, He—Chad," I said narrowly avoiding saying Heft.

"Hechad? What is that, Middle Eastern?"

"No. His name's Chad. Just Chad."

"Just Chad? No last name?"

"Preston. Chad Preston."

"Uh huh. So he's not from the Middle East and he's not some one-name-only celebrity like Prince or Sting. I see. I see. And how is it you know this Mr. Chad

Preston?"

"School."

That was the first thing he'd heard that he'd wanted to.

He nodded with just a smidge of approval. "Good student?"

"One of the best," I said. "Honors. The kind they make the bumper stickers for."

"Bumper sticker material. You don't say?" he chewed his lip as he considered it all. "And are you two, like…?" He twisted two fingers together.

Thank God the doorbell buzzed. I threw open the door and had myself caught in a Chad, Dad sandwich. A Dandwichad.

"Daniel Tobin, Chad Preston," I said, surprising Heft with the introduction. Being the type of guy he was, yanno, alpha, he recovered immediately.

Heft extended his left hand. "Please excuse the cast, Mr. Tobin."

"Clipped your wing, Mr. Preston?" my dad said.

"Please, sir, call me Chad. No, just a little spill. Nothing major. The docs were able to rebuild me."

"You don't say. And such manners. Maybe you can let some rub off," my dad said with a nod my way.

As my dad gave me another look, I couldn't be sure if he knew about Chad's subway fiasco, or if he was still just fretting to know his little girl wasn't the cloistered nun he'd forever thought she was.

This brief encounter was over. I'd revealed Heft to my dad. Baby steps.

"Whelp, as the rabbit says, I'm late, I'm late, I'm late," I said pushing Heft back out into the hall to make good our escape.

"And, as the dad says, don't be late, late, late, getting back home tonight. Nice to meet you, Chad. You'll have to stop by and we'll do it again sometime."

"Sure thing, Mr. Tobin. Really great to finally make your acquaintance," Heft said.

"Yes, *finally*," my dad was forced to throw out through the quickly closing door.

I guess it was a day for introductions. We ran into Tweed coming up just as we were almost down the stairs to the lobby. We stopped on the second floor landing when we did, something that never would've happened if Heft hadn't been there. The two of them started their little hand-smacking ritual.

"Hey, wassup?" Tweed said to me.

"Not much," I shrugged. "You?"

"You two know each other, right?" Heft said. "You must."

Tweed and I answered in unison, "Sure." "Yeah." Then Tweed said, "Sorta," as I said, "Just from, yanno...." and I waved a hand around. We all nodded to agree that that was saying enough.

"Well, hey, I'm Tweed," he said and pursed his lips in this funny way.

"Chloe," I answered. I quickly added, "Yeah, Tweed, I know. Your tag, I've seen it around. It's ubiquitous. That's one of my SAT words for the day. Ubiquitous. But yeah, I've seen it. *Tweed.* My dad's seen it too," I teased. I'd lied about ubiquitous being a SAT word. Just, after I'd thrown it out there like that, it sounded kind of...I dunno. So I'd covered with a little white lie.

"Yeah...about that...." Tweed said, referring to the tagging.

Heft looked perplexed so I explained. "Tweed here tagged our car."

"I didn't..." he started to say, followed quickly by, "Okay, okay, but just the hood."

That kind of broke the ice and we all laughed.

"So I finally get to say thank you to Heft's famous subway hero," I said.

"Oh he's been thanked enough already, believe you me," Heft said.

"Yeah, says you," Tweed said.

Outside the landing, on the ledge of the little grated window, a pair of pigeons pecked at the plastic owl that was mounted there to keep them away.

"Well I haven't had a chance, so..." I leaned over and kissed Tweed on the cheek. "Thanks. For reals. That was like the bravest thing I've ever seen anybody do. Ever."

"God, okay, Chloe," Heft said. "You can give him the key to the city later. We have to run." He tugged me by the arm.

"Let's not be strangers from now on, okay...neighbor?" I said to Tweed and gave him a little wink. I don't know why. I never wink. To anybody. About anything. But I did. Thankfully, before I could regret being so kind of cheesy, Tweed smiled and nodded. And blushed. And when he did, I was glad I'd done it.

When you're pregnant you tend to notice other women who are in the family way. Don't ask me why. Then again, it's sort of obvious, isn't it? You notice strollers and babies in their little urban papooses. You especially notice the newly initiated to mommy-hood who have a man at their side, pushing that stroller, wearing that papoose.

As we left Tweed behind and were exiting the building, we passed just such a couple. I guess I stared a little too hard, too long.

When I looked back to catch Heft watching me, he said, "Yeah, I know."

"Know what?" But it was weak. He just cocked his head and threw me his 'give me a break' expression. "How?" I asked.

I followed his eyes as he looked back to my building. To Tweed.

"Yeah, I guess that figures," I said.

"It's going to be okay. Let's go someplace where we can talk."

...

Keeping track of Pops was beginning to kill me. The only good thing I could count on was the old guy either being over at the bar or rambling on and on to some poor bastard he'd cornered on our street.

I no more than got up to the apartment then I realized I needed to go look for him. That was okay. And--get this--the front door wasn't even locked. But even that didn't really set me off. I kind of was preoccupied with thinking about Scissors for the time being. It was pretty cool of her to thank me. To give me that little peck. She was really something.

As could be counted on, Pops was holding court at his local dive. His was the only voice in the room other than the game going on over the bar when I came in. Nobody even gave me the time of day.

"No, you see," Pops was saying, "After I showed up at Lachlann's, the gentleman seated at the bar recognized me. He was never scared. Never dropped his gun or wet his trousers. All that was a bit of fabrication on my part. A little cover story. No, and would you believe, somehow he knew I was the Saturday night dealer over at my employer's club. Just the one table in the backroom. Private game. Very hush, hush. Restricted to certain clientele. And so a man was told of me and I was taken into the back of Lachlann's to a nice private office. An office with a great mahogany desk. Behind that desk, the kind of man you'd expect to find there. On the desk, this violin case." Pops wrapped the lid of this violin case on the bar in front of him. I nearly flipped when I saw

Pops had the thing with him. The case normally stashed way back in his closet, all hidden. Thank God he hadn't opened it. And this wasn't the story the way I knew it. Not the way I'd heard it a hundred times.

"This man, he did not mince words." Pops said. "Men in such positions seldom do, I've learned. I suppose that's how they get to such places to begin with."

While I tried to decide what to do, Pops went on.

"'Normally, under such circumstances,' the man behind the desk explained with a nod to the cake box I'd been sent with, 'the mealworm who delivered such a package to me would be sent back with his scrotum stuffed in his mouth. That's the common courtesy one extends for such a thoughtful gift as yours.' And he said just that, 'mealworm.' Can you imagine?"

"With only his pinky finger, he pushed this very violin case just a few inches across his great big fancy desk towards me. This very violin case." Pops tapped it with a shaking finger.

He was flanked on either side by his little barfly Dominican girlfriend and this other dude. Skinny weasel looking guy with neck tats and gold chains. Middle-aged loser type. The breed you watched your wallet around. He fit right in with the place.

Pops was full tilt. Even the Bourbon Monkey was engrossed.

"'But I'm going to give you an opportunity,' the man behind the desk said. 'Deal of a lifetime. Deal of the century. Maybe the best deal anybody, any place, any time, ever got. You go and play this little song for your boss,' he said. 'For this, not only can you keep your balls where they belong, between your legs, but I'll compensate you nicely for the trouble of this return-receipt. Are we understood, messenger boy?' this man behind the desk said to me."

"Oh Papi," that's so crazy!" Pops's little barfly squealed.

He didn't miss a beat.

"I finally figured a few things out once I got back into the cab with the violin case. One, was that my employer, this particular gentleman I think I mentioned, he had sent me into the proverbial lion's den. Can you imagine? At first I couldn't. Then somewhere around 145th Street I realized it must be because he thought I was a crook. A cheat dealer, you see. Skimming, or in cahoots with one of the regular players. No good. He wanted me out of the picture. The other thing I didn't so much figure out as discover. It was no violin I'd been given. Inside the case were two snub-nosed, nickel-plated revolvers. Loaded revolvers."

Bourbon Monkey raised an eyebrow to Pops. Then he spotted me. Gave me his best stink eye before turning back to Pops. The old man went on, happy to have everyone's attention.

"This man behind the desk was sending me back to kill my boss, the particular gentleman who'd double-crossed me to begin with. What a mess. To this, I must confess I got a little sick at the stomach. The cabbie kicked me out when I churned up lunch all over his backseat. None too happy, you see. That was peaches and cream with me because I needed some time to think."

"Okay you," Bourbon Monkey said, taking advantage of Pops's pause to rat me out. He pointed to Pops and with a whistle and a finger snap directed us both to split. "That's enough for today," he finished to Pops. "And if you come back, don't bring that with you," he said with a nod to the violin case. "Just to be on the safe side. For all I know, might be a fiddle today but a butcher knife tomorrow."

"Hey, Pops is okay. Just run the kid outta here," Weasel Guy said. "Let the old man finish his story. Have another drink or two."

"No, dice. There's no such thing as a finished story with this guy. He gets to the end and then backs up to retell a whole different version, twice as long."

I ignored the Bourbon Monkey. Weasel Guy, not so much. "Fuck you, skinny," I said.

"You got a lip on you, hero boy." He started to get up. Wobbled under his liquor.

"Leave the kid be or you're outta here too," Bourbon Monkey said. "Not running a daycare here for chrissake. C'mon, Pops, we all had a good time, but now you should head home with your kid, okay?"

"Fine, yes," Pops agreed and got up to leave.

He'd made a few steps from his stool when his little girlfriend reminded him not to forget his violin. I couldn't help but notice asshole Weasel Guy was more than miffed when she did.

Chapter Ten

I was glad it was Tweed who answered the door. I just didn't feel like the whole awkward talking the small talk with Pops thing. He was a nice old man and all, but you know how they are. There's no such thing as a brief conversation with some old bored guy.

"Hey," Tweed said, trying to act all laid back although I could tell by the way he threw the door open he hadn't expected it would be me.

"Nice pajamas," I said. He was wearing an old ratty Toucan Sam t-shirt and PJ bottoms covered in this Han Solo and Chewie print.

"Pops keeps the AC cranked up to like arctic climes, so…."

"No, that's cool. I just figured you to be more of a Luke Skywalker man."

"Luke's a wuss."

"He was man enough to eighty-six Darth."

"The Emperor iced Darth."

"After Luke stomped him like a grape and light-sabered off his hand."

Tweed conceded the point with a shrug. I could see he was a little shy, so I cut to the chase.

"I was going to go for a run. Wanna come with?"

"You run?"

"What's that supposed to mean?"

"Nothing. I don't know. You just don't strike me as the running type."

"You saying I'm fat?" I said playfully.

"You? Hell no. You're smokin'. I mean, you know. No, you got a great body. I just…."

"Yeah, yeah. You're off the hook. So?"

"So…?"

"Do you want to come with? In or out?"

"Sure. I don't know. Yeah. In."

"Great. Meet you downstairs. Unless you plan on going in your jammies."

"Ha, ha. Yeah, just give me a minute to change into my Incredible Hulk running shorts."

"Tasty."

...

"I...got...to...stop," I gasped to Chloe and did just that.

We'd made it all the way to the bay at Inwood Park--I'm not sure of its name, but I suppose it has one. It was the hills that were killing me. If we ran along Broadway, where things were flat, I'd be okay. But Scissors had us running up and over, through the Tryon, and then straight, way into Inwood, both of which are mad with steep grades and twisting stone stairs and whatnot. Brutal. Scissors said she didn't like the traffic fumes out on Broadway or along the Henry Hudson Parkway--which had a jogging and bike path running along it for Christ's sake--and besides, running on the inclines was better for us anyways, she argued. Sure didn't *feel* better. I collapsed on a bench and playfully asked Scissors for a smoke. I'm a real card that way.

She punched me in the arm as she sidled down next to me and I used my spent condition as an excuse to lay my head on her shoulder. Okay, I'll admit it now. I sort of was developing this thing for the girl. I guess it was a crush or something. I don't know. Whatever.

"I know you know," she said. "About me being pregnant and all. And, like, the cutting too...but mainly the pregnant thing."

It was right out of the blue like that. No preface, no preliminary bullshit. I thought about playing it dumb. Maybe saying something smartass. But when I looked up at her and saw the way she was staring out over the water, well, that just changed things. I sat up and noticed it wasn't just sweat dripping down her face.

"Yeah," I said. "Jeez, sorry."

"Why are you sorry? You don't need to be sorry. I'm the one who has to be sorry. I'm the one who fucked things up. Royally."

"Okay, true. But hey, let's not let Heft off the hook here," I said.

"Chad has his own problems. He's scared to death of starting NYU. His parents, they ride him pretty heavy, expect too much. He's talking about going to Europe to backpack for the rest of the summer. Maybe a year. If they'll let him."

Europe for a year? That was news to me. I wondered why.

"You going with?" I asked.

Scissors scoffed. "Yeah, as if. When my dad finds out I'll be lucky if he lets me go to the corner deli alone…much less Barnard…or jeez, anywhere, already."

"Heft. What an asshole."

"He's not. He's just…a kid," Scissors said.

After we were quiet for a bit, and after I kind of held her while she cried a little and all, I asked her, "Do you know what you're going to do? Is there, you know, anything I can do?"

"I dunno. I thought maybe if I didn't think about it it'd just go away," she said, snorting a muffled laugh at her own expense.

"Should you even be running? That can't be good for the baby, can it?" As soon as I'd said it I realized how stupid I'd been. We hadn't been out here running for our health. And the real reason we'd laced up was the same reason that she'd wanted me to come along. I might be slow, but I'm not a complete moron.

She just shrugged and we were quiet again.

People passed us by. All different kinds of people. I mean the full spectrum. And, as they did, it made me wonder what kind of problems those people might have. Because to them Scissors and me probably looked picture-perfect. Just two young people, maybe in love, sitting, holding one another on a park bench on a beautiful summer day. Not a care in the world and it our proverbial oyster. But, man, what did they know. A picture might be worth a thousand words, like they say, but who knew so many of those words could be lies? So that got me thinking, who knows just how fucked up all these other passerby's lives might be? You just never can tell. Am I right?

"I think there's something wrong with that duck," Scissors said.

"What?" I thought she was making a joke I didn't get. Sure sounded like one.

"Out there," she said, pointing out across the water. "I think there's something wrong with him."

Sure enough, there was one of those brown woodland ducks kind of thrashing around and acting all out of sorts. We went over to the water's edge to get a better look and quickly discovered the thing was all tangled up in one of those plastic six-pack rings. It not only had it caught around its neck, but worst of all it'd managed to get a leg caught up in the same loop. It seemed like it was all it could do to keep itself righted on the water.

"Somebody should do something," Scissors pleaded.

I learned a long time ago that if you wait around for somebody else to come to the rescue, you're going to find yourself with a lot of time to twiddle your thumbs.

I would have, under any other normal circumstances, taken my shoes off to go into the water. Unfortunately, the bay edge where we were wasn't so much water as it was a sludge of muck, crazy water weeds, and like a million tons of disgusting refuse. It was the kind of shit only a drunk guy would go into on a bet. So that's where I found myself, sober and with nothing to gain, up to my knees and heading out.

The duck must have been exhausted, because he didn't put up much of either flight or fight. One wing was caught up too, I discovered, and so between that and his free foot, he was reduced to bobbing and making little circles. He was living at the intersection of sad and ridiculous. And doing that just barely, and not for much longer, I imagined. Not really sure how to proceed, I got the idea to throw my shirt over him--which turned out to be pretty damned clever--and I got him back up on dry land with no trouble except for leaving my left sneaker behind when it got sucked off by the bog.

"Oh poor thing, poor thing," Scissors repeated as we sat down on the shore, me with the tangled duck in my lap.

The duck, wanting to make sure he didn't go out quietly, I guess, started quacking up one hell of a ruckus and so a pretty good crowd gathered to make sure I wasn't some kind of sick duck molester.

I was having more trouble than you'd think trying to break the plastic loops. I was especially concerned about hurting old Daffy or freaking him out any more than he already was. That's when an old guy in the crowd offered up his penknife. That was cool. A few seconds and snips later, and Daffy was free and literally flying out of my hands.

The crowd burst into applause and cheers and a handful of little kids started whooping it up, running in circles and hollering their lungs out as if the freed duck symbolized the abolishment of school forever or some shit. The duck kept things going for a minute, acting like he was taking his curtain call, kind of standing out on the water, showboating, flapping his wings and quacking like mad. People patted me on the back like I was some kind of hero and Scissors kissed me on the cheek. Then, like it was all part of some mystic script and the drama concluded, the duck flew off, disappearing around the bend of the Hudson tree line leaving us all to finish our smiles and handshakes before moving on as well.

"You gonna get some tonight!" One of the crowd--this potbellied dipshit--said in a booming voice to me, more than just kind of ruining the moment.

I gave Scissors a look to let her know I thought the guy was being an ass. And even though he was, and even though I was all wet and nasty and kind of smelled a little something like sewage, she took me by the hand and smiling real sweetly said, "Let's go home." So to all those mugs it sort of looked like the guy was right.

I got pretty tired of walking like Quasimodo before we'd even left the bay behind and so I took off my other sneaker and sunk it with a three-point shot into a garbage can along the path.

"It's alright, you and me, we have to stop running anyway," I said.

"Sure. You say so," she agreed.

She was typical Scissors then and took off her sneakers and tied the laces together so that she could carry them over her shoulder.

"Nothin' but socks. It's what the cool kids are doing this summer," she said.

And so we walked home in our socks together that way and that was that. Pretty cool and all.

Chapter Eleven

The mute television, locked in a test pattern of broad strips of color, cast a ghostly blue light around an otherwise darkened room. Me and Pops's living room. Old photos of strangers framed upon every wall and perched along cluttered shelves. A countless mob of mostly black and white, a few in faded colors scattered here and there, and others still, sepia-toned and obviously much older. Some of them from the old country Pops had explained. Women with mustaches, he liked to joke. Some others, actually most I guess, were from his mail route. His work-adopted family he called them. So here they were, muddled faces too dimly lit to recognize even if I had known any of them, which I didn't.

I woke up on the couch. Pops was still asleep in his recliner just within arm's reach. I thought about waking him only to fall asleep again before I could make up my mind and stir myself into action. Not that it mattered. Nothing much had changed when I woke again a little while later.

I grabbed the remote as I sat up and flipped the channel to an actual program. I kept the volume off. It was still a pretty shitty hour for viewing though and so I found myself staring dumbly at one of those home-shopping shows.

Knives. Hunting knives, pocket knives, butcher knives, crazy ninja knives, knives with skulls for pommels, knives with two blades, three blades, knives for throwing, knives with serrated teeth, knives with fake bone handles, knives for divers, knives for chefs, knives for scouts, knives with hidden compartments and compasses. Knives. These bastards had knives. And they were very excited about having all those knives. And even with the volume muted, I could see just how badly they wanted all of us viewers to have their knives too. These two guys with bulging neck veins and animated faces. Stabbing knives into the tables, tree stumps, planks of wood. Running the blades through melons and aluminum cans. Stabbing and cutting everything on the set but each other.

I was pretty zoned out with knives when Pops spoke up. I hadn't noticed when he'd woke up.

"Who are you?"

There was fear in the old guy's eyes. Even in the room lit only by the television, or maybe especially so because of it, I saw the fear. But it wasn't just in his eyes. It was in his voice. Even as he tried to demand again in anger I heard it there. Sneaky little fear creeping around his tough guy voice.

"Who are you? How did you get into my house?"

"Pops, what are you--"

"Get out! Get out of my house!" he yelled.

And there was the fear in his hands as he lashed out at me. He couldn't get to me, but he made this pathetic little jab just the same. The skin seemed translucent in the flickering soft blue light, the veins on the back of his hand like one of those Rand McNally maps I'd sat in the back seat and read to pass the miles all those years ago when I'd came up with Mom and Dad from Florida.

"Pop, Pops…hey, c'mon now," I said, looking to calm him.

Water on an oil fire. He was having none of it and just got worse. And yeah, like some kind of growing fire, it freaked me right the fuck out.

"Get away from me!" he carried on.

He grabbed for the phone, knocking it and the TV tray he kept it on over onto the floor as he fumbled with the old style rotary. Shit spilled everywhere. First time in my life I was glad we had a model from the turn of the seventeenth century or whatever. It wasn't like we needed him dialing 911 just at this particular moment.

Pops made to crack my head open with the handset he'd managed to hold onto, throwing it at me, but when he did, the cord kept it from hitting the mark. Otherwise, it was a really impressive throw for an old guy. The end with the mouthpiece cracked and pieces skeedled and danced across the room as the handset joined the rest of the phone on the floor.

Pops leapt to his feet, took half a second to look for more ammo and then bolted when he came up empty-handed. The whole scene would have been mad funny, except it wasn't. This wasn't some screwball movie. We weren't zany actors hamming it up. This was me and Pops. This was our fucked up life. The old guy was screeching like a nut job as he rushed down the hall and barricaded himself in his room. Literally. The second after the door slammed I heard his dresser being shoved in front of it to block the way. Then everything went silent. That was a good thing, because otherwise somebody in the building was going to be phoning up the law if he kept at it. Probably old bat Goldstein was already doing just that.

...

I wanted to talk to my dad about things. Yanno, everything.

Instead I sat in my room and toyed with my latest razor blade. I didn't make any cuts. I just flipped it between my fingers kind of like a magician with a coin. I expected things would end in a cut if I kept it up, but then that wouldn't really be my fault. Something like that couldn't really be considered, like, intentional.

I thought about the girl at school, the one who had caused all the trouble. I wondered if she was someplace now where they kept her sedated and scoured her rooms for anything sharper than a blunt eraser. Probably. I wondered if those rooms were really all white like they always make them out in the movies. Probably not. Movies hardly ever get anything right in my experience, which is limited, I admit.

I'd sort of forgotten about the razor blade when my dad opened my door with one of those cheating little knocks. Yanno, the kind where they open the door while they're knocking on it. That doesn't count as a knock as far as I'm concerned.

He poked his head in and I could see he was in his tuxedo. I'd forgotten that tonight was the big night.

"Hey, kiddo. Time for me to run. Opening night," he said and held up his French horn case.

The razor blade was motionless on the hand out in front of me.

"Oh, hey yeah, I'd almost forgotten."

"Listen, you don't have to wait up. If it goes well I'll be in late."

"And if the play bombs?"

"Even later," he said with a grin and pulled the door shut.

My dad broke out in song as he left the apartment. It was from the play his orchestra was opening tonight. I knew because he'd been singing it on and off for the last few weeks. I guess that was a good sign; it meant there was at least one catchy tune in the production. That or my dad was just lusting after the actress who sang the lines, "That man of mine is a fine man this time. As sure as the sunshine, shiny as a dime, that man of mine." He was still at it as he left the building. I could hear him as he headed down the walk. I got up and went to the living room window to see him off.

As I watched him leave the family car where it was parked and head for the subway instead, I knew he hadn't been kidding about getting back late. That was okay by me. Poor ol' Daniel didn't get out often enough as it was. Maybe at the cast party he'd woo that actress and really have something to sing about.

He'd been so excited he hadn't even noticed the razor blade.

My dad's a good dad. A great dad. But we all live in our own little worlds, don't we? I read or heard somewhere that we really are all alone. Yanno, no matter how many people are in your life, in the end it's just you. I tried not to think about things like that too much, because all you can think about something like that is how true it is. We all only have ourselves and our own lives. Like the actress my dad was probably going to be getting hot and bothered over from his seat down in the orchestra pit, we all have our own parts to play, our own cues to play off, our own entrances and exits, and that's it.

I stood in my window and looked over to Tweed's. His light was out. That didn't necessarily mean he wasn't home, so I called out to him. I got no answer.

"We really are alone, aren't we?" I said.

I squinted to pierce through the darkness. I don't know if that really helped. Convincing myself it did, I was sure I could read where it said "TWEED" on his bedroom wall. I called out one more time hoping that was maybe all he needed for his cue, but I guess it just wasn't Tweed's turn to take the stage.

But I couldn't screw around anymore. I had bags to pack.

...

The plan to take the bus had been Heft's contribution, going had been mine. Sort of. We weren't eloping or anything even remotely romantic, but that was fine by me. The second Heft mentioned it I was all over the idea. He didn't care where we went, he was just glad to be getting out of the neighborhood. He was, like, petrified that the CC181 were going to get him again, so leaving was a great solution and the sooner the better. Me, I was really starting to show, that's why I was ready to split. I hadn't left Manhattan since the last family vacation when my mom and dad were still together. I'd done a good job of forgetting about all that, but with the schemes Heft and I were formulating, the memory of that little family drama, that disaster, kept creeping back around. Dramaster. I hoped this trip wouldn't be a repeat.

I guess I'd made a mistake a few days before when I mentioned Tweed saving the duck. Heft kind of blew up. I'd never seen him that way. He accused me of having something for Tweed. I told him I didn't but he just kept on. He cursed Tweed and even threatened to kick his ass. I guess it was a good thing he wasn't there. Heft finally calmed down after I agreed to leave town with him.

Anywho, if it'd been up to me, and if we'd had the money, we would have flown. But Heft was footing the bill, so I left it up to him. He was persistent that the bus was better anyway. He was still going down his list of pros for taking the bus as we sat in the George Washington Bridge Bus Terminal at 175th Street waiting for the 10:20 pm announcement to board.

"The road trip is an American tradition, a rite of passage, practically an institution, Chloe," Heft said. "This will be something you'll remember for the rest of your life. A plane? Phewff, forget that. The only way that'd be exciting would be if we crashed."

"Nice."

"But a road trip?" he kept on, "Riding the bus across the country? I'm telling you, we're going to see things, places, people, the real America. It's going to be an *experience*."

Heft was poring over a road map he'd picked up in the gift shop. Yanno, comparing it to the bus schedule and itinerary and stuff, running his finger along the little lines of highways and turnpikes like he wanted to be prepared in case the driver succumbed to zombies or terrorists or something and it was suddenly left to him to get the bus to safety. It was really cute. He sort of reminded me of my dad.

It's funny how people can surprise you. I dunno, you think you know somebody. When I'd talked to Heft about being pregnant, instead of this crazy blowout I'd anticipated, the worst I got was, "Yeah, we were stupid." He elaborated with no prodding whatsoever that Tweed had told him. And while I blathered on and on, he listened, really listened, only interrupting to correct me that it was more PC to say *we* were pregnant. I almost said something stupid about how was he so sure he was the daddy. Yanno, just to bust him a little, or maybe to, I dunno, lighten the situation, but then I just sort of clammed up. Thank God. Instead of the fight I'd been so worried about, he was so sweet. Until like a week later, that is. After the deal with the duck and all. So we fought about that, and then we made up, and then within the half hour we'd put the final touches on our "escape from New York" plan. That's what Heft dubbed it. Just like that old cheese-ball movie all the guys like.

We still had almost a half hour to wait. I was munching on a bag of caramel popcorn and chewing my nails, nervous I guess that my dad was going to come bursting into the place with like a bazillion cops and my guidance counselor. If I could have pulled it off, I might've gone to the bathroom and maybe done a little cut or two. Just to take my mind off things. I guess I could've gotten away with it, but mainly I didn't want to stoop to being caught dead in some Port Authority *facilities*. I mean, how sick.

"What's that?" I asked when Heft pulled a paperback out of his backpack.

"This?"

"Nooo," I said. Yanno, sarcastic like.

"This is what my people call a book. It's a rather clever invention involving wood pulp that's been processed into very thin sheets upon which text and images can be printed. It comes nicely bundled and bound by both a front and back cover for ease of conveyance. Pretty nifty, huh?"

"Ha, ha. You're so clever, Mr. Preston." I punched him in the arm. Just a love tap. "Give it up."

"Jesus, but you primitives sure rile easy."

"Give it," I repeated, and took the book from him without waiting.

"I wanted something on childcare and baby stuff," he said. "I looked. Zip. I guess the day-to-day clientele frequenting Hudson Books here in the fabulous Port Authority creates little demand for the subject. So instead I got the next best thing."

Raising an eyebrow of condescension I held it out to him and read the title aloud. "*Death Train*. Really?"

The author's cheesy, made-up name, Neil Goreman, was in this medieval dagger font, stabbing about dangerously above your run-of-the-mill hurtling, demon train. Of course it had a giant skull for an engine, and a gaping maw of blood-dripping teeth for a cowcatcher, and long, gangly subhuman arms cranking the wheels. So then, it was just a bit more inviting than Amtrak. The blood was embossed and leapt out in a shiny metallic scarlet, same as Goreman's name, of course.

"I can't believe trees died for this. Should be a law," I said.

"What? It's spine-tingling," Heft defended, pointing to the cover blurb that made the same claim. "And it seems so fitting. I mean, sure, if it was *Death Bus* then that'd be perfect, but it's still pretty close."

"Great, tree-killer supporter," I said. "When you're finished with it you can mail it back to my dad. Make him your accessory or accomplice to lumbercide or whatever they call it. He loves that kind of tripe."

Heft was staring at me for what seemed the longest, and I was wondering if I had popcorn stuck to my face or something, when he said in this quiet voice, "People are going to be falling in love with you your whole life."

It was one of those out-of-nowhere type things. For a boy who couldn't get around to saying the three little words every girl supposedly wants to hear, Heft sure knew how to do one even better.

I tried to get away with pretending like he never said it. Or, that if he did, that I hadn't heard him. But he just sat there with his beautiful little dopey eyes, cleft chin, and confidence. He could be irresistible that way.

"Yeah, people do a lot of stupid things," I said, the words kind of tripping over one another as my tongue evicted them from my mouth.

Heft just smiled and let it go. "I got this for myself," he said, passing the most recent copy of Cosmo into my lap. "But I guess sharing is caring."

"My Romeo."

"There are some tips for keeping me hot and bothered in there. Expect a quiz later."

"I forgot my number two pencil."

"That's okay," he said with one of his trademark winks, "you can take the oral."

"You wish. Really. You are so broke."

Across the station, through the crowd of usual whack-jobs and whatnots, I spotted a homeless man putting down cardboard and blankets and stuff on the floor. He was making himself a little bed right there in the corner of the bus station and nobody paid him the least bit of mind. Not even the cops or the janitor types. People just looked right through him. And like that comment Heft had just made about how people would always see me, I realized people would never see this sad homeless man. He'd just have to do the best he could to keep living until one day he wouldn't be around to not be seen anymore. I guess that scene troubled me and maybe I started to cry a little. Things were stressful, yanno?

"Hey, you scared?" Heft tried to console me.

I shrugged him away. "Me? Naw. I get pregnant and run off with my boyfriend all the time. I'm all but a professional at this sort of thing. Nothing to it."

"That's a relief," Heft said, slumping back in his seat. "Because I'm a little freaked."

I was thankful Heft wasn't going to try and play up being macho or whatever. Maybe later, I dunno, but right now just wasn't the time. As I watched the homeless man finish getting ready for bed, he caught me staring. It kind of startled me too, because although I'd been staring, I'd also been like everybody else and really more like just looking through him. The man paused, kind of surprised I guess to see somebody looking right at him, and that's when I realized he wasn't a man at all, but a woman.

She turned away from me and disappeared into her bed of blankets and cardboard.

Clickity-click.

...

Someplace upstate, in the Allegany Mountains, nestled up in the woods of one of the larger state parks, my family, or really my dad, I guess, had discovered a bunch of quaint little cabins available for rent. It was one of those serendipity things that just happened during the final days of our vacation. Six or seven simple little cabins huddling close together, all picturesquely bordering a stony brook that meandered and babbled like in the fairy tales. Honest to God, it was like something stolen right off a greeting card. A sappy greeting card, yanno? The kind your grandmother would choose from the rack with an approving little sigh of delight.

Smitten with the place on sight, my dad pestered and pleaded with my mom like a kid wanting a candy bar until she acquiesced, and so that was the setting where the Tobins would bring the curtain down on so much family drama. It would be our last vacation together as a family of father, mother, and daughter under one roof.

I admit it. I probably recall the place more sweetly than it deserves. I even cheat with the old brain camera. But that doesn't hurt anyone except maybe me, providing more angst for my blahs.

Anywho, the cabins were identical. Sure, each one had its own charms and individuality, maybe a slightly sagging front porch here, or maybe a missing window screen there, you get the picture. And each was painted in a faded, almost melancholy, olive green. If not melancholy, then perhaps a bit military. Probably too military for some, but very park-like just the same. So they were these simple little things offering only the most basic comforts; a roof overhead, a fireplace to keep warm by, and a mouse of a kitchen that was really no more than space for a sink. A sink with no faucet, I might add. Very little else. Not even bathrooms. For that business you had to tromp over to this small building just off across the dirt road. Gross, huh? Not wanting to tarnish things I'll call those amenities rustic and leave it at that.

The cabins didn't have furniture, unless you wanted to count a pair of single-mattress cots in the bedroom. These were thread bare and worn, and, in my mom's opinion, "Depressing as a malodorous old couple wasting away, and best left to die," or something like that. To me they were cute, fitting, and smelled more of slightly damp hay. That last detail was something I always found cheerful in my own twisted fashion. I dunno, maybe something to do with all little girls loving horses or something.

One detail that did set one of the cabins distinctly apart was way cool but you'd never have known it unless you went inside. In what would otherwise have been the nicest, since it was closest to the gurgling stream and probably in the best condition, this one cabin had countless graffiti covering every wall inside. I'm talking thick bold marker, ballpoint pen, pencil, paint, carving, scratched, you name it. The worst was all but cleaved into the wall by knife, or maybe Freddie Krueger's claws, or something.

Most of the graffiti was your old tried and true testaments to those who'd passed that way before us.

On walking in, my dad read from over the fireplace, "Bobby Wuz Here 1971," and then he just stood there like he was in a gallery of the Met or MOMA or something.

We spent the next few minutes--even my mom--checking it all out and even reading it out loud to one another. I took a ton of brain pictures to boot.

"Claire n Teresa were here!" In the kitchenette, that is, and apparently very happy about the fact.

"T-bass in da house june 89" In this case I suspected Mr. Bass used a hatchet or machete, as the inscription took the whole of the living room wall and was at least an eighth of an inch deep where it went shallow.

Others recounted how time had passed for the previous occupants.

"We came We drank We got drunk as Hell! Dave Jim Tony Matt Annie Spring Break Class of '77 Baby!" My parents' peers and scholars to the last, no doubt.

The ones that said something of their time there, they mostly were these declarations of discovery or some kind of adventure.

"I caught a two pound trout in the stream. Hank N. Carolina"

"my daddy seed a bear jinny"

"Mama got lost in the woods Terry Wilson."

"A skunk live under this cabin!" And in the same crayon, "I hided a quarter somewheres in this cabin! Michael Purdy"

So young Mr. Purdy thought to send us on a treasure hunt, I suppose. Too cute.

A few messages had been left behind to give a shout out to a favorite band or musician. And for some strange reason, that to this day I have never satisfactorily fathomed, these were mostly to be found in the bedroom and were either country or heavy metal.

"Ozzy Rulz!"

"Black Sabbath" This too in rather a machete-like font.

"Hank Williams is the man" In cursive, and pencil no less.

"Iron Maiden I am Eddie!"

"Tina Golby loves David Hasslehoff!" This followed by, "NO SHE DON'T!"

But there was also your run of the mill, true proclamations of both love and heartache.

"Ken & Holly"

"Wendell loves Venice"

"Karen -n- Tim 4 ever!"

"Ward hearts Julian" And this matched sweetly by, "Julian hearts Ward"

"I love Heather Walters even if she don't never love me"

"MATT + ANNIE"

And, almost hidden away, squeezed into a small valentine heart was "Annie + Jim."

I say, "almost hidden," because protruding from the wall--straight out of the heart that contained the two lovebirds' names--was the better half of a bent nail. It was really rather ominous the way it pierced through Jim's name, obviously having come *after* the valentine, jutting out from the right cheek of the heart as if pinning it there. I don't know much about nails except to say it was a serious shank that would've required a good pounding to have crippled it so. Nasty business love. Creepers.

My dad was in the bedroom using the ballpoint pen from my mom's checkbook to add "George Frideric Handel" to the wall. That's when the storm broke.

"What're you doing?" my mom asked him, appearing in the doorway.

"Adding Handel. The classics are sorely underrepresented amongst this lot."

"Daniel Tobin, you bitch and moan night and day nonstop about the graffiti in the neighborhood, and now here you are.... Is that my pen?"

"I don't *bitch*. And besides, this is different."

"Different how?" my mom wanted to know.

"Well...it's indoors for starters."

"Just, do me a favor, put my pen back when you're done," she said.

He probably shouldn't have offered, "I don't think it works anymore."

My mom shook her head in exasperation and left him there, inkless to dot the umlauts over Handel's A. Poor old Danny boy.

We didn't speak through dinner. Or, I should say, my mom didn't speak...to either of us. Don't ask me what I'd done.

Although I suppose I did escalate things as the three of us cleared the table.

"I'm bored," I said.

"Me too," my dad played along.

"I wanna do something," I said.

"We are doing something," my mom snapped.

"Something fun," my dad countered.

"I know," I said, "We can find a good spot and carve all our names in the wall."

"No," my mom said, and that was that. And that was the last she spoke for like the entire vacation. Okay, probably not, but it felt that way.

I don't mean to imply that my mom went mute. A few words were said here or there. She still could muster up "yes" and "no," and even the occasional "thank you" punctuated these. Frequently a "fine" or an "I don't care" was substituted in her limited repertoire of truncated replies after that initial night of coldness that I guess my dad and I thought would blow over.

It wasn't the writing on the wall that led to the writing on the wall, as my dad had explained to me much, much later, but more the straw on the camel's back, to be more precise with his clichéd metaphors. He'd go on to tell me their failed marriage was a long time in the making, fading like a final note, decaying bit by bit until the two of them were merely sitting alone in a darkened theater pretending something was still out there in the stale air to listen to. My mom, he said, had broken their stupor and decided to usher herself away. That had been told to me by him three years and two bottles of red wine later.

As we were all loading the car to go home.... Actually, just as we'd finished loading the car, my mom found her voice. She thought it was safe to talk alone to my dad, that I couldn't hear her from inside where I'd been sent to do one last sweep of the cabin for our things. I could. I watched them from the living room window, framing them like they were my own private soap opera.

"I'm leaving, Daniel."

"If you don't mind I'll be coming with," my dad offered with a smile.

"No. I'm leaving *you*. Us. After we get back I'll be going to Denver. Chloe starts summer camp. As soon as she's off I'll fly out and get things settled and be back before she comes home. We can break the news to her then. I'll stay until the school year starts."

"Beth, what are you...."

"I can stay with my sister while I look for a place. I've made up my mind."

"I--"

"I think Chloe should stay in New York. You can keep the apartment...for Chloe's sake. Maybe after she's on her own we'll deal with it then. I don't want to uproot her, make matters any worse than they might be," she said.

My dad tried once more, despite the finality in her voice. "Beth, where is this--"

"I'm calling it quits, Daniel. I tried to make it through to seeing Chloe off, until she was through school, but I don't think that's even for the best anymore. Certainly not the best for me. So that's that. I want out. I hope we can make this painless for all of us. For Chloe."

"Out? You make it sound like.... Where did this come from, Beth? Don't you still love me?"

It felt like I was watching a bad actor, to stick with my soap opera metaphor. I wanted my dad to have better lines. Or, at the very least, better direction. I gave the episode two stars.

"I will always love you, Daniel. But not in the way...this, what we're doing, it just doesn't work anymore. You know that. I know you do. Stop being the wounded, helpless romantic and let's just do what we should have done years ago."

"I'm not helpless."

And then she smiled. Not like a cruel thing, but a genuine sliver of happiness, brought about I thought--hoped--maybe by her remaining affection for my dad.

"Daniel, remember whale-watching out at Montauk, when I told you I wished I could be that great, incredible finback we saw that day? How I wished I could trade places?"

"Yes. Of course I remember."

"And you said that if I was, then you'd be the sea, and so that way I would never be away from you?" she said.

"I meant it."

"Daniel.... Really now."

I didn't think it then, but I'm not a kid anymore and so I know it now. She was right. Not that being right mattered a whole lot. But, about that stuff, she was right.

My dad told her he needed a minute and would meet her back out at the car in a couple minutes. I busted it back to the bedroom and I heard him go into the kitchenette. Pretending I didn't know a thing I went in there a second later and found him leaning his forehead against the little space of wall that didn't have shelves. It was the spot where "Claire n Teresa" had let the world know they'd been there before us. He hadn't noticed me come up and suddenly he started pounding on the wall. Then, really weird, like some sort of a response from heaven or something, a coin plopped down from the slats of the wall and fell to the floor. It was a quarter. I watched transfixed as it rolled in a wobbling little circle like it was caught in orbit around my dad's ginormous feet, until finally it came to rest against the toe of his shoe. He looked at it and then he noticed me. His face red, his eyes really sad.

"What do you know," he said. "Little Michael Purdy's hidden quarter. All found."

Later, like for the next few years later, whenever my dad was cornered into the awkward explanation of his status as a divorcee, he'd say he was down a wife but still up a daughter and twenty-five cents. Nobody ever got that one except me. It was surprising, or maybe more like disappointing, how many of those people still pretended to laugh like they had gotten his little joke though.

People can be so fake.

...

Estranged is one of those great words that really kind of sounds just like what it means, yanno?

Heft was snoring along with what seemed like the rest of the bus. Except for there was this little girl a few seats behind us in the gloom who kept letting her frazzled mother and everybody else know that she was wide awake and planned on staying that way. I'm talking a real brat. A few times over the past hour the man just in front of Phone-it-in-Mommy and Princess Intolerable had bitched and moaned about how the little girl was kicking the back of his seat. Each time he did, Phone-it-in-Mommy pleaded with Princess Intolerable, "Maya, sweetie, don't be kicking that man's seat no more." But all that accomplished was nothing.

I didn't really care though. Like the little princess, I was wide awake too.

The pungent smell of an orange being peeled by one of the other passengers drifted over us. Talk about your pleasant surprises. It was way out of place, far too clean and fresh for the stale and icky stink of the bus and the kind of people that rode it. I guess now I was officially one of those people. A bus person. A burson. Thanks, Heft. I elbowed him and he chortled-snored but didn't wake. I wondered how long the stench of the bus stayed with you after you got off. A lifetime, I imagined.

I was letting myself get as midnight blue as the city we traveled through, welcoming and exploring my inner landscape of depression along with the sprawling urban decay the bus jostled and wrestled with. I felt poetic. I felt maudlin. I felt like one of those girls who found the drama in everything and wallowed in it. One of those girls who jots every melancholy thought down in a diary.

I thought a lot about what I'd say to my mom when we got to Denver to pass the time.

Maybe we weren't officially estranged. I mean if you went by the dictionary definition of the word. But we were definitely emotional strangers to one another. Yanno, like, emostranged. I might as well have been someone else's daughter; her, nobody's mother.

So I cried quietly, throwing my own little private pity party, and watched my reflection in the window. Tears migrated either down my face or through the passing collage of the city, all depending on which way I focused my eyes. Ratty boarded-up buildings, vacant lots and the drunks, meth heads, and crack whores who called those places home were all one with my tears. Seemed about right. I think it might have been Pittsburg.

These people we passed on those dark streets were what my dad called bad pennies. So I called them bennies. I could relate to that because when I was little I used to collect pennies and so I picked up every penny I came across; unless, that is, it was face down. Everybody knows those pennies are bad luck. So it was no surprise that so many of the people outside my window seemed to all keep their faces down. Why did there have to be so many bennies in the world?

I wished Heft had asked me why I wanted to go to Denver. He hadn't. I mean, yeah, my mom was there and he knew that and all, so that would seem to make sense, except for I'd explained to Heft the situation between her and me a million times. So I figured he might think it was sort of odd me wanting to run away to see her there and all, but, no. Boys don't really listen, do they? So there goes your reason for me looking to hook back up with old Moms.

The way I saw it, my mom probably was the best person in the world to help me with my predicament. I'd figured it out a long time ago that her real problem wasn't with my dad. Her real problem was that she never wanted me. Well, not me in particular, but any kid. She was one of those women who simply didn't have the whole maternal thing.

Between that and the fact that I was her daughter, that made her the perfect candidate to help me sort things out, yanno? If anybody could sympathize it would be my mom.

It wasn't a perfect plan, though, I'll admit that much.

I was kind of bummed, worried about my dad, for starters. I knew he was probably going out of his biscuit with worry, him being one of those high-strung types and all. There was no way getting around that though. First off, there was no way I was going to tell my dad I was preggers. Second, he would never have let me head off to Denver with no good reason. Not in a million. At least not without running the whole thing by my mom first, and I was pretty sure she would have said pass, thank you very much. And for certain I couldn't call my dad until we were there. I knew my dad, and he'd have every law enforcement agency on the planet chasing us down if he had even a clue of a clue of where I might be.

But being not a complete waste of a daughter, I did leave him that clue. Well, not even a clue really, since it was a note that pretty much explained things. It was a postcard that was years old and never used. From our family vacation. I found it when I was going through one of my shoeboxes looking for this other picture I had that I needed. Anywho, the postcard was from this make your own cider orchard upstate. On the back I wrote:

"Don't worry. I'm okay. I'm going out to see Mom in Denver for a little while with my friend Chad. I'll call when we're there. Love, Chloe"

I didn't want my dad to find it right off and so I hid it in his underwear drawer one pair down.

Just like the card explained to my dad , we'd worked it out that during our escape from New York plan that I'd call him just as soon as we were safe and sound at my mom's. Like Heft said, what're a few days? I wasn't too keen on the idea at first. But Heft kept repeating that it would be no biggie. After a bit, I caved. Yeah, before I knew it I was thinking just like him. So until we made Denver, Daniel Tobin was just going to have to fret. Play his French horn extra loud. Drive the neighbors bonkers. Sorry, Dad.

Then there was my mom. I was actually on my way to see her face to face for the first time in what seemed forever. I kept thinking about how I treated her with the photo albums I cut her out of right before she'd left us. When you're hurting, sometimes you lash out and try to make others hurt too. Or so that's the story my dad tried to sell me.

Truth is I was really just kind of a bitch to my mom when she left. But I was a kid then. I was way more mature now. So, I dunno, maybe out in Denver I could find a way to make it all up. I had one starter idea.

Chapter Twelve

The next morning Pops was fine. Like nothing at all had happened. Go figure. I fixed us our late breakfast of eggs and refried beans and then I split out to go goof around. I thought about asking Pops about the big stink the night before. Yeah I was almost that stupid. He was better and so I got smart and left it at that.

I went over to Heft's. His sister Preenie, home from college or wherever, told me Heft had gone out to the Hamptons the day before to stay with some friends for a while. So he was ducking me. What a lump.

Razer's mom, or "Moms" as he called her, said she didn't know where Razer was either, so that was no help. One of his little sisters, Lily, pestered me to take her to the corner store so she could spend the seventy-six cents burning a hole in her pocket. So, with mom Rodriguez's permission, I took Lily by the hand and we made the corner store and back. I got me a nickel Tootsie Pop out of the deal without even asking. Not too shabby. She's a sweet kid.

After that, I thought about going back up to the apartment to see Scissors. Thought about it, but didn't. And I don't know why I didn't. I hadn't seen her lately and she pretty much occupied a lot of my thoughts and all. Whatever. Instead I grabbed a train up to the Bronx to look for suitable rooftops to bomb. I got off at the end of the line, Van Cortlandt Park, where I wasted the day tagging here and there and doing a bunch of nothing. Had Chinese for lunch and worked on my tan. Talked to some girls who, turned out, were pretty snooty. Threw the football with these two noisy kids I didn't know from Adam. Read the paper. Shit like that.

It was around eight or nine when I headed home. The sun was spent. The old Dominican dudes were breaking out the folding tables and chairs to play dominoes and get drunk out on the sidewalks of Broadway. By chance I was passing Pops's dive hangout and thought I'd save myself a return trip by sticking my head in. Sure enough, the king of the neighborhood was holding court. And it must have been good because they even had the televisions turned down for a change.

"The room reeks of Pine Sol," Pops said. "My boss, this particular gentleman, he likes it that way. He's got a thing about germs and he likes that the stench of the cleaner makes the other card players ill. So it's a win-win. Like anything, you get used to it. You get used to it that is until somebody reminds you about it, starts harping on it."

Hanging on Pops's every word are the usual suspects. Band of losers. Weasel Guy, Little Dominican Girlfriend, Bourbon Monkey, this other old guy at the end of the bar.

Pops went on. "My boss says he's gotta tell the woman to stop using so much Pine Sol. He keeps pestering the other players with 'Can you smell that? Jesus, mother of Mary. I got resin collecting in my sinuses here,' he'd say. Across the table the fat asshole from Detroit blinks. I think maybe he's not looking at his cards so much as through them.

"My boss keeps up his magic. 'You in? What, that damned Pine Sol giving you the vapors? Make up your mind. You in? You out?' But the asshole is wise. Too wise."

"Tony Two Diapers is out, so what does he care? Except for the fact that he's the fix, that is. So Tony does his part fiddling with his colostomy bag like he'll be doing all night. Part of the act. No one likes to watch a man fiddle with his colostomy bag, so it makes for a nice muck, a place to stash cards. And Tony not only has that working for him, but he also has the good sense not to slip the big action into his hand. A guy remembers when he gets beat with aces, queens, and kings, but far less the wiser when they lose to a full house of sevens and nines."

Bourbon Monkey wagged his finger at me when I went to sit at the end of the bar. So I walked over to Pops who smiled but kept on with his story.

"Mike the doorman dropped the ball. He didn't stop this woman. When she barged in, I was surprised not just by the woman, but also by this child she brought with her, this boy with heavy eyelids. She clung to him and him to her as if he were an infant, even though he wasn't. Big boy. And the thing about this woman, the thing I remember most about her now was her sad lips. Sad because they were thin, hardly there at all, offering nothing for a man to kiss. I've always remembered thinking that."

Little Dominican chimed in, "Oh Papi, that is sad. More sadder is when they got no butt." She laughed like a hyena. Weasel Guy laughed too. Loudly.

"No, no," Pops said, getting a little agitated. "This is serious now. This woman, she is demanding to know which one of us 'bastards' was the particular gentleman I worked for. Of course she asked for him by name but she did not know which of us was him, you see."

"Well I can tell you, the card game came to an abrupt halt. I paused the dealing, placed the deck on the felt, put my hands palms down. They were sweaty. The game brutal. For the eighth or ninth time of the night, several thousand dollars in chips rose up from the middle of the table."

"Big rock candy mountain," Bourbon Monkey mused.

Pops ignored him. "Tony Two Diapers, he's folded. The monster pot is a contest between the fat bastard from Detroit and my employer. Another man called Stan--which wasn't his real name--he's already been run out of the game. As usual, gone home to lie *to* the wife, never *with* the wife. Little did he know, his bad luck at cards, best luck he ever had. Things were about to get real ugly.

"Eight people were in the room when the woman burst in with her son. Let's see, there was fat bastard from Detroit, him and some muscle he'd brought along named Mitch, I think, a small, gimpy fellow who liked to clean his fingernails with a penknife. Sometimes muscle is found at the end of a steady gun barrel, see. Then there was Tony Two Diapers, like I said, Ed the bartender, Del and Ernesto, the Guirelli brothers who were my boss's guys--they shared a brain between them--then there was myself, and my employer. Everyone except the asshole from Detroit they was all watching this woman. Dashing in right behind her followed Big Mike, the private room's doorman.

"Between my feet, the violin case fumbled around. I'd told my employer I found it in the cab. 'Lucky you,' he'd said. 'Those things can be worth money. I'll have a look at what you have in there later,' he'd said. So now my feet kick at it nervous like and I just wish to forget it's even there. Wish I'd never brought it in with me.

"Of course my employer was surprised when I'd come back. He thought I couldn't tell. As if I were blind to the pinched look of his face, fumble in his voice, the unnecessary scratching behind his ear. Dealing cards has me noticing those little somethings, little tells, when they show, you see. 'Big game tonight,' was all he'd said after asking if I'd made my delivery. 'You up for it?' I'd nodded and he'd played it off like that'd been that. It hadn't, I knew, but what was I going to do? I played along until I could get a fix on things. Now here we were with a monster pot and an unexpected interruption.

"Big Mike the doorman claims the woman tricked him, his thick finger stabbing accusations, a puckered up wounded expression stealing his manhood. Looking like a kid in the back seat complaining to mama that sister pinched him. I remember music from the bar down the hall started up behind Big Mike, his feeble excuses drowned out before he could finish. A tune I don't know anymore, I can't recall. Probably something good. We always had good bands, great music, in those days.

"This woman kept shrieking, 'Which one? Which one?' She's demanding to know which of us is my boss, you see, the particular gentleman I worked for, a man who was certainly not going to be pleased by such a poorly-timed, ear-splitting interruption. Big money on the table. Monster pot. Like the tenth or eleventh time for the night. Shrieking. Oh, the shrieking. Big Mike letting this banshee barge in. Guns on the table. Can you imagine?"

"Guns on the table?" the Weasel Guy butted in. "When did guns get on the table?"

Pops was never one for being called out on one of his stories. Looked like he wanted to give Weasel Guy a poke.

"You see?" Pops said. "That's what happens when you take off your comfortable shoes…. Everybody notices the stink."

"You had guns?" Little Dominican Girl asked with wide eyes. She squeezed up to him.

Bourbon Monkey was acting like a human being for a change and fixed me a coke. "Here ya go, kid."

"Thanks." I slid a dollar across the bar to show him I knew how it worked. Maybe a bit of bridge building.

"Knock it off," he said, and waved the bill off. "On the house."

"Yes, there were guns! That's how they all got themselves killed!" Pops suddenly pounded the bar.

Drinks spilled. I noticed the violin case under Pops's barstool as he teetered about in his excitement.

"Can I finish the story now? Can I? Forty-something odd years people have wanted to know the truth and here I offer it no strings attached and no one wants to listen?"

"Pops, Pops," Bourbon Monkey said soothingly, "tell your story. We're all pins and needles here."

More soothing than his voice was the drink he poured for my old man. He really knew his turf. Pops heaved like he was letting go of a heavy load and downed the glass in one gulp. Like nothing at all, he dove back into his story.

"So my employer, this particular gentleman, scolds Big Mike. But this tips his hand, you see. The woman, this woman who I remember now had the saddest lips, thin, almost not there, very sad, she steps forward with her boy pressed to her hip. 'So it's you then, is it? You run this bunch of hooligans,' she says.

"'How can I help you, miss?' says my employer. Don't you forget, the most dangerous men are the ones who take the time to be polite when they are angry.

"Me, I can't say just why, I think this woman is about to pull out a rod and start making a holy mess of the place. I slide down almost out of my seat. My violin case like the egg I've laid. Big chicken.

"And then the fat bastard from Detroit, he starts in, 'What is this? What is this? Some kind of hustle? Some kind of distraction game? I'm not a, some, some lump of cottage cheese, you know!'

"To some people, everybody's a cheat when they're getting beat. Never forget that." Pops tapped the point home on the brown-skinned girl's arm where it is nested in his.

"'I got some business to attend,' Tony Two Diapers says, which probably referred to his colostomy bag, I'll never know. He starts to leave the table. Big Mike paused opening the door, still not sure what to do. Poor simple bastard. The band in the bar blasting in. Big brass section. Percussions. The works. They were really jumping in there. You can imagine.

"But Detroit, he's having none of it. 'No, no, no. Everybody, relax,' he says. 'We're settling this freaking hand here before everybody starts doing the Cincinnati shuffle.' He turns to Big Mike, 'You, big knucklehead, you stay put. Shut the goddamned door.'

"Mitch, the fat bastard's gimpy muscle, he exchanges his pen knife for a rod from beneath his jacket, puts the piece on the table in front of him as if he were anteing up."

Bourbon Monkey interrupted this time. "There's your gun."

"Listen here you, who is telling the story here? There's a good boy. You know I like you, but you interrupt too much."

"Sorry, Pops," Bourbon Monkey said.

Pops, satisfied, went on. "My boss held up one steady hand. 'Let's everybody ratchet it back a notch, shall we?' he says. 'Mike, take a seat.' Raises a hand. Points to the chair just beside the door. 'No sudden movements, see?' Big Mike, he just shrugs, shuts the door--muffling out the music--sits himself down. Got these giant hands rubbing his eyes. I don't know if he was an overly-sensitive gentle giant or if the Pine Sol was getting to him too. Little of both, probably.

"But the woman with thin lips just gets worse. Much worse. Screaming really. Something about a debt her husband, Avery, owes. Something about how is she going to feed her child? Something about something else she never gets to finish demanding as the fat bastard from Detroit picks up the pistol on the table, gimpy Mitch's ante. Shoots her dead."

My Pops understood when this detail shocked his little audience. He didn't mind the gasps and grunts. He let them quiver for a few seconds and then continued.

"Shoots her dead and then, 'Be quiet,' he tells her. Very calm like. Like a bored father talking over his Sunday morning newspaper at the breakfast table to his unruly children. 'Be quiet.' There is no need. She slumps to the floor. She is dead. Now people are screaming and other guns are coming out. I can't see much because now I'm down on the floor. They're screaming, threatening one another, everyone screaming; the boy the worst of all. The boy screams and screams and now fat bastard says he'll make him quiet too. A real hullaballoo.

"That's when more people begin to die. Gunshots like fireworks. I can't see them, but Del Guirelli cries out for his brother, Ernesto, who is howling like a kicked dog, and then I don't hear anything more from either of them. Still at the door, Big Mike hits the floor loud enough that I hear his head crack even over the gunfire. A splatter of blood grows from his back quickly making a lake all around him. Gimpy Mitch spills down onto the floor to join me under the table after what seems like forever. Now he has three nostrils.

"There is a strange quiet now. Quiet but for little sounds, whimpers and wheezing, a tinkling of broken glass and somewhere something is spilling onto the floor. All I can see from my roost under the table are the fat bastard's trousers and a momentary trickle of poker chips sprinkling down from the table above. It would seem that as quick as it started, it's over.

"The boy crouches, weeping over his mother. The fat bastard from Detroit scolds him, 'You want something to cry about? I'll give you something to cry about.' A pistol cocks.

"The violin case is open on the floor in front of me. I don't remember opening it. Still, here it is, an opened clam with two great chrome-plated pearls nestled in its crushed velvet innards.

"All I can see are the shins of his trousers and his shiny black shoes. So I shoot them. I suppose I could have shot up through the table, but I don't think to do that. It doesn't matter. He falls down beside me, the glass eye I didn't know he had pops out and rolls away. All the while I shoot and shoot, again and again. The chambers are empty and the guns merely click like toys. The fat bastard from Detroit is unrecognizable.

"The woman is dead. Everyone in the room is dead. Everyone, that is, except myself and the young boy. He huddles with his mother's ghost. I put my pistols back in the violin case. Somehow a dismembered finger with a ring just at the stump has found its way into the case as well. I recognize that it belonged to Tony Two Diapers. I close the case on it and take the boy by his hand. A bit out of sorts, I guess. Stepping over the mound of Big Mike where he sprawls by the door I hear the boy gasp. Big Mike is still alive. I lean over the large man to hear his dying words. They are words as simple as you could expect from him. I will never forget them. 'Can you imagine?' he says, and then Big Mike is gone.

"I take the boy out of the place. No one's the wiser as to the bloodshed in the backroom. The band doesn't bother to stop. The dancing goes on. The drinking and the laughter are oblivious of us. Perhaps a bit blood splattered--quite a sight to be sure, not that anyone notices--we pass through the crowd and step out onto the sidewalk. The three men who work the door pause to watch as the boy yanks himself free from me and bolts off into the night. I mumble something about cigarettes and move off in the other direction. They are back in their heated conversation about race horse tracks before I cross the first crack in the sidewalk.

"You got away, Papi?" Pops's Little Dominican Girlfriend shrilled.

"He's here, ain't he?" Weasel Guy answered for him.

From the far end of the bar, the other old guy woke from his stupor to add, "I always knew that was you. I told 'em. Yeah, I told 'em. Nobody believed me."

We watched this other man for a moment then to see if he'd say any more, waiting for some unexpected twist, only to be disappointed. Clearly, his part was played out. His words disappeared along with his will. Everything about him drowned in the amber drink between his swollen fingers.

Pops nodded. "Me? I go scot-free. No one talks. No one dares utter a word about the bloodiest mob hit man they ever had the horror to cross paths with. Assassin. I will hear it whispered for years. Besides, there are bigger fish to fry for the moment. The papers scream with banner headlines. Gang war erupts. Men die in the streets, the barbershops, the restaurants, even the churches. Lachlann's, the very nice bar where I delivered my cake box and received my violin case for my trouble, is burned to the ground in a blaze that spreads to three other buildings before it is snuffed. Can you imagine?"

Pops paused at his drink while we all sat quiet. Children gathered around grandfather for his campfire horror tale. Waiting for the old man to say something more. Not sure if he's finished his story. Little Dominican Girlfriend sighed with impatience. Not a sigh of irritation, but nervous anticipation. I don't know if Pops even heard her, but regardless, he went on.

"There is a man at my door with a parcel for me. A delivery man in a three piece suit. *Here is the real assassin*, is the thought that I am sure will be my last. With a smile, this man, he announces he has something for me. I almost close my eyes in anticipation. But there is no bullet. Instead a parcel filled with so much bound cash. Crisp hundred dollar bills that seem to have never known a man's touch. I suppose blood money should be this way. It is what one might call a windfall. The man at the door, he calls me Pops as he hands the parcel to my shaking hands. Pops, even though I'm a young man and he is decades my senior. Pops, because as he says with a wink, 'You do a nice job of taking care of people what need taking care of.' His hand over my breast pocket just as he turns to leave. Like a magician he's left me with the glass eye from the fat bastard from

Detroit. A souvenir I guess.

"So you see, these men have decided that I am the real deal. I am a killer of men. Dangerous men. Perhaps, they no doubt consider, such a man could be of more use. Perhaps they will not kill me after all. This is what my nervous thoughts come to at any rate. Who can know these things with certainty?"

I'd heard enough. "Pops, you're telling these people you killed somebody?" I said. "Man, you can't be doing that. That's messed up."

"Mind your business," Pops said.

"Yeah, mind your business," Weasel Guy butted in.

"You don't know what you're doing. This is nothing to brag about," I said to Pops, ignoring Weasel Guy altogether. "Especially to these people." To the Little Dominican Girlfriend I added, "No offense."

"Oh, none taken," Weasel Guy hissed as if I'd spoken to him.

"Hey, Pops," I said, "Whatdaya say we get out of here? I need to fix you some dinner."

Suddenly Pops exploded. It was like the other night all over. Except, this time, he was more angry and hardly frightened.

"Who are you?" he demanded. "Why are you pestering me?"

"Pops, c'mon, quit goofing." I made the mistake of touching him.

"Get your damned hands off me!" He lurched back, nearly falling off his barstool. A bottle of beer on the bar, the Little Dominican Girlfriend's with a straw in it, gets toppled over and started gurgling foam everywhere.

"Whoa, whoa!" Bourbon Monkey shouted, "Hey now, settle it, settle it!" He pointed at me. "You! Outta here! Now!"

"Fine. We're leaving," I said. And then to Pops I whispered, "Pops, don't do this. Don't make a scene. You should come home. You don't need these losers." I guess the last bit wasn't as subtle as I thought.

"Who you calling losers, you snot-nosed punk," Weasel Guy said.

Little Dominican Girlfriend wanted in on that too. "Losers? Losers?"

I ignored them. Pops was cleaning his sleeve with a bar napkin. I swear to holy macaroni you'd think he'd already forgotten the whole incident.

"Whatdaya say, Pops? You ready to go?"

"I don't need you," Pops scolded me. "You think I'm some kind of old feeb? I don't need you. Go. Leave me alone."

"Pops, hey…."

"You heard him. Beat it," Weasel Guy said.

Pops turned his back on me.

"Listen kid," Bourbon Monkey said, "you gotta go. Pops is fine. He'll head home when he's good and ready. But you, flip side, you gotta go now."

"Loser," Little Dominican Girlfriend added.

"Pops," I pleaded one last time.

The old man held up the back of his withered hand to me and waved me off without a second thought.

So I'd had enough too. "Fine. Whatever. Hang out with these degenerates if you want to. Let them look after you. Fuck do I care?" And so I was a dot. Outta there. Gone.

Chapter Thirteen

The scent of oranges is an old memory now and the bus rumbles on through the night. Through the city. Through the city night. Through the *cight.* Or maybe those oranges still hang on the air masking the stink of the musky bus and the sun has risen. There is no way to know for certain since I am asleep. Asleep and dreaming. Dreaming but aware that I am in some fantasy corner of my slumbering mind. It is no fantastical world, however. Apparently my subconscious mind is content to entertain itself with the place where my for reals world body currently resides. I am on the bus snuggled between the window and Heft and the bus pushes on through the *cight.*

When I was just an infant, my father would read to me. Not now and then, but prodigiously. And not from kiddy books, either. He would read to me whatever it was he was reading at the time. As might be imagined, because of that last detail, sometimes his dedication wasn't such a great idea.

I don't remember all of those books now, at least not in my waking hours. How could I? I was just a baby for most of them. But here in my dream state things are different. Here in the tangled corners where my waking mind never goes, all those forgotten memories have made their nests. Camouflaged from awareness, safe in the gloomy forest of forgetfulness where waking mind wouldn't know the way or out. This is a place where it would get lost if it ever tried, and so wisely it stayed away.

My dad read aloud, "Oliver Eckhart tugged at the simple linen curtains in a vain effort to block out the light. His attempts failed. The fabric was far too sheer. Even worse, the curtains were simply too small to accommodate the great bay windows. The noonday sun's radiance made its way not only through them, but around them as well. It poured into the study unabated."

He paused his reading to turn the page with a tongue-moistened finger and adjusted my blanket, taking the opportunity to tweak my tiny toes. I mewed and gurgled. Satisfied, he read on.

"Oliver's knuckles were white with strain. The tycoon's trembling hands appeared jaundiced against the all but glowing curtains. The translucent yellow of the fabric only conspired to add to the strange effect.

"It was in that moment that Detective Vicki Crenshaw saw the light, or so to speak. Not only did the radiant hue of the ill-fitted curtains not match the décor, but in an instant, Vicki realized these were not the same curtains she'd seen before.

"Décor, before? What is this, Dr. Seuss?" my dad said and tickled me again.

"No, on that rainy night just two days prior to Bernice Eckhart's murder, when Vicki had been so rudely summoned to the Eckhart estate, she recalled thinking that the great bay window's luxurious blue satin curtains would have been the choice of Scarlett O'Hara herself."

My dad turned his eyes up to me and chirped, "Carpet doesn't match the drapes." His laugh is a wonderful bass and then he returned to the page. "Lovely curtains, Detective Crenshaw said. Two birds with one stone, eh, Mr. Eckhart? Very quick thinking."

"As she spoke, Vicki Crenshaw raised one steady alabaster finger. She coolly slid an errant strand of her Titian locks from her brow. Her other hand calmly pushed back her coat. Her palm came to rest menacingly on the grip of her backup, a 9mm Glock. It was a coiled black serpent in Oliver Eckhart's perverted Garden of Eden.

"The unexpected appearance of Detective Crenshaw's service weapon proved to be the catalyst that finally distracted the lecherous millionaire's gaze from Vicki's heaving, ample décolletage.

'Begging your pardon,' Oliver stuttered.

'After you murdered your wife, Bernice, there by the window, you wrapped her still warm body in the no-doubt blood-splattered satin curtains. Two birds, one stone. And that also explains the extra box of chocolate strawberries as well,' Crenshaw added, revealing Oliver's wicked act was his secret no more.

'Preposterous! My wife wasn't murdered by me, or by anyone else. Why, you don't even know that she's dead!' Eckhart indignantly sputtered.

'Oh, she's dead all right. Dead and--'"

"Daniel Tobin!" my mom, Beth, howled from my nursery doorway, "You call that a bedtime story?"

"No! What?" Was all my dad could squeak. He was caught as red-handed as the man in his book, Oliver Eckhart.

I want to join my mom in her temper scold, everything is disturbing me now. Milky spit bubbles suddenly frothing and popping in a rush of breaths.

"Good night, moon," my dad said, and closed the book with a slap.

"I'll goodnight your moon," my mom said.

Their voices are angry. Upsetting. I will get their attention. I can speak. I understand.

"Dead!" I shout as loudly as I can.

It is a momentous occasion; my first word. Dead.

"Honey," my dad grinned, "Chloe just said 'Dad'!"

"She said 'dead,' Daniel," my mom whispered.

"Nooo…." he said.

I have their attention. I have a word. This word is magical.

"Dead! Dead! Dead!" I cheered.

I'd found my voice. I can't understand why they aren't happy for it.

My dream returned to the present. Why, I don't know. So now here I was again on this bus. No longer an infant. A grown woman, practically. Or at least a girl enough of a woman to hide her own infant inside her. And did I hear a little voice rising up from my belly? I did. I would've leaned over to hear my baby, but I'm afraid for what her first word might be. I don't want to hear.

In the aisle the little girl from one of the rows behind is standing. She watches Heft sleep. Is it her that is whispering now? Was it always her?

"What?" I ask her. "What is it?"

As she looks to me I see it is not the little girl at all. It's the girl from my school. The girl from the cafeteria. The girl that caused so much trouble. And then there is the floor beneath my feet. Sticky and wet. Looking down I see a swirl of red, of blood, pooling about the green tile at my feet. Blood and milk. Mother's milk? And then this girl whispers again. When I look back to her she has taken Heft's place. Her bare arms laid out on the arm rests. Her bare arms sliced open over and over again. But she is not the girl from the school; she is me.

I only scream the one time, but it's enough that the bus driver is startled into a swerve. Heft is thrown awake with a jolt of his own. Many others on board are cast into a tizzy by my startling disruption.

The bus corrects, people slowly settle, Heft holds me, and I cry quietly as the bus weaves us into the blanket made of gaining morning and rolling farmland.

...

Pops never came home.

When I woke up the morning after he ran me out of the bar, I supposed I just hadn't heard him come in. I checked his room to see if he wanted breakfast and to make up with him and all, but he wasn't there.

I freaked a bit about it. Then I just decided to say fuck it. He doesn't want to come home, then fine. Whatever. I ate my cereal and decided I wasn't going to bother looking for him again either. I was tired of this game he was playing. It was a half-baked decision that would become a major regret.

For something to do I decided I'd head downtown to the library. And I didn't bother with cleaning up my cereal bowl or nothing. I left the whole mess right there on the coffee table. Let Pops do the cleanup for a change. Let him be the one to come home to a mess.

I headed downtown to the library just like I'd planned. I didn't go in when I finally got there though. Even after the half hour train ride, my mind was still racing and tangled and overlapping all out of sorts. My headspace was a knot. I'd started to feel like I was suffocating in the subway--something that'd never happened before--and happy to be back above ground, I decided hanging out in Bryant Park sounded like the thing to do. It wasn't as though I gave the matter a whole ton of consideration. I just thought it another dumb, inconsequential decision. Everyday shit. But it turned out that call was nothing of the sort. Turned out it was something of a catalyst, like the flapping wings of the proverbial butterfly in China. Seriously. I hyperbole you not.

At the west end of the park, close to the cooling spray of the humongous fountain where I knew the derelicts and hustlers conned the tourists at the chess tables, there sat Razer. He was playing chess. And no, I couldn't believe it. Chess just didn't seem Razer-like. And not just playing, but apparently entertaining at least a dozen people by running three different opponents all at the same time. I'd arrived just as the unexpected spectacle was concluding.

As I walked up, Razer declared checkmate on two of his competitors--middle aged men, tourists likely--one right after the other. With those two dismissed, he turned his full attention on the last fellow, an old coot in what looked to be an expensive suit. Looked to be a local. I mean, who else wears a suit in the city in the summer? Am I right? But you can never be sure.

The poor old guy took this new development as an ill omen, I guess, and wasted no more time trying to gnaw off his salt and pepper mustache or prolong the inevitable. He sighed the sigh of the defeated. And with a slightly shaking index finger, he toppled his lonely king. All three defeated players then proceeded to pay Razer twenty dollars apiece. Needless to say, I was knocked into orbit.

Most of the crowd--with the exception of course of the bested and their few companions--clapped hands and congratulated Razer on his wins. He was a big time park celebrity. Okay, maybe not quite duck-rescuing celebrity, but celebrity nonetheless.

Like a butcher sharpening his knives and considering the work set out before him, Razer took on a serious air, resetting the three boards and going about the business of soliciting his next marks. I'd never seen him like this. It was somehow--don't even ask how, I couldn't begin to put it in words--kind of unsettling.

"A beautiful day for a beautiful game, hey, everyone? Who's up for a game?" Razer called out. He zeroed in on a lone fellow with a backpack. "How about you, sir?"

The man smiled and shook his head. I wasn't sure if the fellow understood a word of the crap coming out of Razer's mouth, although it was obvious that Razer was offering him a game. I'm not sure why, but Razer kept at the guy as if he'd settled on him--or more like zeroed in on him--and was determined to make him his mark.

"Tell you what. I'll take two minutes against your four," Razer said, setting the chess clocks and making a big deal of it. "Plus," he said, and snatched up one of his bishops. And then, "Plus," he repeated, taking away a pawn as well when it looked like that first sacrifice hadn't changed the fellow's mind. "I'll give you *both* a bishop *and* a pawn." He smacked the pieces down next to the guy's side of the board. "Whatdaya say? C'mon, take my twenty. We'll have some fun," Razer said and slid a bill under the chess clock. Nothing.

"I'll give you white!" Razer proclaimed, spinning the board around and switching out the sacrificed bishop and pawn.

That was enough. The smirk that suddenly emerged as the guy dropped his backpack and took a seat gave me pause. It was the smirk of confidence. The smirk of impending trouble. Looked like Razer may have just walked into a trap.

Razer had to remind the fellow to ante up his twenty. This elicited even more smirking. The guy quickly produced a hundred dollar bill and wordlessly looked to Razer to see if the raise was going to fly. Razer pursed his lips thoughtfully and nodded back. He pulled out a wad of folded twenties, matched the bill, and the game was off and running.

I'd played enough chess to know they both opened with no groundbreaking strategies, just your general development of pieces. Pawns out. Knights out. The castling of kings. That sort of thing. With the exception, of course, that Razer only had one bishop to worry about bringing out into play. The other aspect that was new to me--although, yeah, I'd seen it before--was how they were playing with a clock. Actually, two clocks. You know, one of those box dealies that have a clock for each player and little start-stop buttons on the top for each one.

Obviously, Razer and his mute opponent were both well-versed in the move-your-piece-smack-the-clock play. So for the first minute the game was nothing but a blur of move and smack. And then the smirking guy moved out his queen and everybody got quiet when Razer didn't have an immediate retaliation. A good ten seconds ticked off Razer's clock in a relative eternity of pause.

"Oh man, that was a good move, huh?" Razer said.

The smirk grew into this irritating grin of smugness as the dude kind of puffed up, pleased with himself to no end. Razer's two minutes were just eroding away.

"Ah, what the…," Razer said with a shake of his head. He moved one of his pawns up a rank and timidly pressed his clock button.

As the grinning fellow moved his queen and took one of Razer's rooks, his face melted. He hadn't hit the clock yet, but he'd made the exchange. His hand was off the piece. He looked forlornly to Razer.

"Oh snap, a trap," Razer said. "Done is done, my friend. Now you just eatin' time wishing you could go back," he added. Then, as though the game was a foregone conclusion, Razer turned to this guy in the crowd behind him--who was our age and looked familiar, but I was too preoccupied to give him a second thought--and started yakking about some movie the two of them should go see later in the day.

The poor bastard across the board from Razer blinked a few times and pressed his clock button to finish his turn. Razer only bothered to pause his conversation long enough to slip in, "Check," as he moved a knight to mount a fork attack, threatening both the opposing queen and her king. The crowd muttered and murmured. This was major. The smirking guy was now the frowning guy. He'd truly blundered. Twenty seconds later by Razer's clock--which still had thirty odd seconds of his original two minutes remaining--and my boy was sliding a rook across several rows and shaking the bewildered fellow's hand with, "Checkmate."

The crowd applauded politely and Razer waited patiently as the guy spent a few lost moments confirming defeat and letting it sink in. You could tell it wasn't something he'd expected or was used to.

"Malcolm Sarsgaard," the dude said, jumping up and shaking Razer's hand again. The way the guy snapped to his feet and sort of announced his name made me think he expected some kind of recognition from Razer. Whether he did or not, he got none.

"Razer," my boy said, leaning back and casually crossing his feet. If I hadn't been so impressed I would've called him out on the spot for acting like a broke tool.

"Yes. Razer…umm?" Malcolm Sarsgaard asked, searching for something more.

"Just Razer, Malcolm, my friend. Just Razer."

The guy Razer had been bullshitting with about going to the movies--the one I recognized from somewhere, maybe school--chimed in, "The Razer of castles, yo! Leveler of yer shit to the ground, baby. You can't defend against the Razer!"

Malcolm Sarsgaard, whoever the hell he was, had had enough. He collected his backpack and was trying to lose himself in the crowd as Razer called after him, "Hey, welcome to New York. Enjoy the sights, Malcolm. Good to meet you, my man! Good luck in the tournament! Come back anytime! I'm here all week!"

With that, Razer and his compatriot burst into a series of high fives and bullshit antics.

Suddenly the guy with Razer yelled out to no one in particular, "CC181 represents!"

That's when I knew where I knew him from. It all came together. I'd seen him from the halls at school. I'd already known that right off. He was one of the Dominicans that Razer ran with that I didn't have time for. But that wasn't it. Where my brain had been racking, trying to place him, was from that day on the subway platform. The day Heft nearly got put down. This kid was one of the CC181. Not the one who'd nearly killed Heft by sucker-punching him onto the tracks, but one of the other misfits that'd been with that goon that day. And, as the guy looped his tattooed arm around Razer's neck and repeated his chant, that's when the first blast from that distant butterfly smacked me hard. My boy Razer was one of the CC181.

Chapter Fourteen

I felt like some kind of wet-noodles for legs astronaut by the time the bus finally rolled into the Denver bus station. The road trip had been no great experience as Heft had promised. No astonishing discoveries. Not one iota of soul-opening revelation. The near infinite two-day journey had been nothing more than a dreary study in maintaining sanity while forced into hours upon days of too close quarters with these other...humans. We were the bursons, the bus persons; a nomadic people of limited soap and deodorant, forced to subsist on a strictly fast-food diet. Well, at least for some of the bursons the food was maybe something different and disgusting. Yeppers, journey from hell. A miasma of poor sleep, bad food, cramped legs, sore butts, stinky bodies making stinky air, and endless highway thrusting and humping across land that was so tired, boring, and unremarkable, even the balding white guys in charge of it in some room somewhere with buzzing fluorescent bulbs and plastic potted plants had decided it couldn't be put to any better use. Just roadways, billboards, and crops.

Yanno, if we ever plan to colonize Mars, a good litmus test for the potential crew would be the Greyhound bus run from New York to Denver. Any spud making it as far as North Platte, Nebraska just might have the right stuff.

I was doing my antsy dance and Heft finally noticed.

"You need to go to the bathroom?" Heft asked while we waited for the porter to get our bags from the underbelly of the bus.

"You kidding? My kidneys are floating over here."

"Again? Really?"

"I guess it's a pea in the pod thing."

"I thought that was pea like a bean, not P with a double E," he said.

"No, it's bean like in upside your head, funny boy."

"Okay, okay. No need for violence. You can go first then. It's right through there. See the sign? I'll wait on the bags." Heft pointed through the glass doors to where I saw the restrooms.

"Killer," I said. I gave him a peck on the cheek for thinking of me.

I was only gone from Heft for like a handful of minutes, so I got kind of confused when I came back and couldn't find him right off.

"Hey, Miss," the porter called to me. I noticed my suitcase at his feet.

I thought Heft had gone to the restroom too, leaving my luggage for the porter to watch. "What, he couldn't wait to go himself?"

"I don't know not a thing about that, but this here's yours, ain't it?" he said, meaning my bag.

"Yeah, thank you." I wasn't sure, and he looked like an honest sort, so I asked, "Do I tip you? Did my boyfriend tip you?"

"No, yes. Is to say, you're fine, thank you," he said and held up a twenty dollar bill that I guess Heft must have given him.

"Yeah, I'd say so. Have a nice day."

He smiled with like a bazillion super bright teeth. "You too, miss. You too."

I grabbed my suitcase and looked for a bench to wait on Heft. He'd left his *Blood Train* paperback on top of my suitcase. Not so much like my dad after all, I thought, since my dad always took a book with him to the bathroom.

I'd waited about ten minutes or so before restlessness led me to open Heft's book to the first page: "Chastity Delgado's awareness slowly parted from the gauzy stupor of her disjointed and haunted dreams only to discover a terrifying reality. Wherever bare skin met any part of the sleeper car, the flesh, her flesh, had become irrevocably fused with the train."

"Yuck. Cool," I said aloud.

Out of boredom I flipped to the envelope Heft had been using for a bookmark. It was a plain blank envelope except for where the address should go, in Heft's handwriting, it read:

"Chloe, I'm sorry, but I just can't. Take care, Chad"

Inside were two twenty dollar bills.

Clickity-click.

...

I was glad I got out of the park and away from Razer and his CC181 homey before either of them spotted me. I didn't want to risk any chance of a run-in and so I skipped the library altogether and bee-lined it for the subway back home. The day was a scrub.

When I got back to the apartment only to be greeted by the mess of breakfast I'd left behind and still no Pops, well, I got kind of pissed. I headed over for a visit to his little bar hangout. I was fed up with the shit. And what the hell was Razer's problem anyway? How stupid you got to be to join a gang. I had half a mind to go over to the precinct on Broadway and report Mr. CC181. I really did.

The thing that stopped me was when I realized I actually said that to myself. "I have half a mind…." Seventeen going on seventy from all the stress.

The dive bar was even more dive than usual. Mostly empty except for the diehard half-dead, middle of the day zombies. No Pops, no Weasel Guy. It was just Bourbon Monkey and Little Dominican Girlfriend along with the other old guy at the end of the bar. Looked like Pops had been replaced.

Bourbon Monkey gave me the stink eye. "Your old man isn't here, kid," He said before I even stepped in. "Shoo, you're letting out the AC."

"Yeah, sorry I let some nasty fresh air into your crypt," I ragged back and split before he could mouth off.

Sometimes shit just happens. Not to quote that dumbass bumper-sticker or nothing. But, anyways, I kind of hurled this trashcan through the bar's glass doors before I'd really given it a whole lot of thought. Maybe no thought at all. Seemed like the thing to do.

The double glass doors of Pops's dive bar had been painted black on the inside. This to keep out the filthy sunlight and for the sake of beauty. Even though the trashcan, one of those mesh wire dealios you see on every other street corner, only went through the door on the right-hand side, both doors shattered into an explosion of glistening black shards like some kind of bomb had gone off. The impact being pretty vicious and all.

I stood there as the last bits of broken glass gave up the ghost and tinkled from the aluminum door frame down onto the concrete. From beyond came the screeches of Little Dominican Girlfriend. I'd never heard "Oh my God" repeated so quickly. So there was that and this parade of profanity from Bourbon Monkey. Otherwise the city was eerily quiet. Sort of in shock by what I'd done I just stood there like a lump as the profanity parade worked its way around the bar and headed towards me from the dark maw of the doors. Felt like I was staring into the gates of Hell as some Satan spawn rushed up from the depths.

"You fixed his wagon."

It was some homeless dude that'd sidled up to admire my handiwork who'd spoken. As Bourbon Monkey emerged through the shattered doors, pulling them open as if that was still necessary, the homeless dude started cackling like a nut.

"Fixed your wagon! Fixed your wagon!" he sung as he started dancing around.

"You crazy son of a bitch!" Bourbon Monkey said, "What'd you do that for?"

Except he wasn't talking to me. Bourbon Monkey, I realized, was screaming at the homeless dude. For a reply all he got was more dancing and a second and third verse of, "Fixed your wagon. Fixed your wagon."

I ran.

Well, first I just backed away. Slowly. But as Bourbon Monkey began trying to wrestle the homeless dude up against the wall while Little Dominican Girlfriend was gingerly trying to come out through the threshold of broken glass, that's when I broke into a little trot. By the time I heard Bourbon Monkey raging about how the homeless dude was going to pay to fix the doors, and while Little Dominican kept up her beseeching to God, me, I was at a full clip. And I ran that way for four long blocks.

I stopped when I saw the cop and he saw me. Cops are like dogs. You run, you're going to get yourself chased. No questions asked. So I went from a fist-pumping sprint to a dead stop just like that. No matter. He'd seen me and so here he came. Before he could start on me I pointed back down the street.

"Hey, man, some crazy homeless dude…is like going crazy. He's fighting some dude…I think the bartender…out in front of the bar…around the corner. Breaking windows. Crazy stuff," I said between gasps, winded from the excitement.

"Yeah?" he said. "So why you runnin'?"

Cops are always suspicious.

I could tell he wasn't buying it. I couldn't think of what else to do when all the sudden I got saved by the walkie-talkie strapped on his shoulder. In a crackle of garbled cop talk the voice on his radio reported somebody had called in the trouble at the dive bar. John law needed to get on the scene.

"I tried to tell you, man," I called out after him as he headed off to go deal. He didn't even run. Just sort of a get-out-my-way, I'm-in-a-real-big-hurry, walk. Cops.

...

I guess I'd been crying and that was why the officer came over. He was too overweight to be on the force. Or so you'd think. I guess that was why they had him on foot-patrol at the bus station. That, or maybe it was because his superiors knew his heart was as big as his waistline, and that made for a good fit with the kind of place where teenage girls routinely popped up far from home with teary eyes.

"How are we doing over here?"

"We? You look like fine," I said.

"Oh...I see," he said as he took a knee at the end of the bench beside me.

Under normal circumstances if an adult had gotten down on their knee to speak to me, I'm pretty sure I would've felt a little offended, like I was being condescended to, like I was some kind of child. But here, abandoned by my boyfriend, pregnant and alone thousands of miles from home, it didn't offend me at all. In fact, it was a pretty big comfort, him being so nice and all, because the last thing I needed was trouble with the police on top of everything else. Not that I'd done anything wrong, but, yanno, still. When he bent down and got on one knee like that though, I knew he hadn't come to be an aggressor; he'd come to offer his help.

"My boyfriend left me. Just split out," I said.

He nodded knowingly. I guess I didn't need to be surprised. I imagine he'd witnessed this scene more than once on his beat at the good old Greyhound bus station. Probably like every other day. He stood and asked if I'd mind if he took the seat next to me.

"You'd think I was a K-9 patrol, my dogs are barking so bad," he added.

"Free country," I said without looking up at him. When he didn't move I finally met his eyes. That did it. They were those big brown teddy bear eyes ginormous guys like him sometimes are lucky enough to have. So I quickly added, "Sure. I could use some company."

"Great, because I need some advice and you look to be the very person who might be able to help," he said as he sat.

"Huh?"

"Yeah, see, here's the problem…." He paused to shift his weight around, taking a few seconds to find a comfortable position. Once he did he leaned his head back and sighed, "I got to get me some better shoes."

"You need shoe advice? Contrary to the feminine myth, I don't think I can help you out there. I'm mostly a sneakers gal." I rubbed my swollen eyes with the back of my sleeve.

"What? Oh no, no," he said and chuckled with amusement. "No, I don't need shoe advice. Well, maybe I do…or just better shoes. No, it's more just a woman's perspective that I need. Kind of love-life stuff."

"I think we'd have a better shot with the shoes."

"No, no. And don't worry, it's nothing I could lose my job over," he explained with a smile. His nametag read "BARTELL." He had a cleft in his chin a little like Heft's. Not quite as pronounced. Still, ugh. I tried to let it go.

"Shoot," I said.

"Okay, here's the gist of it. "I'm kind of overweight." He paused for me to remark. I guess I was either supposed to argue the fact or I don't know what. I only shrugged. "And my girlfriend always said it didn't bother her. Said she loved me just the way I am."

"I see." I said, feeling very clinical and all. "Go on."

"But it's worse than that."

"That's not a bad thing. She's loving," I said.

"Well, maybe," he nodded in contemplation.

"Maybe?"

"I always thought she was just saying that to be sweet. You know, the whole 'I love you just the way you are' thing."

"Right…."

"But a few months ago I decided to go on a diet," the giant bear of an officer said.

"Good for you," I said.

"That's what I thought," Officer Bartell said. I could tell he was really delving into the personal stuff. He sighed a few more times. Being the good listener, that's all I did, listen. "After about four months, I'd dropped eighty pounds."

"Outstanding," I said. I even patted him on his ginormous thigh. The good officer still had a ways to go.

"That's what my superiors said. Beatrice, on the other hand, she doesn't quite see it that way."

"Come again?"

"Beatrice, she's my lady. She confessed to me the other night that she likes me big."

"So…she's been straight up with you all along. What's wrong with that?"

"She said she wants me to put the weight back on."

"For reals?" I guess I was a little too enthusiastic. Officer Bartell's big brown eyes looked to the floor. "I mean…wow," I said. "You wouldn't expect that."

"When I told her no, she said that she didn't know if she could love me if I lost any more weight. She gave me what I guess you'd call an ultimatum."

Okay, I have to admit, it was at that moment I thought maybe he was yanking my chain. I even looked around for the cameras to see if this all wasn't some elaborate punk set up by Heft. For like a millisecond I thought the joke was on me and that actually came as a relief. Relief to think that I hadn't been abandoned. Relief to think Heft would stay in my life.

And in searching the room for Heft, there stood my mom. "Hi, Chloe," she said. I turned back to Officer Bartell. I was pretty shocked. It was quite the trick.

"How'd you do that?"

"Me?" Officer Bartell defended, "I didn't do a thing."

My mom closed the gap between us slowly giving me time to come out of my shock, time to think of what to say.

"Hello, Chloe," she said when she was finally within arm's reach. But neither of us did any reaching out at all.

I was speechless.

"I'm her mother," my mom offered to Officer Bartell. "Has there been some trouble?"

"Trouble?" I said. "Thanks for the vote of confidence. Off to a great start, Mom."

"No trouble," Officer Bartell said. "Your daughter and I were just taking a break to watch the world go by, is all. I guess I'll get back to the grind. Was nice meeting you, Chloe. Thanks for letting me bend your ear." Turning to my mom as he left, Officer Bartell lifted two fingers to where a hat might have been if he'd had one. "Ma'am. You two have a nice day now."

"Officer Bartell," I called to stop him.

"Yes?"

"You spend a lot of time on your feet. You should wear shoes that are like a half a size too big. That way, as the day wears on and your feet swell, they have room to breathe and all. That, and my dad, he gets sore feet, he swears by arch supports. Says they help. So make sure you get something with arch support."

"Bigger shoes. Arch support. Gotcha. Thanks."

He started to walk away again.

"And, hey, while it is a lot more important you love somebody for what's on the inside…if Beatrice can only love you for your body, well then, maybe she's like the shoes. Yanno, bad fit, no support. You could probably find better…like you deserve."

He smiled and tipped his absent cap again before heading off back to his beat as the bus station's patron saint for wayward little lost girls.

"Gosh, Chloe, look at you go," my mom said. "That certainly was sweet. And mature."

I just watched him go and wondered how it would all work out for him. I would never know, I realized, and that made me feel really weird. My mom coughed, one of those fake mom coughs and so I turned to stare at her.

"It's good to see you," she said. She had this ridiculous smile plastered from ear to ear. I couldn't tell if she was serious and just nervous or what. I let it slide.

She couldn't decide how to or even whether to hug me, and I guess I wasn't too receptive. I didn't offer any help. Finally she just wrapped me up in her arms. So we did that whole thing for a minute.

"How'd you find me?" I said as I eased her off.

"What? Well, you came out to see me, didn't you?" she said, all confused-like. I didn't respond. "Your boyfriend, Chad, he called the house yesterday, said to meet you both here…at…well, I'm early, I guess," she said looking at her watch. "So, in any event…. Where's this boyfriend of yours? Where's Chad?"

"He's not my boyfriend."

"He's not?" She looked even more confused.

"Nope. Just the father of the baby."

Chapter Fifteen

Used to be, I loved that summer days were the longest of the year. During the summer it was nothing for it to be light out right up to say nine or so at night. That'd always meant a sliver more of freedom. One last, long game of romper. A feeling that you were getting away with something even when you weren't. Made youth seem eternal. Like it'd always be summer. Me, Heft, and Razer, we'd always be kids. Always be friends.

The sun had gone down behind the Palisades on the far side of the Hudson. The day had ended in a sky pummeled and swollen. My hands ached. I wasn't sure why. Maybe I was the one who'd bruised those clouds so badly. There was still a bit of hazy light, but for the most part the twilight had been eaten by time. The day was gone. Gobbled up. The headlights of cars on the bridge above flickered one after another, a trail of luminous ants gathered and coming to collect up my corpse, bit by bit, bite by bite. I sure as hell didn't feel young anymore. Heft had split out without even saying a word. Scissors seemed to have done the same, to where, I didn't know. And Razer, that sorry son of a bitch was a goddamned gangbanger. Worst of all, the granddaddy of worst of all, it'd been days and days and Pops had never come home. I lay back in the grass beneath the bridge getting drunker on my last beer and wondering what had happened to the old man. What would become of me if he stayed gone, if he never came home?

Before, I'd been toying with the idea of not going back to school. That plan had sure seemed a lot sweeter when it'd been a choice. But if Pops was gone, like for good, then I had no place to live. No place to live meant I couldn't really go to school even if I wanted to. And yeah, I'd thought about running away before. What kid doesn't from time to time? Just your usual fantasies. But now, well let's just say the reality of being on the streets wasn't such a romantic notion. I'd heard there was some kind of band of street kids that lived someplace down around Hell's Kitchen, somewhere in the abandoned subway line there on the West Side. Before all this, the thought of joining them, or maybe thumbing my way out West, had seemed intriguing and all. Definitely something to daydream about. But now? Oh hells to the no. I didn't want to live in no filthy freaking tunnels. I didn't want to find myself hustling tricks at midnight in some diesel stink truck-stop out in Wyoming or some shit.

I might have been drunker than I'd thought. Or maybe just lightheaded from getting up too quick. Or maybe I was just tired. Whatever the case, I sort of bum-stumbled my way up from the little park down under the GWB. I didn't have any place in particular to go. I kept telling myself I wasn't looking for Pops. Which, in a twisted sort of way, meant I really was. So I followed thc bridge back into the city and found myself staring at the entrance to the bus terminal.

It was the usual crowd of delinquent, wanna be teens. Young kids probably just in middle school, when they bothered to go. Punks grinding their skateboards on the curb out front of the bus station doing their best to looked bored. A pair of cops sat parked in their cruiser looking like they were trying to decide who was pissing them off more, the punks, or this grubby homeless dude brazenly panhandling at the terminal glass doors not twenty feet from their bumper. I just smiled as I strolled by with the flow of pedestrians. Figured I'd head inside and see what was what. Keep up my non-search for Pops.

So I was going in and he was coming out when Heft shouldered right into me.

Normally I wouldn't have bothered, but being a bit lit, I mumbled, "Watch it, ass." I hadn't recognized him. Probably would have said it louder if I had.

"Tweed? Hey, man, what're you doing here?" Heft said.

He looked at his watch and then me and then looked around all stupefied. We were both surprised to see each other, I guess, and so I followed him and his rolling suitcase back out onto the curb. Heft lowered the extended grip on his luggage and sat down on it after the first cabbie honked to get his attention. Heft waved the guy off and asked me again what was up. I drunk shrugged.

He looked a little…no not a little, but a lot…haggard. Clearly he hadn't shaved in a few days and so his nappy little faux-beard was in full sprout and he smelt like he hadn't been within twelve feet of a shower in at least five days. I probably looked and smelled just a little bit worse.

"What's up, man?" Heft kept up. "You comin' or goin'?" He nodded back over his shoulder to the terminal.

"Ah…I don't know. Little of both, I guess."

"Dude, you're vicious wasted," he said. This really amused the shit out of him.

"Ding, ding, ding. We have a wiener." I said.

"No doubt. So where's my prize? What're you holding?"

"Got nothing for you," I said. I pulled my front pockets inside out to show him they were empty, and then added, "Unless you wanna kiss my bunny between the ears."

"Dude...."

"C'mon, kiss the bunny. Kiss the bunny. Kiss The Bunny!"

I guess I got a little out-of-hand because I sort of stepped on the cop's foot when he came up behind me to gauge what all the hubbub was about. Heft, tool that he was, didn't give me any warning, of course.

"Better get a hold of yourself there, son," the cop said as he grabbed me by the shoulder and turned me around.

I made the mistake of slapping his hand before I realized who I was dealing with. "Yo, what the...get the fuck off me," I said. Or maybe barked.

"Best cool your jets," the cop who had a hold of me said. He gave me a little shake to bring his point home.

"Hey, hey, sorry."

The other cop was coming up from behind his overeager partner. As he did, he said, "Whoa, Murray. We know these two."

"Yeah?" Murray said all suspicious-like, not taking his hard stare off of me.

"How are you doing tonight, officers," Heft said.

I tried to accuse Heft of being a sycophant, but all that came out was, "Sick-o."

"Somebody's had too much," Murray the cop said. "Somebody who shouldn't be having any at all to begin with."

His partner eased him back.

"These are the two what went under the A train while back," Good Cop said. He tapped Heft on his cast. "How you coming along there, champ?"

"The doctors all think I'm going to make it," Heft said with a broad smile.

Me, I didn't know these two cops from Adam, as Pops would say. Then again, that day when we played hide and seek under the A train, well, that day there'd been a lot of cops to keep track of.

Heft kept it up getting all chummy-chummy with the cops and made like he remembered them. I doubt he really did. That was Heft for you, Mr. Kiss Up. Always laying it on heavy. Bad Cop Murray diffused just a smidgen. I kind of pulled myself together. Fingers combing through the hair. Straightening of the shirt. Put my inside-out pockets back in. Concentrated on a street light across the way to keep my balance. When I met his eyes again, Bad Cop Murray couldn't help but say something.

"Yeah well, any kid that'd jump down on the tracks for his partner is alright in my book. And that's the only reason I'm not citing you for underage drinking and public intoxication. You listen up. You only get one free pass per act of heroism. Got it? So unless you plan to start wearing a cape and patrolling the city streets saving old ladies and babies from burning buildings and whatnot, I suggest you not come out here looking like the mess you do ever again. We good? We understand each other?"

"I'm understood," I said.

I guess he didn't like my tone or something.

He turned to Heft. "It's your turn to make sure he gets home safe. And when he's in a place where and when it'll sink in, you may want to remind him of what I just told him. And that goes for the both of you. Got it?"

"I got it, officer," Heft said. "Most definitely. No, seriously, thank you. He's usually not like this."

"Beat it," Good Cop said, and then turned to whistle at the grinder tweens. "You guys. Yeah, you. Hoof it on out of here. Not on the boards. Hoof it. Walk. Outta here. What have we told you about this traffic? Next time we're confiscating those things," he said, referring to their skateboards.

One of the younger ones, skinny little dude that had himself more piercings than Pinhead, and wearing a t-shirt with a sheep getting electroshock, captioned with "*Puck the Fope*," which seemed about right for a kid his age, mouthed something I didn't catch.

"Try me again, Mr. Buber. Just you try me," Good Cop said to him.

I wanted to sincerely thank Officer Bad Cop, and started doing my best at just that, but Heft drug me off before I could fully articulate myself.

Back at me and Pops's place Heft was knocked for a loop to see how the mighty had fallen.

"Man, Tweed, what the hell happened in here? Indoor twister?" he said followed by a long whistle as he surveyed the mess.

"Whatever. Cop a squat and shut it. Better yet, clean something up. Ya spoiled rich bastard, wouldn't know a sponge from a…." Still tanked, I couldn't think of just what it was his privileged, upper-class, silver-spoon upbringing might afford him knowing a sponge from. "Spaghetti," I finished.

"Wouldn't know a sponge from spaghetti?" he said. "Maybe. What's the context?"

"You want some spaghetti or not?" I said.

"Nah…I'll pass. Don't think I'll risk what might end up on the plate in your present condition."

He was smarter than he looked. That was something else Pops would say. 'Smarter than he looks.' It seemed my mind kept in orbit around Pops no matter how hard I tried to break free. Maybe it was like one of those Chinese finger trap dealios where the harder you pull, the tighter it gets.

By the time I got back on the couch with my nuked noodles, Heft had dozed off. Being considerate I turned on the television to wake him. I had to crank the volume twice though before he finally came around. He started to bitch until he saw the beer I'd brought to the couch with my dinner. He sat up and tried to drink the damned thing in one gulp without even asking.

"Have some manners," I said.

With a burp he said, "Thank you," and left me the last third of what had been a full bottle.

"That's better."

Heft pulled himself up and wiped his eyes. "You're drinking at home now?"

"My house, ain't it?"

"Isn't it. Isn't it. I swear, my amigo, you have to work on your grammar and speaking skills if you want people to take you seriously. If nothing else, for the ladies. Thug speak is so…guh-het-tow," he said, turning 'ghetto' into one, long burp.

"You need to see a doctor about that. Disgusting."

"Pops doesn't mind if you drink now? I mean, like, here, in the apartment?"

"Aw, you know how it is, man. Everybody is AWOL. Pops, you…. Speaking of…you seen Scissors? What, did she go out to the Hamptons with you?"

I chewed a mouthful of pasta waiting for his reply. I got nothing so I shoveled another forkful and added, "Because I ain't...I mean, isn't...I isn't seen her around, lately."

"I wasn't in the Hamptons, Tweed."

"No, it's cool. Preenie hipped me. Don't worry...I isn't mad you didn't invite me. Whatever. I know you got better friends from your fancy school or what have you."

Heft snatched up my beer and finished it.

"Dude...." I said. "Not cool."

"Is there more?" He got up and walked into the kitchen. Since he was heading that way I didn't bother to answer. Spaghetti was already getting cold. Guess I didn't nuke it long enough. I heard him clink around with a couple of bottles and was satisfied when he came back to the couch with one for each of us. A true friend indeed.

"Last two. Hurry up and finish and we'll hit the bodega," he said.

"You're buying. My stash of cash is all dried up," I said.

Which was true. Almost. I still had a shoe box full of rolled quarters and dimes back in my room, probably a couple hundred dollars' worth. And actually it was Pops's box of coins, but whatever.

"Sure. Fine," Heft agreed.

"So what did ya guys do out there? Eat lobsters three meals a day and talk about polo ponies and shit?" I asked.

"What?"

"The Hamptons. Whatcha do? I never been. C'mon, let us mugs like yours truly live vicariously for once." I couldn't believe I'd put 'vicariously' together correctly and felt pretty good about my drunken condition.

"We didn't go to the Hamptons."

"WE? WE? See. See. I knew she went with. I knew it. Because I haven't seen her around."

"And you're not going to be seeing her around," Heft said all nasty like.

"Do what, man? What's that supposed...?"

"And why have you been trying to hang with my girlfriend anyway, Tweed? What? You working on stealing my girl now, Mr. Hero? That it?"

"What do you mean 'won't be seeing her around?'"

"Just what I said."

"You killed Scissors?" Admittedly it was the stupid conclusion of a soused brain. And yeah, I know I already said I was drunk. Drunk, drunk, drunk. Drunk enough to repeat myself…like drunk people do.

"Don't be an idiot," Heft said.

"I'm not an idiot. I'm drunk. Shut up."

I slid my half-finished, way-too-cold plate of spaghetti onto the coffee table and just sort of melted back into the couch. I might have zoned out if Heft hadn't spoken up. Made his little absolution.

"I took her out to live with her mom. I took her out to Denver."

"Did what? You did what now?" I asked. And asked again.

"I couldn't have my parents finding out. She wants to have her baby, she can have it out in Denver. And keep it out in Denver."

I sat back up. Some things just slap you in the face. Get your attention but good.

"Whose idea was this?" I asked.

"Hers," he said. I wasn't buying. He saw I wasn't buying. Changed his story. "Okay, it was mine. What does it matter? Only thing that matters is she's gone. She stays gone."

"So you talked her into moving to Denver?"

"Something like that."

"Something like…what's that mean? Did she want to go?"

"I told her she'd be better off out there with her mom. You know, babies are women's stuff anyway. How was her dad going to be any help? Or me for that matter?"

"So you two are broken up? I don't understand."

"What's to understand? I convinced her to do the right thing. She doesn't need me. Better off with her mom."

"And she agreed to that? To you taking her out there and leaving her?"

"Not entirely," he said. "I didn't tell her I wasn't staying."

"So what did she say when you told her that?"

"Didn't."

"Whatdaya mean, didn't?"

Heft shrugged. "I didn't tell her. When we got to the Denver station I made sure her mom was there and I split."

"You abandoned her in Denver?"

Heft got real defensive. "I took her to be with her mom…where she needs to be. I'm starting college. I don't have time for a baby."

"You shit," I said. "You complete shit."

"Oh, now you're the high and mighty one. Tell you what, Tweed. If you ever get laid, ever, and it turns out you get the proof you're not sterile, then we'll see how you deal."

He started to mumble something. Some kind of insult or smartass something. I don't know. I didn't care. The plate of spaghetti flew from the table to my hand to his face all in one frame. Pow! I thought it was spaghetti sauce at first, but then I saw it was blood gushing from the bridge of his nose as well as his nostrils. Served him right.

…

Making conversation with someone you're supposed to be close to, or used to be close to but really aren't anymore, or maybe never were, is truly awkward. It's much harder than just shooting the breeze with a stranger even, since with a stranger there's no guilt or expectations.

On top of everything else, I hadn't seen my mom in a while. Even after being there a few days she didn't seem very familiar. And nothing from the multitude of little brain photos I had stored away looked anything like the woman sitting across the dinner table from me, or on the couch while we pretended we were interested in some movie. All my pictures looked like the woman I'd cut out of the Tobin family photo albums. She'd been kind of a frumpy, got to get my kid to soccer practice, kind of gal. But this woman? Not her. This one, she was just different. No resemblance. Different hair color. Blonde now, brunette before. Bob cut, not shoulder length. Her teeth whiter and maybe even straighter. How's that even possible? This woman was definitely in better shape. And tan. This woman looks like she must have herpes, because she strikes me as one of those rock-climbing, jet-skiing, competitive bicyclers you always see in the commercials for herpes medication. Whatever. I'm just glad she hadn't gone and got a boob job. At least, as far as I could tell, the girls looked the same.

My mom was playing it cool too. Yanno, not pressuring me to talk. I hadn't gotten the first real question from her yet even after three days. At first that was a nice break, but after some time it just added to the sense of uneasiness. I mean, were we ever going to really talk? Or would we just be like actors in a play with a very limited script? How confused would she become if I stepped out of character and said something real? I imagined her eyes going wide as she stared out to the audience that wasn't there and in her stage fright she'd go on choking out her lines regardless of what I said. Then it'd be surrealism for sure:

"Chloe would you like chicken or fish for dinner?"

"Mom, I've been cutting myself and I can't stop."

"Fish would be quicker, yes."

"It's like this conversation I keep having with the pain to keep from feeling lonely. The pain is my best friend now and I can't say goodbye."

"If you want to play Scrabble, sure. I'd forgotten how much you loved it. I always get the worst tiles though. Ugh!"

"I've been cutting ever since you left, but it's not like I blame you…even though it probably is your fault. You abandoned us."

"Oh, I'd say about half an hour or so. Why don't you watch some television and I'll call you in time to set the table."

Then Rod Serling would step into frame and explain how we were two people living in separate realities whose lives had collided at an intersection known as the Twilight Zone. I dunno, so maybe it was like we were living more television than stage play.

Anywho, I was a bit more confused than usual even. I don't know what I'd expected. I suppose it was that Heft would be here so it wouldn't be like I was on my own no matter how strange things turned out with my mom.

How could Heft have left me, abandoned me, like this? First my mom and now him. That was my reoccurring thought as I padded around my mom's home. *She* sure wasn't alone. She had her new husband, Jim, a retired orthodontist and about five gazillion pictures of the two of them along with his two sons trotting the globe to prove it. Apparently orthodontists have it pretty good, because the house where they kept all their framed photos was like a mansion; two sprawling, and I mean, sprawling stories and a basement that wasn't like any basement I'd ever seen or heard of. It had the rec room to end all rec rooms, plus a laundry room, a room for the maid, and Jim's workshop. Three days in and I was still getting lost. I'd run into Jim every now and then as I wandered around taking it all in, and it was like bumping into an acquaintance on the street. You felt obliged to make small talk before you both wondered off to the other realms of the house.

Back home in our apartment we had an intercom for the front door and lobby, and if my dad wanted to know if I wanted black beans or refried beans with my tacos he'd call from the kitchen and I'd answer him from my bed or desk or the couch. Out here in Denver, they had an intercom for the entire house and yelling was frowned upon, if you were even heard, that is.

Jim was older. Not ancient, but he had some years on my mom. But he was fit. Sort of a health-nut from what I'd gathered. Judging from the pictures, his sons were probably finishing up college, if not starting families of their own about now. The first wife? I didn't know her story. I supposed she might have died tragically, since there were plenty of pictures of her and she seemed pretty happy if not kooky happy in all of them. Probably a car wreck, or cancer, or something horrible. Maybe a lion. Jim had a whole slew of him and his first wife on safari. Those were all along the wall of the main stairs to the second floor, making them pretty tough for my mom or me to overlook. The other big thing I gathered from the photos of the sons and the first wife's hair style and fashion, was that they'd clearly done the safari thing two or three times over the past few decades.

I wondered if Heft was home by now.

"Chloe, I'm in the laundry if you need me," my mom's disembodied voice ran through the house over the intercom.

"Thought you had a maid," I said, but didn't push any talk button. "Okay!" I yelled instead.

I wondered if she could hear me. A moment later Jim's voice floated through the house, emanating from all the various speakers. "Please use the intercom, Chloe. That's what it's there for."

I found the nearest panel at the top of the stairs and pressed my lips right up into it.

Using my most melodious late night radio DJ voice, I breathed, "You're listening to Chloe radio…all Chloe, all the time. Cha-shh-ssh…." The last bit being my lame attempt to imitate the sound of soft rain.

"Chloe, please don't play on the intercom," my mom said. Not on the intercom, she'd suddenly appeared on the landing below.

I guessed it was as good a time as any. "Is this why you left us?" I asked pointing to no one photo in particular. "World travel, hobnob and rub elbows with the jet set in Aspen and Monte Carlo?"

"Jet-set? Chloe…."

"I mean, not that you're in any of these. These are all Jim's first pick, from what all I've seen. He's got your gallery limited to less prime real estate down the hall."

"I was wondering when we'd get to this," my mom said.

"Get to what?"

"Your anger."

"Me? I'm not angry," I said.

"It's not quite lunch yet. How about some tea?"

That sounded good. "Sure. I guess," I said.

Twenty minutes later over our chamomile my mom dropped a bombshell on me.

"I had a long conversation with your father last night. He's been worried sick about you," she said. She bobbed the teabag in and out of the steaming mug in front of her. I waited for her to go on, but she just kept up torturing the little baggie along with me.

"Yeah, so?" I shrugged. Two could play at this game.

"You really put him through the ringer on this one."

"Praise from Caesar."

My mom smiled this weird little smile. One of those, I know something you don't, kind of smiles…maybe.

"You've really grown up haven't you, Chloe. And I mean that most sincerely. That's just the kind of barb I'd expect from Victoria or Denise down at the tennis club. Well done."

She'd finished with the teabag except to give it one last hard press between her thumb and spoon. She winced as she did. I wasn't sure if the baggie scalded her or if it was something else.

"Chloe, your father was going through your room after you left…trying to get some idea of what's going on with you."

"It's his house," I said. I could tell she wasn't expecting that. More proof that she didn't really think I was so grown up.

"Long story short, he found some razors and some bloodied things…a towel or something, pliers, he said…hidden away behind your dresser."

My chickens had come home to roost. My own fault. I don't know why I hadn't thought of ditching that junk before I left. Stupid.

"Yeah, so…what'd he say?"

"He didn't say much of anything, Chloe. But he's…we're…worried. What's going on? What…?"

I didn't know that'd been overcast outside, but just at that moment I guess the skies parted, because the whole kitchen was suddenly illuminated, bathed, I guess you'd say, in sunlight. It was as if God himself was saying something to me. And that was fine. The truth be told I was tired of the secret. All the secrets. They knew about my baby, so how could this make things any worse?

"Did he mention anything about the stuff that happened at school this year, right at the end?"

My mom shook her head.

"We had this big incident. This girl in the cafeteria."

"Oh, wait," my mom interrupted, "he did mention something. A girl was cutting herself or something horrible."

"She came into the cafeteria during second period lunch. That's the girls' lunch. And she took out this ginormous like hunting knife and started slicing away on her arm right there in front of everybody."

"Dear God…."

…

The screaming of the fleeing student body was only drowned out by the pounding and roar of the bright red blood as it fell, sledgehammer drops from the girl's forearm and fingertips, exploding onto the emerald green linoleum at her feet. With each new slash of the knife the volume increased steadily to a deafening crescendo while the students' cacophony retreated with them. Finally, but for the nervous chatter of two teachers pleading for her to drop the knife, the girl and I were alone.

"I think her name is Sarah," one said to the other. I couldn't hear her, but it seemed to be what she'd said as I read her lips.

"Sarah, please drop the knife, Sarah," the other mouthed ineffectually all while the deafening bombardment of blood continued striking the floor. She now stood at the center of her own little lake, an island of isolated flesh.

I doubt Sarah, if that was her name, could hear them either, and she wasn't bothering to look at their quivering little mouths. But she did look to me. I was still sitting at my lunch. Tomato soup. Ham sandwich. Crumpled ball of aluminum foil.

I could hear her.

"I can't stop," she said. "No one knows. No one understands. I can't stop." She slid the knife along her arm creating the deepest gash yet. We were both enthralled.

Perhaps one of the teachers said something to me. I can't be sure. My little brain camera and I were focused only on this girl.

Clickity-click. Her arm. Clickity-click. The knife. Clickity-click. The blood on the floor.

But I had to stop this. I couldn't let her cut anymore. Someone had to stop this destructive behavior, this pitiful and pathetic cry for help, for attention.

The teachers were helpless. One fainted into the other's arms. Too much blood.

"You can stop," I said.

"No...."

"And I do understand," I said.

"No you don't. How could you?"

...

"Chloe? Chloe?" my mom asked for me like she wasn't sure where I was. Her voice was like a child caught down a well, small and nervous.

"Yes," I said.

"Chloe, are you okay? You kind of fainted there...a little spell," she said. At first, I thought we'd slipped back into our surreal play where nothing either of us said had to do with the other. That's when I realized my mom was holding me. Her face was etched in the furrows of a mother's worries.

"I showed the girl proof that she wasn't alone," I said. "That I understood."

Just as I'd done that day in the cafeteria, I eased the hem of my skirt up ever so discreetly to reveal my inner thigh. There could be no missing the rows of fresh cuts. They lined up like claw marks.

"My God, Chloe…sweetheart…."

"It's okay. None of the teachers saw. They were too distracted. And I got the girl to put down the knife. I think she went away someplace, yanno, mentally. Come to think of it, so did I, huh?"

My mom started to cry. Then, weirdly enough, so did I.

Chapter Sixteen

With Pops missing, Razer being a gang boy, and Scissors gone off to Denver for probably forever, Heft was the only friend I had left. So the more I thought about it the more I thought I should just kiss and make up with his dumbass. It was going to happen anyway, so sooner rather than later, like they say.

After a few days of stewing I caved. I grabbed a few rolls of quarters from Pops's shoebox stash and caught up with Heft like I'd been thinking about. And we made up too, I guess. Not that doing that required anything more than ringing his apartment buzzer and saying it was me. I mean, we're guys, after all. It's not like we were going together. And we'd been friends almost all our lives. Anyways, maybe he was just happy to get out of the house.

Since he already had the cast on his arm, the bandage across the bridge of his nose and the swollen eyes didn't really seem out of place. I'm sure most assumed it was all part of the same package. I wanted to tease him a little, just bust his balls a bit, about how he was really falling to pieces. Wise for my time, I held back.

The two of us spent the morning rooting among the foul moments of the city. Broken bottles--mostly beer and Snapple, but also tenacious plastic, still intact and sealed with hard working cabbie piss--yellowed condoms, discarded clothes, shoes, whatnot, and always, always discarded batteries like the bums and junkies ran on them. That was just a short list of the endless crap that littered the tucked away places where we searched. We hadn't talked about what happened with the CC181. I guess Heft wanted to keep that near-death experience out of his mind, and who could blame him? When you're young you think you're invincible, immortal. A hundred tons of hurtling train coming down on you tends to shake those ill-conceived notions a bit.

Not talking about it was just fine by me. You know I didn't want it coming up. Lying is a good deal easier when you don't actually have to speak about it. Nobody was the wiser to the part I'd been playing setting up Heft for the fall--literally, it turned out--and I was meaning to see it stayed that way.

We'd been looking for Pops. I'd managed to convince Heft that getting out would do him some good. He had to walk the streets again someday, am I right? To tell the truth

I didn't even have to make that point. I think the conversation went something like I said, "C'mon, let's go screw around." To which Heft got all gregarious with, "Sure. Whatever."

We sure enough hadn't found the old man, Pops, but all the same, it wasn't a total waste. Turned out to be a real lesson in urban discovery at its finest. The pair of us were a modern day Tom Sawyer and Huck Finn. I even told Heft as much as we walked along a dirt path we'd come across that wasn't even in any park. Yeah, a dirt path in the city. Can you believe it? A wild place, real unexpected like. It was this trail running along the wilds of the Hudson's choppy edge, hidden down in the armpit of the Westside Highway. If you ignored the constant roar of the traffic, it was easy enough to imagine we were forging our way someplace along the ol' Miss-i-sip. Reeds and bullfrogs. A place for the boy in me that used to run amuck in the Tryon.

"I'm not your Huck," Heft said.

It was a remark right out of the blue.

We'd paused at the sight of a baby snake zipping across the path ahead of us. The place was just that wild. But our minds were so heavy that even a thing as crazy as a baby snake didn't really budge us. I'd heard what he said. I didn't say shit though. Instead I played with an old bottle top with the toe of my sneaker, freeing it from the earth where it was nestled in. With a good kick I sent it skipping and rolling off the path and into the weeds chasing behind the long-gone baby snake.

Then I looked at him. "What?" I asked. And not all pissy like. I sincerely didn't know what he was getting at.

"I'm not your Huck," he repeated.

"I guess I'll pretend I get you."

Heft turned on me almost like he wanted to start some shit again. Add a split lip or something to the collection.

"You think you're the hero, Tweed. The first person. The only person. The world's your stage and the rest of us are just insignificant dust motes in the wake of your glorious, ongoing soliloquy. The rest of us, not even bit parts. Just props."

Holy macaroni, but he was on his game. I didn't offer a thing when he paused to catch his breath. Pretty pleased with himself, I guess, he went on.

"You're wrong, Tweed. Just plain wrong, dude. I'm not your Huck. You're not Tom Sawyer. And I know what it's like to not be wanted. To have even your own family not care."

I'd heard enough.

"Listen, *Heft*, if it's too much to have your help, then just say so. Okay? Don't gotta be a dick about it," I said.

A pair of those little brown birds you always see--the ones forever playing in the dirt-- they whizzed by overhead, all tangled and twittering. I didn't know if they were fighting, mating, or just cutting the fool. All nonchalant-like, I watched them go. When I got back around to looking Heft in the eye, well I could tell I'd gotten near the end of his rope with all my shit.

I needed him.

"Huck had his own book too, you know," I said.

The birds came back and this time it was Heft who watched them while I waited.

With his eyes still following them he said, "Yeah. Yeah, I know. And it was the better of the two."

"Without a doubt. Classic."

Heft considered me coldly for a moment, but then smiled. It was that handsome bastard smile that too often made the girls on the subway blush. Even busted up he could still pull it off. I smiled too. I guess we were both relieved to have given and taken a bit of ground in putting our little previously unspoken turf war out on the table.

"Bridge," Heft said with a nod to the skyline.

Sure enough, the great span of the GWB had snuck up on us and come into view. Not such a wild place after all.

"I'm buying," I said. It didn't really mean I was paying, just shorthand for let's go to the hole of a bodega that sold beer to us minors. So I marched off and Heft tagged along. A good while later we were up along the Tryon getting stupid.

We'd been shooting the shit about much of nothing. To keep from spilling the beans about how it'd been me that'd tagged Heft's name over the CC181 and all--something I felt pretty guilty about of late--I pressed Heft for just what he meant by it when he'd said he knew about not being wanted. Even before I asked I thought he was going to tell me he was adopted or some other Dickensian load. Instead he started telling me about his dead brother's leukemia and some family vacation they all took to some godforsaken place in Florida back in the day. Not like your typical Florida vacation. No, they were like in the swamps of the panhandle or some shit. So Heft's all into his tale of ennui and before I know it, I don't know what in the hell he's jabbering about.

"So we finally make it to this beach house we're going to be staying at for the summer," Heft said.

We were sitting with our legs dangling over the wall at a place in the park that we called *the spot*. The sun had dropped away, and in its place headlights from the highway traffic gouged the dark at our feet.

"Should've seen it," he said. "It was real cool. One of those houses up on stilts out over the water. So we first get there, me all sick from the ride and all, and I hear this, 'Ya'll Yankees?' squeaky like, like--"

"One of your sisters?" I asked, tired of listening, but, you know, to make a show like I was interested.

"No, dude," Heft moped. With his one free hand he thumb-zipped the bottle cap he'd been idly playing with, snapping it off down in the direction of the cars whizzing by below. Not too bad considering it was his off hand.

They were still a good ways down there though, the cars, what with the long slope of wooded hill between us and them, so it wasn't like he was being a delinquent and targeting them or anything. Still, only the Big Guy Upstairs knows how many bottle caps, firecrackers, and butts we'd sent down that way from the spot over the years. I started trying to put a number on it--anything to ignore Heft's story--must have been in the hundreds. The footprint of our aimless and idle adolescence. We were just so much litter for future archaeologists to ponder. Maybe even as high as the thousands, I figured.

Heft went on.

"I'd just rolled out of the backseat, pretty carsick and all, so I wasn't really paying attention, wasn't even sure who or where this kid was."

"What kid?" I asked.

"This kid. Just listen."

"I was," I lied. Heft ignored me.

"I was busy yuking, car sick, like I said. Then, all the sudden, my sister, Preenie, she screams. She's all, 'Ahh!'"

"Preenie," I added with a shake of my head.

"Yeah, Preenie. Typical, huh?" Heft said, all sort of happy with me for agreeing with him. I just nodded.

"And you know, at first, I thought maybe she's screaming at my barf or something. Trying to make a big scene out of it for Mom. But then I'm thinking, nah, that'd be a bit much in the hysterics department. Even for Preenie. So I got my shit together to see what all the mayhem's about."

"Mayhem?" I chided. But Heft just chugged at his beer. So I added, "You sure have a vivid memory."

That got Heft a little bent.

"You wanna hear the fucking story or not?"

"Yeah, tell your story, Homer. Jeesh," I said.

"You know something, Tweed, you've been living with your Pops so long you think nobody else thinks straight either," Heft said.

"Yo, Heft. Don't go raggin' on Pops."

"Yeah, yeah," he said, with one of those *whatever* waves of dismissal.

But I meant it. "Don't be raggin' Pops," I said again, and this time I let him know things were going someplace he didn't want to be.

"I'm not ragging Pops," my boy said. "I'm out here helping ya look, aren't I? C'mon, dude, just calm down. You want to hear the story, or what?"

I finished my beer and let the bottle slip from my hand to go plunking off down below us. That really pissed Heft but good, because somehow there was a big difference between his beer caps and my bottle, as far as the litter goes. All the same he passed me the last beer even though that made the count five to seven and he'd paid.

"All right, but that's all I'm saying," I said, and let the matter drop too.

"All right, yeah, so," Heft went on, "so I was sick and all wiping my mouth with the front of my shirt, and all of the sudden there's this kid, five, six, maybe seven years old. I can't be sure, but, trust me, Preenie was right to scream."

Heft cupped his good hand over his head. "This kid, crazy orange fro. I'm talking a bird's nest of hair, all kind of balancing all up here," he said, still cupping the crown of his head with his good hand. "I mean, seriously, worse than any bowl cut you've ever seen. Ever. Obviously, like a little sister butchered this kid's style. Way too small of a bowl," Heft started laughing.

"No shit?" I laughed along to make Heft feel better. I can be cool that way.

"No shit," Heft confirmed. "Oh man, you don't know. But it gets better. And his face, you know, his face was stained bright red by whatever he'd been eating. I don't know, must have been like a popsicle, or, man, I don't know. Looked like he'd been trying to eat it with every part of his face except for his mouth. And he had these mad-long fingernails with enough black filth and crap under them to pot an orchid."

"Nooo," I laughed. Perhaps a bit too sarcastically.

"What?"

I gave him a look. "I mean, really, c'mon? *Pot an orchid*?"

"Screw you. Mom came up with that," Heft said. Thinking about it, he added, "It's a good one. But listen, that wasn't it either. He had this harelip--"

"That ain't funny," I cut in. "Gina, at my school, she has a harelip. Shit ain't funny. She's a sweet girl."

"I know. No, listen, I'm just trying to paint a picture here. This kid was...just listen."

I shrugged my indifference and my boy went on. The way Heft was slipping into his past reminded me of Pops. I was surrounding myself with nostalgic weepers. Yeah, weepers. Believe it or not--I certainly didn't--Heft's eyes were starting to pool up and he tried to play it off when I noticed by turning away and sucking at his beer all sloppy. Still he kept talking. Or trying to.

"He had so many freckles and bug bites all over him, it...man, you just don't know."

"Yeah, I'm listening," I said. I was hoping this story was going somewhere. I was starting to think Heft was just making it up. You know, just some bullshit to get my goat since I used to live in Florida when I was a kid and all. Back before I came to live with Pops.

Heft manhandled his beer again, gulping it down like some demented legionnaire who just crawled in from the desert. As if that wasn't bad enough, between pulls, he started absentmindedly plugging and unplugging the mouth of the bottle with his index finger all while blathering on. "No, what made this kid, Peter Botche--that was his name. I remember--no, what made this kid a mad crazy sight was, get this, except for these ratty sneakers, not even laces, and a pair of homemade goggles dangling around his neck--,"

"Homemade goggles," I interrupted. But Heft ignored me. He was there now.

"The kid was naked. Buck-ass naked."

"Completely?"

"Naked," Heft said and guzzled down the better half of his beer like he'd earned it. When he finished he belched and added, "Oh, and he had this makeshift gig. You know, like a spear, a sawed-off broom handle with an exposed nail at its tip for a barb."

"I know what a gig is."

Heft shrugged and put the empty back with the rest in the twelve pack carton.

"So what happened?" I asked.

"Whatdaya mean?"

"Whatdaya mean, whatdaya mean?" I countered. "You said you knew what it was like to know your family didn't want you. So what the hell does some naked redneck you met on some Florida vacation have to do with any of that?"

But something had struck a chord, and the grin on Heft's face just kind of washed away.

"Nothing, I guess," he finally said.

I felt a little pissed at Heft. It seemed like he was just running his mouth when I was feeling in a pretty shitty place, so maybe I didn't feel so bad for all the crap I'd put him through with the CC181 after all. But then all out of nowhere he told me something that was, well, the kind of thing you don't tell just anybody.

"One afternoon," Heft said, "about a month into our vacation, I snuck up under the back porch where Preenie and Hanna were sprawled out sunbathing. I remember the tide was so far out you wouldn't even know the Gulf existed. The Sun driving up this fishy stink out of the muck. I was alone you know, and I snuck up because I could hear them talking. I had this dead, smelly blue crab in my hand, and I was planning on throwing it on them. Make a real big fuss. Well, that'd been the plan. But as I got right up under them, just where all I had to do was this simple hook shot lob, that's when I heard what they were saying. I can't really explain it, but there was something in their voices, all conspiracy-like, so I started to eavesdrop. Sounded like a couple whispering mice. You know how girls are, and my twin sisters were…and…."

I wanted to ask Heft what they said, but I just gave him room.

After a good long pause that made me wonder if he'd gone completely Pops on me, Heft finally said, "And so Preenie said, 'I wish it were Chip instead.' That's what my sister Preenie said. My family, they used to call me Chip. You know, like off the old block,"

"Instead? I don't get it," I said.

"Neither did Hannah…or me," Heft said. "So Preenie straightened us out. 'I wish Chip had leukemia instead of Freddie.'" Heft's voice shuddered like a dying thing and the tears broke out for real. "Not, 'I wish Freddie didn't have leukemia.' No. No, she said she wished I had it instead. And then you know what?"

I stared at him. I guess kind of stupid like and so he screamed. "And do you know the fuck what?"

I shook my head.

"Guess," Heft demanded.

I didn't and thankfully he'd had enough. He took a deep breath and looked away and all but whispered, "Hannah told her, 'Yeah, me too.'"

He turned and smiled at me. "Yeah, me too. That's what my sister Hannah said. 'Me too.'"

"Jeesh," was all I could think to offer. I admit, it was pretty broke.

"Yeah, 'jeesh' is right. So quit thinking you got the market cornered, okay, Tweed."

"Cornered? Man, I never--"

"Never mind," Heft said, coming to his feet off the wall so fast that he made me startle a little. "C'mon, it's getting late. Let's go see if maybe Pops hasn't found his way back to your place. Order some pizza," he said. "I must be crazy. Shouldn't even be out here. Fucking gang after me. I should probably go ahead and blow town again."

"You're right," I said. He stopped and looked at me hard. "Get some pizza. Good idea," I said with a shrug.

After we'd walked a good long ways, when it seemed safe, I threw out the question that'd started bothering me. "Say, so what was the deal with that naked kid?"

Heft didn't miss a beat. "Jaybird? He was all right. He taught me how to catch crabs."

"Taught you to catch crabs?" I said. I wanted to add a smart remark about prostitutes, but being kind of buzzed it didn't come to me fast enough.

"Yeah, tasty critters. Maybe I'll share the secret someday," Heft said, with a toss-away wink like I was his little nephew or some shit.

Heft had taken the lead, marching along with a purpose. It was clear he didn't care if I kept up or even followed at all. And, for the first time that night--if not in my life--I found myself padding along behind, all huff and puff, just so much background churning in the great Huck Finn's wake.

And so there was the irony. Maybe if Heft had been beside me, or behind me, the CC181 thug who'd been after him, that big fucking goon, wouldn't have gotten the jump on Heft the way he did. As the dude stepped out from behind this parked van when we were just a block from the bodega, I was too far behind my boy to do anything but yell.

"Knife!"

Chapter Seventeen

Dinner had been kind of strangely and silently awkward and so I was surprised that my mom had waited until we were alone in the guest bedroom to start in on me. Really getting to the point she came in and said she wanted to talk about my pregnancy.

"And so you're sure this young man is the father?" She nodded to the door as if Heft was just on the other side and not long gone back to NYC.

I didn't answer my mom so much as let my eyes burn stakes through her heart.

"I'm sorry, Chloe, but you need to be certain and…well," my mom said, all pausing dramatically and taking in, like, a big deep breath so that I knew *it* was coming, "I have to say, I'm disappointed in you."

"Yeah, good, let's get this out of the way. I'm sorry, Mom. Okay? What do you want me to say? I got knocked up. I messed up. Majorly. I know. Okay?"

"Oh, Chloe," she said and scooched up closer and ran her hand through my hair. "That's not what I mean. Well, of course I would've rather you not made this mistake. But that's not what I'm talking about."

"No?"

"Chloe, please don't take this the wrong way, but I don't really understand what you're doing here."

"Don't take *that* the wrong way? My own mother doesn't want to see me. But I shouldn't take *that* the wrong way?"

"That's not what I meant. Not at all," my mom said, placing one hand over her heart and holding up the other palm like she was swearing herself into the witness box. "Chloe, your father has been there for you always. Hasn't he?"

"Yeah, I guess," I said. She dropped the stink-eye bomb on me with a hardness. So I amended my testimony. "Yeah, fine. Yes, yes he has."

"Then, sweetie, why did you run away? Why didn't you let him help you? Why didn't you, I don't know, trust him? With everything." She said, with this, like, duh-tone in her voice flavoring the last bit.

I thought about it for a few seconds although I already had my answer. "I dunno," I said. "He's a guy." I thought that would be enough.

I wasn't trying to be funny. Still, my mom laughed. "Daniel Tobin may have all the right equipment to qualify to be one of the guys, Chloe, but you and I both know he's far from ever being pigeon-holed by that pesky Y chromosome."

"Yeah," I agreed. "He's a weird one all right."

"He's one in a million," she said, and quickly corrected with, "A billion."

"Then why'd you leave him?"

I was glad she took a second to answer.

"Oh, I don't know. It's not so easy to say. Maybe because I wasn't."

"Does that mean--" I started, but my mom cut me off.

"Whoa, we're getting way off track here. Let's get back to *you* and your father."

Somewhere in another of the upstairs rooms a phone rang.

"Is that what this is about?" I said, gesturing to the sound of the ringing phone. "Did you set up some kind of pow-wow for me and Dad?"

"No. But I think that's a great idea, don't you?"

I paused for a moment. I was just blank inside. "Sure, I guess," I said.

"Chloe, I just don't want to see your father hurt by this. You know him. And this is big stuff. Don't crowd him out. I think you'll be surprised."

"I don't need him telling me what to do. This is my decision. You're a woman, Mom. You understand that. I mean, that's the reason why, like, why I came here in the first place."

"It is your decision. I agree. All I'm saying is that if you'd only give your father the chance, I'm certain he'd agree too."

"So? What now?" I asked.

"Now? I suppose you could call him. Talk."

"So I can go back home?"

"Or stay. Your choice. But if you do decide to go back, I'd like a promise."

"Yeah?"

"Next time you want to come out, call first. That way you can avoid the whole bus ordeal, since I'll spring for the airfare. Greyhound. Must have been a nightmare."

"Mother, you can't imagine."

We hugged and it was really good. Then I remembered the present I'd packed along.

"Hey, I got you something," I said.

As I rummaged through my bag my mom was doing the whole, 'you didn't need to get anything for me,' blah, blah, blah thing.

"Here ya go, stranger," I said. I handed her this framed photo. The frame was real simple, just silver, probably aluminum, with a print of leaves stamped into it. I admit it was pretty cheap, but so what, because the picture was the important thing. It was of me and her and my dad, from when I was a kid and we were all spending the weekend at this crazy cabin upstate.

"I'd saved this for myself because I thought you looked pretty…and I always liked how Dad has his arms around us. I got the frame in Kansas City on the way here. I hope you don't mind, but this is just a copy I had made right before I left. I still wanted to keep the original for myself. I wasn't sure you'd even want it, so…. But you can't tell. It's on real good paper, the best I could find and everything. And I'll send the original if you really like it."

My mom started to cry so I jabbered on. "Remember that crazy cabin? It had all the--"

I shut up pretty quick though, because it was hard to talk the way my mom buried my face in this ginormous bear hug all the sudden. It was pretty good and all. So clickity-click, yanno. Now I'd always have this really in-tight, almost out of focus shot of my mom's blouse. Immediately, like in that very moment, I knew it was one of my favorites.

I didn't want my mom to let go. But after a minute I started to wonder if she ever would. I was just thinking I'd give her a little bit longer to acquiesce. That's another of my SAT study words. Acquiesce. I don't care for it though. It's one of those words that sounds great in, like, maybe a history paper or something, but it's way too pretentious to ever use in real life, so I don't know how it snuck in here.

My mom was still in hug-mode and so I'd moved on to thinking about how 'pretentious' is fine enough, because it sounds like 'precious' which is what I imagine snooty types that actually use words like acquiesce really are. All the vocab gymnastics to distract myself from the never-ending bear hug were cut short when a knock came at the bedroom door.

My mom's new husband Jim stuck his head in. "Um, Chloe, the phone…I'm sorry to interrupt you two, but that was your father, Daniel. I'm afraid your friend…Chad, is it? I'm afraid there's been a rather horrible incident."

…

Heft died in my arms. He'd said my name twice. Not Tweed, but my Christian name, and then he asked for his mother. He was gone before I could reply that I'd get her, before I could assure him that he was going to be okay. Just like that, my best friend was gone.

After spending the day with the police, first at the crime scene, then at the 34th Precinct, even as wiped out as I was, I didn't go home. I'd already seen practically everybody from the building anyways as news of what'd gone down had spread. Along with everybody else, David, the super, and Daniel, Chloe's dad, came by on the street to gawk and get the gory details. How Heft had died. How this CC181 guy had stabbed him three times in a flurry and was gone before Heft hit the pavement. How I had been helpless.

At first, Daniel kind of freaked out a little. He wanted to know where Scissors was. Had she been with us? Had I seen her? All that jazz. I guess the last he'd known was that she and Heft had run off together out to Denver. As I set him straight about Heft taking her out there and ditching her with her mom, Daniel just glazed over. That was odd. I'd been sure he was going to get angry about it. He had to. I mean, I had. But he just stared off across the street looking at much of nothing, nodding here and there as I told him what I knew. What Heft had said. People can be so weird.

David and Daniel were cool though. Daniel let me know he'd phone out to Denver and give Chloe the news of what'd happened while David stuck around for me kind of like moral support until it was time to go with the cops to the precinct. Then he said he'd go and let Pops know what was going on too. I quickly lied and said Pops had already been by and gone home to rest so he shouldn't bother him. I hoped I was convincing. Like a criminal I watched David's concerned expression from the backseat as we pulled away in the patrol car. I was sure the jig was about to be up on Pops's disappearance. I'd be going straight from the police station to some foster home or orphanage. My Dickensian nightmare was really starting to come together.

Not that the cops had been abusive. Anything but. They were actually way cooler than I ever could have thought. They'd known all about what had gone down before with the subway, but back then we'd played dumb and hadn't ever mentioned nothing about the CC181. Heft had especially been more concerned with those gangbangers getting more riled up to get him if he snitched them out. And I guess I hoped it would all just blow over. Of course there were other witnesses there that day, and the news had reported Heft's brush with the A train was suspected to be gang-related, so I never knew what the cops really knew.

I hadn't been sure if I just wanted to run or throw myself down and bawl as I watched them load Heft's body into the ambulance. The thing I was sure of was that I'd be catching a lot of shit from the cops about me and Heft and gangbanging. And knowing that was my immediate future didn't help me as I tried to keep it all together. I imagined the bare room with the two-way mirror. Cold, circulation cutting-off handcuffs. A real disgruntled cop with stinking breath right in my face. Threats. The old police straw-grabbing routine.

Turned out I'd seen too much TV.

The detective in charge, Robinson, he didn't play that game. He was this big Russian dude who'd obviously Americanized his name. His accent was still majorly thick though, so it was going to take a lot more than a name change. I wondered why he even bothered. Yet another proof that people do some funny, unfathomable shit, sometimes.

There was no interrogation to speak of. We sat in Detective Robinson's office. He chatted me up with what seemed more like small talk than anything else. Even talked some baseball. All the while, I wolfed-down some Chinese delivery that he'd gotten for me. I don't know why. I wasn't even hungry. Maybe because while I ate everybody but this small-talk detective left me alone.

He said he knew me and Heft were good kids and that it was a tragedy that we'd somehow gotten our paths crossed with this 'bad element.' The good cop routine, if that even was what it was, wasn't necessary. I gladly ratted out the CC181 this time around. I even admitted it was them in the subway before. I didn't implicate Razer though. Just the big dude, as best I could describe him with his tattoos and all, along with the couple of tools I'd seen hanging with him. I still didn't know what I wanted to do about Razer. I supposed I might be doing enough already with just that.

Robinson said he understood why we'd kept quiet. He told me the cops were aware of the CC boys through their tagging, but admitted that they knew nothing else about them. He seemed pretty frustrated about that and asked me several times over if there wasn't anything I was leaving out, anything at all that might give them more of a lead on the CC181. It was almost like he knew I was holding out about Razer. He could smell my deception. I didn't rat Razer out though. And I didn't rat myself, either.

No, I didn't come clean about the tagging I'd done, the tagging that got Heft in trouble with the CC181 in the first place. I might have been dumb enough to start this mess, but I wasn't so moronic that I was going to roll around in it. When it was all over, Robinson called for Pops to come get me. No answer, of course. The burly Russian Detective left a message and after I swore up and down that I'd have Pops call him, he let me skip out with an escort to see me home. Close call. I waited for my boy in blue escort, who was actually a chick, to leave the building after she dropped me off. Then I headed back out myself.

In an effort to avoid David, or more questions from the building neighbors, I made it straight for Pops's dive bar again. I was being a glutton for abuse.

"Hey ya, kid," Bourbon Monkey said when I walked in. I waited for him to tell me to leave, sort of like that was the whole reason I went there these days, because Pops sure wasn't looking like he'd ever show up again. Instead Bourbon Monkey popped a beer, slid it across the bar towards me, and nodded for me to have a seat.

There was a little bit of a crowd. Maybe it was my imagination, but it seemed like I'd gotten the place's attention. Even after I couldn't really pinpoint anybody paying me any mind it felt like all eyes were on me. Little Dominican Girlfriend emerged from out of a group of guys as I sat down. She shimmied up to me and smiled one of those sad smiles.

"Oh, little Papi, I'm so sorry about your friend. We all hear it on the news. That's terrible. So terrible," she said and hugged me and left a lipstick deposit on my cheek.

"Thanks," I said. I looked to Bourbon Monkey and then to the beer he'd put in front of me and repeated the same thing to him.

"It's alright, kid. Don't you worry none. They'll get that scum. On the house," he said, rapping the bar with his knuckles. "Now drink up and get the hell out," he added with a smile.

Little Dominican Girlfriend added something in Spanish that I didn't understand. Probably a curse or something like that, judging by her expression. Then she spit on the floor to punctuate it. Not a mimic spit for effect, either. She actually spat out a frothy white wad onto the floor.

"Thank you, Teresa. That was lovely," Bourbon Monkey said.

"Have either of you seen Pops today…lately?" I asked.

Bourbon Monkey pursed his lips and thought for a second. "No…" He looked to Little Dominican Girlfriend who was shaking her head. "No," he said again. "Matter of fact, I was meaning to ask you where he's been off to. Haven't seen him in a good while."

Little Dominican agreed. "He no been around, little Papi."

"Last I've seen of the old fella was a few weeks ago when he was in here with Wallace."

"Wallace?"

"You know," Little Dominican Girlfriend said, "He a big rat-looking man. He a real asshole, that one."

"You mean Weasel Guy?" I said.

"Yeah, come to think of it, he does have sort of a rodent thing going on, don't he?" Bourbon Monkey agreed. "Yeah, no, that's been a while since the two of them were here tying one on."

The news that Pops had last been seen with that lowlife really drove a stake into me. I finished the beer by chugging it. "If Pops comes in, will you do me a favor and call? I'll give you the number."

"Sure, kid," Bourbon Monkey said and handed me the pen that he kept tucked behind his ear.

"You let him know we miss him," Little Dominican Girlfriend said.

Weird thing, I believed her.

I had one last beer in the fridge back at the apartment. The last, lonely soldier, Pops always called it. I chugged that one too. In the half a dozen seconds that'd taken, I'd made up my mind about Razer. It was one of those decisions that just happened without any upfront thought. Like some part of the back of my mind, some primal part, had taken over and done the legwork to get there.

I went to my room and proceeded to gird myself. Knee pads. Elbow pads. Weight-lifting gloves. Goalie mask. My heavy-ass tweed overcoat that'd I had for years and years. Thing was like padded armor. I'd had more than a few scrapes in it to know. From Pops's room I raided his shoe box of rolled coins again. What had once seemed like an endless supply was now down to the dregs. I snatched up the last roll of quarters and settled for the next best, a roll of dimes. Pennies would've probably been heavier, but none of them were rolled. Pops only saved the wheat pennies and they slid around the bottom of the shoebox loose. I stuck the quarter and dime rolls in my overcoat pockets, making sure the quarters were on the right side, and tucked my hockey mask up under my left arm on the inside of my overcoat. I was ready.

Razer just happened to be out on his building's front stoop. His street, 184th, was a steep hill that shot up the minute you started heading over on the east side of Broadway. Razer's building was midway in the block ending at the top of the hill. He didn't notice me right off. His little sisters and three other girls about the same age were playing some version of hopscotch with multi-colored chalk lines and boxes they'd drawn on the sidewalk. Razer was watching them and talking on the phone.

One the girls squealed before Razer saw me. "Tweed!"

As I passed them another one remarked on how stupid I was to be wearing my coat.

Razer looked like a ghost that'd seen a ghost. He said something quickly into the phone and then laid it down on the doorstep as he jumped up to greet me. He was real agitated and my adrenaline was mad pumping. I wasn't sure what he was about to do but I damn sure knew what I was bringing.

"I just heard, man," he said, "I just heard. This is some crazy messed up shit, man." Then he was truly at a loss as I quickly put on my goalie mask. "What the fuck, Tweed?"

My hands dug into my coat pockets and found their coin rolls. Heavy and hard-fisted with dimes and quarters, I dove into him. I guess the mask wasn't the best idea after all, since it kind of warned Razer. A sucker punch with the quarter roll probably would have been a better start. Hindsight and all that jazz. Regardless, my coin-filled fists were wailing home a full day's supply of hurt. I couldn't be quite sure where the blows were landing. Fog of war. Flurry of battle. Goalie mask slits for eyes. But I was putting it to him good. He fought back, of course. Mad cussing me the whole time. My heavy overcoat proved to be worth it. Like I said, growing up, it always had. That was actually one of the many reasons I loved it. Getting pounded to the body didn't hurt nearly as much with the old tweed on. It was only a detriment if we started wrestling. If I hit the ground.

I hadn't paid the girls' shrieking any attention until the roll of quarters exploded in my hand. I'd landed a savage blow I got in to what must have been Razer's forehead. Their high-pitched yells rose above Razer's continued vulgarities, and I realized they were now crying out not in fear for Razer, but in joy for the rain of quarters dancing around our feet, rolling madly down the hilly sidewalk to the busy Broadway intersection below.

Razer got the better of me just then and somehow managed to both tear off my hockey mask and violently flip me onto my back all at the same time. My head cracked the sidewalk hard. The world spun and I began to drown in my massive coat. I think the back of my left hand smacked the sidewalk at the same time, dislodging the roll of dimes that had at some point split open as well. A slew of shiny dimes exploded like shrapnel, striking us both before quickly joining the scrambling quarters. More squeals then as no doubt the little girls thought I was some sort of quarter and dime filled piñata that Razer was beating the unending silver stuffing out of.

"What's your problem man? What're you doing, Tweed?" Razer shouted, inches from my face.

I tried to get up. Not a chance.

"Hit 'em again!" someone shouted.

I hadn't realized it, but Razer's sidekick from Bryant Park was there. I don't know when he'd arrived on the scene. Maybe it was him who'd flipped me. Whatever the deal, at the moment, he was holding down my legs while Razer straddled my chest, pinning my arms under his knees.

"What is your F-ing problem?" Razer seethed again. His bottom lip was split open and the blood was dripping onto my face. I tasted blood and assumed it was Razer's. It wasn't.

The little girls had wrapped up collecting all the on-the-loose change, and so they moved to the curb to excitedly count their booty. Much bickering and giggling was taking place between them. Surprisingly, no one else had gathered to witness the disturbance except for one elderly woman watching us from an open window on the second story of Razer's building. She poked her head out and tossed her scolds down onto us in Spanish. No one paid her any mind. What a surprise.

"CC181," I said. "You fuckers killed Heft. I know. I know you're a fucking CC boy, Razer. I know. You guys killed him. You killed Heft," I spat the blood in my mouth back into his face and clenched for my beating.

"Oh, snap. No dice," Razer's partner said.

"Tweed, you got this shit all wrong," Razer said. He wiped my blood spittle from his cheek with his sleeve. "We gonna let you go. But you gotta promise to listen." I didn't say anything. "I sit on you all night, my man. C'mon, we let you up you let me talk to you. Nothing crazy. You let me explain. Promise?"

I didn't have a lot of options and so I nodded.

...

"CC181 is a chess club, Tweed," Razer said through a mouthful of fries. He winced as the salt hit his split lip.

"Chess club?" I said. He'd repeated himself and I still wasn't believing my ears.

"Chess...C...Club...C...181...One hundred and Eighty-first Street," he spelled it out like I was broke. "I'm the president."

"President?"

"What can I say? I'm the best, my man."

"But you said they were a gang. A real badass gang," I said.

"Whatever. Like you never talked no trash before." He had a point.

Razer and I had wandered over to this hole in a wall diner joint he said was the best in the Dominican neighborhood. He'd sent his buddy off on some kind of mission, and as a sort of peace negotiation between us, said we should go someplace quiet to talk things out. That is, once he was sure I wasn't going to go off on him again. I lost my knee pads and elbow pads as well as my hockey mask on the way there. Just tossed them all in the garbage. I folded my coat up and carried it. It was torn and bloodied now. I used it for a seat cushion when we got to the place and discovered they used overturned stacked milk crates for chairs.

So there we were. The place was cramped, noisy, crowded, and chaotic, just like my current state of mind. My head throbbed and I had a pretty nice goose egg where my skull had kissed the sidewalk.

"So if CC181 is a chess club," I said, pausing to sip my drink and buy enough time to make sure I didn't slip up and say something stupid to give myself away, "then how come those guys threw Heft on the tracks in front of the train?"

"Man, that was just Rollo. Rollo be crazy. He ain't no part of the CC boys. He's just a wannabe."

"That so?"

"Most definitely."

"You're the president, why don't you put him outta your gang then?"

"*Club*," Razer shot back.

"Club. Whatever. Why'd you even let him join in the first place?"

"Man, you ever see that ape?"

I shrugged. "Yeah. So?"

"So? So it's like this," Razer said. "You know the joke about where does the five hundred pound ape sit?"

"It's a gorilla," I corrected.

"What?"

"The joke is, 'where does a five hundred pound gorilla sit?'"

"Who are you, joke police? Shut the F train up. So you know what I mean. Wherever the hell he wants, that's where he sits. Rollo wanted to be in the chess club. Thinks it makes his dumbass look smart for the chickas."

"So he isn't really CC181?"

"No way, man. Asshole thinks Alekhine's gun be something you rob the corner store with," Razer scoffed.

"No shit," I said. I had no idea what he was talking about. "Then listen. As president of Chess Club 181 maybe you best talk to the authorities, don'tcha think? Turn his ass in."

"Man, Tweed, do you seriously think I ain't six moves ahead of you, bro? Rollo is about to be mated."

"Mated?"

"Checkmate. I got a plan. I was already putting it together on the phone when you jumped my ass. Bishop's taking care of things as we speak."

"Bishop?"

"Benny. The kid that was just helping me calm your ass down? You met him at the park before. Hell, Tweed, he goes to our school."

"I know. Just didn't know he was 'Bishop' is all."

"Lot of things you don't know."

"Obviously," I said. "Since when did you belong to a chess club?"

"Ah man, Tweed. See that's what happens when you only be interested in yourself. When you think everything revolves around you."

"Yeah?" Sounded like Razer had been talking with Heft.

"I've been playing chess for years now. I take lessons with a coach after school. I'm a ranked player, my man."

"Ranked?"

"I never mention this to you because I know you wouldn't care. All you do is rag. Tear down. Besides, you and me, we ain't been tight for a long time. It was just you and Heft anymore. You never even hang with me at school this whole past year. So, whatever."

"That's not true," I said. Razer raised an eyebrow of derision. "Okay," I admitted, "but you're still a best friend. It was always the three of us. We just…things change, I don't know. Still friends," I mumbled.

"Forget it, man." He checked his watch. "As Heft's friends, we got us something to do. I have a plan."

"A plan? What plan?"

"Taking Rollo down. And I need your help. That fool is history."

"Rollo? That freaking ape? Fuck a plan, let's just call the police. I got the detective's number," I said.

Razer paused and shook his head. "Dude killed Heft. Jesus, Tweed. I can't believe this, man." I could see his eyes were glazing over with tears. "You just call the police who knows who else might get hurt. Maybe one of my boys. My friends. No. No, you made this, you fix this. I'll help, for Heft's memory but this is how it's going to be. That's all what I know right now. Dude is history."

"What if something goes wrong?" I asked as the voice of reason. "Or, what if he comes after us? Ya know, when he gets out? I mean, you're ratting your own gang."

"Comes after us? What? When he's seventy-two and out on parole? He committed murder. He ain't no juvie. He ain't getting no punk-ass wrist slap. And he's got a record. Rollo, he's history. And I told you, fool wasn't in the CC181, and the CC boys ain't no goddamned gang. We're a chess club. Straight up. Legit."

"Still...." I said.

"Man, Rollo is going down for the count. Yeah, that game is locked. The man is going to bury that big ass ape under the prison. And good riddance," Razer said, dusting his hands both of fry salt and Rollo. He dabbed his split and swollen lip with his napkin. As he winced and the water from his eyes spilled down his cheek, I wasn't sure if it was from pain or for Heft. Probably a little of both.

"I can't believe all this crazy shit. Who would've believed this would happen?" I said.

Razer ate a few more bites from his sandwich. Gingerly little nibbles like a mouse. He had that vacant expression on his face that I'd thought I knew so well. Like when he huffed. I thought it meant there was nothing going on up there. Now though, having seen him sit behind that same dull expression while trouncing all those guys in chess, now I knew I'd been wrong all along. It was me. I was the one who'd been in a stupor. Suddenly Razer spoke up.

"Since you started all this mess doggin' the CC181 with Heft's tag, you got no choice. You the one got to fix this mess and make things right, homes. You gonna help me bring Rollo down. That's what you got to do. Least you can do."

"Me? Dogging your tags with Heft's? What? How'd you know that?"

Razer popped a single fry in his mouth and the twinkle that came to his eye was the same one I'd seen when he'd given Malcolm Sarsgaard his chess lesson in Bryant Park that day.

"I didn't. Until just now. So let's go."

I was halfway to the door when I realized I'd forgotten my great tweed overcoat. I turned back to get it, telling Razer to hold up, but then stopped myself. I stood for just half a nanosecond in a flurry of thought. The coat was an old, tattered thing now. It was blood-stained. It was good in a fist-fight. But I was through fist-fighting, or any fighting. I hoped. Even though it was still too big for me, I'd outgrown it. Or so that's how I felt just then. I left it there folded on the milk crate. Never saw my old coat again.

Chapter Eighteen

I crouched in the recessed gated entrance at the corner of the churchyard at the intersection of Fort Washington Avenue and 181st Street, busy watching a dead-end alley just down and across 181st that the CC181 called 'The Castle.' Their main turf. Headquarters. Not a squeezed-tight garbage alley like was so common, but a pretty fair-sized sort of mini-courtyard between two buildings. This was where they hung-out and played chess. Just so happened, it was the dead-end alley between Razer's chess coach's building and the Mexican restaurant owned by Bishop's uncle. The restaurant was nothing fancy. One of those order-at-the-counter places. Menu board overhead with illuminated photos of what the dishes looked nothing like. Two or three wobbly tables. So most days they were there, Razer had explained as we'd trekked over, the CC181 boys got their fill of chess tutelage as well as chicken and black bean burritos. Pretty sweet set up.

"You keep out of sight right here," Razer had told me, pointing me to the church wall. It was a knee-high stone dealio topped with wrought-iron bars ending in spear-tips. Offered some concealment. Not much. There were a few poorly trimmed bushes to boot. They helped. That is, if I hunkered down behind them like I was up to something. "You see Rollo go into The Castle, you make the call to your detective." He'd handed me his phone. "Make sure you let that man know me and the CC crew is in there with Rollo. And don't forget to tell 'em Rollo ain't got no gun. And CC181 ain't no gang. Better yet, don't even say nothing about the CC. Just let 'em know there are innocent bystanders in there with Rollo. I don't wanna get caught up in no crazy-assed cop crossfire."

"Yeah, yeah, I got it. Nothing to it."

"Nothing to it? Nothing to it? Easy for you to say, Tweed. You'll be kicking around out here on blessed, sacred ground. Pretty good ways from what'll be the shit going down. Meanwhile, yours truly, other hand, is going to be trapped in a dead-end alley between Rollo and a bunch of trigger-happy New York's Finest. I don't want to die in no alley, Tweed. That'd break my mama's heart."

"Razer, Razer, don't worry, my man. Detective Robinson, he's alright. You'll see. We'll be cool."

But like all sorts of best laid plans, ours worked like a Times Square Rolex knock-off. Good for about an hour.

I don't know if he always carried himself like such a tool, or if it was adrenaline, or huffing, or whatever the hell it was he'd polluted himself with, but Benny the Bishop was bopping around like a whack job. Yeah, practically dancing around Rollo as the two of them came up the street a pretty good while after Razer had left me to my post and disappeared in The Castle. At first, seeing Bishop acting all goofy got me nervous. But then I considered how it didn't seem to be causing the big, tattooed thug, Rollo, one iota of concern. Okay then. Just as I settled my mind that things were copasetic, the two sauntered right past the entrance of the CC181 hangout. Rollo shoving Bishop through the door ahead of them, they disappeared into the Mexican restaurant instead. Now what? This wasn't something we'd discussed. I wasn't sure if I should make the call. Would they be coming out? Were they sitting down to eat or not? For certain there was a back way through the restaurant into the alley.

Rollo had looked even bigger than I remembered. I wondered if he was carrying his blade. I suddenly wished I'd kept my coat.

"Hey, whatchu doin' there?"

Tucked in the corner on the inside of the churchyard's entryway like I was, the voice called out from the Fort Washington Avenue sidewalk just over the wall behind me. I scowled over my shoulder expecting a cop or somebody connected with the church. Busybody or priest, maybe. Not hardly. This bum, some loser I'd never seen in the neighborhood before, face pressed peering through the iron fence like a kid at the zoo, demanded his answer again.

"Whatchu doin'? Who you spyin' on? A girlie?"

He was a healthy looking black dude. Probably past middle age. Hard to say, really. Street type. A full, scraggily beard, mostly salt and very little pepper, concealed most of his face. The shopping cart full of crap he was pulling like a sled dog with a length of blue nylon rope tethered around his waist told me that much for sure. Not that his clothes alone weren't enough to give him away. Filthy red sweat pants and a matching puffy parka despite the heat. Red with that fake white fur trim on the hood. Or, at least, used to be white. Looked like Ghetto Claus here had been rooting around too many chimneys.

And he sweated like you'd expect a dude in a parka at the tail end of summer would be sweating. Maybe the sauna routine was what was keeping him looking fit even through his hard times out on the streets.

"Leave me alone, Homie-less," I said, and then turned my back, pretending to ignore him. How to get rid of homeless dudes 101.

"Maybe for a dollar I won't blow your surveillance," he said.

"I don't have a dollar. And if I did, sure as shit you wouldn't be getting it."

"Uh huh," he said.

I stood up and walked out of the churchyard to get away. I knew that was the only way I was going to be rid of him. I crossed over to the lamppost on the corner of the busy intersection. Ghetto Claus leaned into his rope and pulled his urban sleigh of crap over to join me.

"You watchin' a girlie, I bet. She cheatin' on you? The ladies, they always be cheatin' a man. Cheat, cheat, cheat."

"What part of 'leave me alone' confuses you?" I said.

I was doing my best to keep my eyes on the restaurant. I could see the blob-like silhouettes of at least four, maybe five, people milling around inside. I couldn't say with any real certainty which, if any, of the blobs were Rollo or Bishop. The homeless dude had decided to pull his shopping cart full of junk right up next to me at the lamppost. He began unloading his cache of garbage at my feet. He'd started by spreading out a blanket. Looked like we were in cahoots setting up a sidewalk sale. As he did this, he whistled. And I mean whistled. If there was some kind of prize or trophy or accolade for whistling, then this homeless fool would've had it in the bag. Or in the shopping cart, I guess I should say. Who knew? What with the plethora of everything but the kitchen sink he was pulling out of his bottomless cart, maybe an award for his whistling was due to pop up out of there any second.

If not for the fact that I had his phone, I could have called Razer to figure out what to do now that our plan had gone down the drain. It was like a game of Romper where the other guy made up some new, crazed rule that just radically changed the field.

"Here you go. This is what you need," the homeless dude said with a tap on my shoulder. He was holding a pair of binoculars. It truly did not surprise me.

"Um...cool...thanks."

I took them, thinking what the hell. As I gave them a shot, doubting they'd make much difference, the homeless guy stuck me with his bill.

"That'll be four hundred," he said.

"Four hundred? Dollars?"

"Cash, please. I no longer accept credit cards," he nodded.

"Are you completely whack?"

I hadn't even gotten the things into focus before I was shoving them back at his grime-caked, grotesquely long fingernails. He waved me off.

"All sales final. No refunds, no exchanges," he said.

I ignored him and tossed the binoculars back into his shopping cart. "Yeah, right."

"You can't...that's a steal," he said. "Thems there, they got the genuine quartz crystal German engineered frost bifocal lenses. Got the haze reduction. Super coat deluxe. Okay, ten dollars."

As the crowd from the intersection crosswalk passed and thinned, I was greeted by yet another request for money I didn't have.

"Mango, two dollars, please. Candy, one dollar," a little girl offered, great brown eyes pleading. She pulled a little red wagon filled with an arrangement of shiny orange mangos, peeled and cleverly sliced to bloom like flowers on stick stalks planted in a cardboard box. "Two dollars," she repeated.

"Sorry, I said and waved her off.

"Them look good," the homeless dude said. "You fix them up like that yourself, sweetie?" She shook her head. "No mind. I'll have me one," he said.

"They're two dollars," I said, maybe with a bit too much attitude.

"I ain't deaf," he snarled back. "Best you mind you own damned business. Even if it is nothin' but mindin' whoever else's business it is you be spyin' on, boy." He pulled a wad of bills from his pocket and freed two. I guess homeless doesn't mean broke. "I'll let you pick," he said, passing the money to the girl.

"This one is good," she said, and handed him his blooming mango on a stick.

"Yes it is," he agreed. "Yes it is!"

I'd let all that distract me long enough that I'd never even seen the trouble coming until it was right there. Two patrolmen stood right outside the Mexican restaurant.

"Aw, no way," I said. "This can't be good."

"No, it's good," the homeless dude said. Mango juice trickled from the corners of his mouth and down through his beard.

I had to think fast. In hindsight maybe I shouldn't have thought quite so fast.

There was a payphone just down the block. Good. I got out a dollar and asked the little girl to make change. She shook her head. I wasn't sure if that meant she didn't have it, or just wouldn't do it.

"I can make change for you," the homeless dude said. "Fifty cents on the dollar."

"Why would I agree to that?"

Across the street, one cop remained out on the sidewalk while his partner went in the restaurant.

"Fine. Good. Yeah." I handed him the dollar. "Give me the fifty cents."

"All right now. Hol' yer horses."

He started rooting around in his endless assortment of pockets and I didn't want to imagine what all his searching, grimy fingers were discovering. The little girl stood transfixed. I guess she wanted to see how this played out. After what seemed forever, the homeless dude found my fifty cents, along with what looked like a dried chicken wing bone. He dropped the change, two quarters, in my hand, and put the chicken wing bone back in the pocket where he'd found it. No surprise there.

"Hey now, that reminds me," he said. "You one of them boys what does the graffiti up around this neighborhood? That spray paintin' whatnot?"

"I need you to do something," I said, refusing to get sidetracked. "I want you to take this phone into the alley over there." I held out Razer's phone and pointed the way to The Castle. He nodded.

"What for?"

"It's a matter of life and death," I said. Which might not have been an exaggeration.

He proved how he'd become the most well-funded homeless dude I'd ever come across. "What's in it for me?" he asked.

I pressed the phone into his dirty palm. "You just take this phone to a guy in that alley named Razer and I'll give you twenty bucks when you come back."

"Let's see the twenty."

"You got to go now. No time. C'mon, go."

The cop outside the restaurant across the street had gotten antsy waiting on his partner. He wandered in front of the alley and cocked his head to get a better look at whatever had caught his attention there. I could only imagine.

"Please, c'mon, man," I was reduced to pleading. I even started to give him a little shove in that direction.

"Don't be touchin' me. I see that cop. You tryin' to set me up." His eyes narrowed to angry little slits. "Some kind of set up. You think I'm stupid?"

The cop at the entrance to the alley fell back and cupped his mouth over his walkie-talkie. Not stopping, he stepped back to the restaurant window and began rapping on it to get his partner's attention. Then he unsnapped the strap over his gun and looked around nervously in his gunslinger stance.

"For fuck's sake," I said.

I started to dart across the street. A cab madly taking the turn onto 181st froze me in my tracks. I locked eyes with the driver and waited patiently through the eternity of a heartbeat as the hurtling mass of yellow played with physics to determine whether it was going to stop in time or mow me down.

Tires squealed. Bumpers smashed. Plastic snapped. Metal crunched and grumbled. Glass shattered. Horns from two, maybe three, directions followed, blaring all at once. Inches from my thigh, the cab came to a jarring stop and then lunged forward two feet when it was rear-ended. I landed on the hood. I landed on the ground. I'd been spared. Momentarily. I stood back up. A spring bouncing back.

The cop at the alleyway entrance jerked around to face me and I thought for sure that he was going to draw down to fill me with slugs. I watched the news. I knew how these things happened. I screamed to him, something kind of nonsensical in my panic, all with arms frantically waving over my head. The cabbie was screaming now too. And so was the homeless dude. I think the little girl with the mango cart was crying. No one seemed to make much of any sense. The cop may have shouted something. Maybe not. We were slivered facets in a kaleidoscope of sensory overload. Suddenly the cop on the sidewalk became two as his partner came barreling out of the Mexican joint. Sirens in the distance as well. Then again, maybe not so distant. Time was whiplashing back and forth between slow and fast, fast and slow, just the same as calm and mayhem seemed interchangeable. The acrid smell of burning tire rubber pierced my nostrils and took root.

As both cops faced me, the source of so much sudden commotion, and as if things weren't confusing enough, Rollo stepped out of the alley behind them.

Rollo could have run. Could have, but didn't. He decided to do something stupid instead. People who do stupid shit are the most dangerous people in the world. People who are compelled to violence and crime that also do stupid shit are way, way beyond dangerous. Rollo stepped up behind the first cop.

I screamed to the cops, "That's him! Get him!" They ignored the message. As they screamed for me to get on the ground, I hoped they weren't about to shoot the messenger.

Even as the first cop's hand hovered just inches above his gun, Rollo slipped his hand in from behind and yanked it from the holster.

Now I dropped back to the ground.

"Gun! Gun!" the unarmed cop screamed as he spun to wrestle with Rollo.

The report was more like one of the firecrackers Razer would screw around with when we hung out in the Tryon.

The cop crumpled onto his knees, doubled over at Rollo's feet. "He got my gun," he whispered. Above all the commotion I heard that whisper. Maybe it was because like him, I was close to the ground. Probably not. I wondered if I'd be the one to know his last words. I thought of Pops's stories. I guess you really do see your life fly by in those moments.

I didn't see the other cop pull his gun, but he must have. As Razer came hurtling out of the alley like a train out of the tunnel, mowing into the unsuspecting Rollo, the second cop let fly with half of his clip. It was a crowded sidewalk. The shots that might miss Rollo and Razer were going to find others. Of that I was certain.

Chapter Nineteen

The day following all the madness proved to be the none-too-proverbial calm *after* the storm. The battered survivors gathered to assess the damage to their lives. Sort through the wreckage. Find the way to move on.

They'd laid him out in a box before us and gave us each our chance to speak. And no matter that some talked a good long while, or that many wept loudly, he never stirred. So they closed him in his box and we carried the box to a hole, freshly and sharply carved into a manicured lawn. Some last words were spoken, and when he didn't pound the lid to say the joke had gone on long enough, they lowered the box to the bottom, covered it with earth, and told us all was concluded. Our friend, our brother, our son, was at rest.

I stayed after all the others had left, waiting until the grave was filled and the wounded lawn was made whole once more by the workmen who patched it with sod. Not that I was the only one who cared so much. Others would have stayed even longer, but they had loved ones to pull them away, to take them home, to share their grief. They had people who cared about them too.

...

I'd come home from Denver a couple of days after I got the news about Heft. My mom convinced me not to rush back the night I got the news, and that I should give myself a day or two there with her to let it all sink in. No sense having a breakdown at thirty thousand feet, she'd said. At first I didn't agree, but it turned out it was pretty sensible advice. She offered to fly back with me in time for the funeral, which probably was good thinking too, but I managed to convince her that I was fine enough to travel on my own. Anywho, I got home the day before the funeral so I expected to see Tweed before all that. I even went to his apartment several times but no one was ever home, not even Pops. I wondered if they'd gone out of town, but I couldn't imagine where they could possibly go. Normally, I could have asked Heft, and that thought actually popped into my head once or twice before I could stop it. How depressing is that? Very.

I kind of kept up a vigil at my window the night before the funeral watching Tweed's window and waiting for his sudden appearance. Every time my dad came to my bedroom to check on me, which was like a bazillion times, I got my hopes up thinking

Tweed had come to our door or called somehow without me hearing the phone ring or the door buzz. I guess I was in some weird place. I dunno.

It was a relief when I got to the funeral service at the church and Tweed and Heft's other friend, Razer, were waiting for me on the steps outside.

My dad and I had walked the last several blocks. He'd wanted to get out of the cab to talk. Not so much that he cared about the cabbie overhearing, but, yanno, for my sake. So that was cool. Funny thing, we didn't go into any of the big stuff like my baby or the cutting or the girl at school. All we talked about really was his current play. Well, it wasn't *his*. He was a member of the orchestra, French horn.

The play was going well, with packed houses since opening and lots of great reviews. I was happy for my dad on this count, mainly because he was one of those very empathetic types who suffered when others suffered. The orchestra would always have a gig no matter how any given play did. They were unionized and all. But the actors, that was another story. Sure they had their guild and all too, but actors were a dime a dozen, even the talented ones sometimes. So my dad had really suffered in the past when nice people, good actors, fell on hard times when a show didn't do well.

I asked him how the actress he had the hots for was doing. He put up this front like he was at a loss to know what I was talking about. I tried to sing the song I'd heard him singing before. I know I got it muddled up, but he knew the score right off. We both had a little laugh and he said she and her very serious girlfriend, the lead actress, were doing very well in their relationship, thank you very much.

That ended the subject nicely and gave him his opening to talk about me instead. So for the last few blocks my dear old dad was forced to listen to my moaning and groaning about how horrendous the bus trip out to Denver had been. I went with that story out of all of them and stuck to that because it felt safe. It involved Heft and all our recent drama, but didn't go into any real hairy territory. I did manage to slip in one worthwhile tidbit, however, right before we arrived at the church.

"Mom has a picture of the three of us on her fireplace mantle," I said and watched him closely for his reaction.

"You don't say?"

"Yeppers. The three of us from when we went on vacation to that cabin upstate. The one with all the graffiti, remember?"

"The cabin...yeah...yeah, I guess I do."

"Yup."

"Funny," my dad said, "I didn't think any pictures of the three of us survived...."

"One did. I can vouch. I've seen it. Noticed it while I was waiting on the couch with my bags for the cab to pick me up for the airport. Right there on the mantle. Primo spot. You two look nice in it too."

"I do remember. That was almost the perfect vacation. Almost."

I noticed Razer then, and, as he stepped aside to let an old lady get past him, I saw Tweed. They were both wearing their black suits and would have looked handsome except for Razer had a split lip and Tweed's left eye was nearly swollen shut. They both looked grave and serious and somehow that made their injuries seem almost respectable. Yeah, but for the thuggish lumps they were sporting, and poor Razer's split lip, they could have pulled off being almost distinguished. I wondered what Heft would be wearing. I wondered how he'd look.

I stopped my dad. "Hey, listen. Would it be okay if I sat with my friends...just for the service?"

My dad looked around trying to fathom, I guess, just who these friends were. Not a lot of girls came by the house. Okay, none.

"Um, sure. No, I don't mind."

I gave him a peck and rushed off to join Tweed and Razer. I glanced back at the last moment and caught the disappointment twisting up his face. I knew it'd be there and tried to give him an apologetic smile to wash it away. He did his best to pretend it was all good. Poor Dad. I guess I was just always giving us something to work on.

Tweed and Razer looked like they'd lived through the end of a super-budget action movie.

"My God, here you are!" was all I could come up with before Tweed and I were hugging each other. He actually lifted me off my feet.

Razer, who I really didn't know, was clearly uncomfortable being left out. He started to hug us too, sort of like a tether to keep us grounded, and that seemed weird until I realized he was the only one crying. That made me feel guilty. We all should have been crying.

"I missed you. I've really missed you," Tweed said.

Like some kind of magical words, Tweed's comment pushed the three of us apart and it was the strangest little look that came over Razer's face. It was the look of suspicion. It was one of those looks that make you feel guilty whether you have anything to really feel guilty about or not.

"I didn't know you guys was so tight," Razer said. Suddenly I didn't care for him all that much. I wanted to cut our tether then and there.

"We live in the same building," I mumbled. Turning to Tweed I said, "Let's sit together."

"Fine by me," Razer said. He was going to make sure he was included.

"See you after, Chloe," my dad said as he walked by. "Boys," he added with his patented fatherly nod.

"What happened to you guys?" I whispered. "Do you get personal theme music to go with all that?" I asked and lightly touched a nasty scrape running over Tweed's brow.

"Tell me about it. You'd think," Tweed said.

"Long story," Razer said.

"Epic tale of the stupid, the stupider, and the damned," Tweed added. "Hip you later."

I kind of felt like Dorothy as they each took an arm and escorted me to the church.

It was a nice service. I'm not sure if it was the flowers, because there were, like, a bazillion arrangements, or the dozens of heavily perfumed elderly women packed into the pews, but the air was super-floral heavy. It was overwhelming even. In keeping with that, it almost seemed, Tweed got up and spoke near the end, reciting a poem by Dylan Thomas that had some mention of flowers. He was very impressive. I couldn't believe how together he was. I tried, but I couldn't recall the poem too well afterwards, except that there was this weird part that went, 'love drips and gathers but the fallen blood shall calm her sores.' It made me wonder if some of what he was saying wasn't solely for my benefit. Tacky, I know, to be at a funeral and have the ego to think things are about you. But, well, that's how it was.

As Tweed spoke, I did the thing with my little brain camera. Clickity-click.

Clickity-click. And as I captured that moment of Tweed up front with all eyes on him, of the room bent to hear his every word, I wondered, who is this boy? I wondered what he meant to me, or what *will* he mean to me. Because I'd gotten this strange feeling that Tweed was going to be someone in my life. Someone special.

I had even more to feel guilty about when I started daydreaming about kissing Tweed. Well, not so much daydreaming, as just musing. Yanno, what would it be like? What kind of kisser was he? I imagined he'd be a good kisser. I imagined more than kissing. Standing up there reciting poetry to a church full of people, and doing it all so effortlessly, certainly made him seem both sensitive enough and confident enough to do other things well.

Tweed, I realized, had suddenly become like that new song you hear. The one you love everything about, but only after hearing it for a few times before you realize it. Out of the blue, it unexpectedly clicks with you. Then you find yourself turning it up and listening to it over and over again. You struggle with the lyrics as some of the passages escape you and you stumble to fill in the spots where the words are sung too fast or too jumbled. But not knowing those lyrics only makes you love the song more, makes you want to hear it more. It's a mystery. It's a riddle to solve. So it sticks in your head and you play it over and over and over again.

Tweed came and sat down beside me again when he was done and I kissed him. Nothing out of place. Just a soft peck on the cheek. Still, he blushed. Talking in front of us like that hadn't shaken him a bit. A kiss on the cheek, on the other hand, and he blushed. He was so sweet.

Would he be like a song? After I knew all his words and his every little beat would I lose interest? Once I knew him by heart would I find myself distracted by all the other new songs that would come along? I squeezed his hand.

I wondered too then, would Heft just become some old melody that would rattle around in my head from time to time as the years flew by? One of those yesterday tunes that sneaks into your head and drives you crazy because you used to know the way it went back in the day but now you can only recall a verse here or there? I guess only time would tell, as they say.

I lifted Tweed's hand up in mine and rested them in my lap so that the back of his hand was pressed against my belly. Clickity-click. And I wondered.

It was crowded on the subway trip out to Woodlawn Cemetery in the Bronx, and so we all had to sit or stand a little bit apart. Tweed and Razer had been offered limo rides in the procession, but politely declined the opportunity to be trapped with the grieving family for such a lengthy commute 'out into the hinterlands,' as Tweed had called it. I suppose that I would've gotten the same invitation had they only known I was carrying Heft's child. Heft and I, we'd done a pretty good job of keeping our relationship under the radar though. So much so, that I hadn't even been approached by any of Heft's family so far. I supposed I'd speak with Preenie or Hannah, his sisters, sometime before everything was finished with if I never got the nerve or opportunity to do so with his mom and dad. Maybe they could help me navigate my way through the Preston family waters. Although, considering the mom's perpetual proximity to emotional collapse and the dad's supporting role as the heavily-medicated crutch, that didn't look like it'd be happening anytime this week.

As the Four train shuttled us along, Tweed reluctantly recounted to me what'd happened to Heft. He kept it sparse. Apparently, this gang thug, the same one who'd shoved Heft onto the tracks several weeks before, had just showed up out of nowhere on the street and stabbed Heft before running off. Tweed had been helpless to stop it.

"It all happened so fast," he said as we were paused at a stop along the way with open train doors as well as open mouths.

"The guy who did it, he wasn't really in no gang," Razer volunteered. "They got the dude. *We* got the dude," he corrected. "Wasn't part of no gang."

The car doors closed, but most of the awestruck expressions remained as the subway car jolted me nearly out of my seat.

"How do you know he wasn't in a gang?" I asked.

The other passengers, not the funeral crowd, but the others, had grown loud, and along with the rumble of the train it was nearly impossible to hold a conversation. I had to repeat myself. The others on their way to the funeral took notice when I practically screamed my question across the car to Razer on the third try to be heard.

He looked around sort of like a nervous dog used to being beaten. For reals he was sporting the cuts and bruises to match that demeanor. Finally, he looked to Tweed.

Tweed shrugged and said something I couldn't make out.

"I knew the dude," Razer said. "Wasn't no gang."

"We set him up. Sort of. The police got him," Tweed added. I guess he spoke a little too loudly.

One of the women turned to us. "You're the boys that apprehended the murderer?"

Heads turned. Lots of heads

Despite his attempt to be inconspicuous, enough of the others in the car from the funeral couldn't help but overhear. For those who hadn't, it didn't matter, the news spread quickly, creating a stir among them. One of the older gentlemen in the crowd asked Razer who he was and what more he could tell them.

Razer bowed his head and looked away. Tweed could see that we had an audience that wouldn't be denied, however, and so he spoke for him.

"It was Razer's plan," he nodded to Razer. Tweed didn't think twice about using their tagger names and didn't take notice at the scrutiny a name like Razer brought them either. "And he's the one who made it work. Get this."

Tweed told his story. After he'd finished, Razer did his best to satisfy everyone that the CC181 wasn't a gang, and that the real members of his club hadn't had anything to do with what happened to Heft. He repeated this over and over through the course of the remainder of the long ride. It didn't seem to matter.

"I can't believe you didn't get shot, Razer," I said. He only nodded and did a silent sign of the cross.

"Lucky a lot of people didn't get shot. But nobody did...except Rollo. Three times." Tweed said.

"Good shooting," an older man, the gentleman next to him, said.

"Saved the taxpayers a trial," someone else said. Others approved.

"And the other officer was alright? The one shot?" another person asked.

Tweed nodded. "Bulletproof vest."

There was a murmur of mutual agreement among the crowd that that detail was, "A relief." "A Godsend." "A blessing all around."

As Tweed had told his story, and as openings in the seats nearest him had become available, those concerned had moved into them to better listen. Now that they'd heard the boys out, it was hard to say whether most of their audience didn't begrudge them as guilty for the whole affair. Regardless of Tweed and Razer's brave capture of Rollo, who'd been shot and killed, the gathered crowd offered no congratulations or condolences for their troubles. Even following more of Razer's impassioned assurances that he and the other true CC181 boys were innocents, kids caught in the middle, the listeners seemed even more sided against Razer and Tweed. In the end, the crowd simply moved away back to the distant seats they'd come from.

"We're a chess club," Razer said. It was probably the fifth or sixth time he'd said it. "Just a chess club."

But everyone stayed quiet.

The attention of all the fakers pretending to ignore Razer was pulled away when one of the elderly women discovered she'd sat in gum. It proved to be just the distraction everyone needed.

She was a frail little thing of really advanced years. Straight out of central casting and picture perfect in her black mourner's dress, she wore a small antique starburst brooch of diamond rhinestones on her shoulder that matched a smaller cluster on her satin black pillbox hat. I wondered how many people she'd seen put to rest in that ensemble. Quite a few, I imagined. Why she hadn't been reserved a ride with the limo procession was anyone's guess.

Several of the older men around her, none of them seeming to have necessarily accompanied her as far as I could tell, did their best to assist with the great gum debacle. One old gent, right out of a Norman Rockwell painting, produced a silver flask from his suit breast pocket and dabbed his handkerchief with it. Before she'd realized what he was doing he'd started blotting the gum residue on the back of her dress while the others fussed to find some paper suitable for discarding the gum. When another of the men suggested his funeral program I thought the dear little old lady was going to snap his neck in two. She snatched the gum from his hand and produced some tissue from her clutch purse. This was when she discovered what the gentleman with the handkerchief was up to. She swatted his hand repeatedly and was really put out that he'd made her 'reek of a distillery.' That pretty much concluded the matter. As she sat back and did her best to reassemble her dignity, I snapped my little brain camera. Clickity-click.

When I turned my attention back to Razer, who'd been riding across from Tweed and I, it was pretty obvious that he was near breaking down into tears again. I wanted to say something, but I didn't know exactly what. So I decided just to let him be. He was quiet for the remainder of the ride. Everyone had moved away and left him alone there in the middle of his bench.

It was a beautiful day that we found ourselves without Heft. It was just the kind of day he would have loved. Ironically, the weather had been as ugly and overcast as you'd want for a funeral when we'd attended the service that morning at the church, but by the time we were traversing Woodlawn Cemetery the skies had parted. I overheard one of the elderly women who'd shared the subway with us say to her companion that heaven had opened up to welcome another angel. Cheesy as it was, that was the first tear I let slip. I don't think anyone noticed.

As fate or luck, two words that combine wonderfully in this case, would have it, there was very little chance anyone would notice my crying; not even Tweed who was holding my hand as we walked the path to the gravesite, since, as we approached, there was something of a spectacle ensuing. Preenie was going off on this woman with a baby. The irony was that Preenie was upset that this woman was creating 'a scene.' As we got closer I was knocked out to discover who she was. Not really quite a woman after all, but a girl my age. A girl I knew.

Lindsey Becker, the source and target of Preenie's outrage, bore the brunt of Heft's sister's attack well, but the baby cuddled into Lindsey's chest, not so much. As Preenie bitched, the baby bawled, and that only made Preenie bitch even louder.

"You have some nerve," Preenie all but shouted. Just over her shoulder, Hannah, Heft's other sister, arched an eyebrow as if to emphasize Preenie's point.

"I'm not try-trying to cause trouble," Lindsey said with a stutter.

"Who's that?" Tweed asked me.

Since he and Razer went to public school, neither of them would have any idea of the infamous Lindsey Becker, the girl who'd gotten knocked up by the debate team captain the year before. I felt a sudden sense of relief that I'd never joined in with the Lindsey bashing at school. That was one rock still on the floor of my glass house.

I couldn't fathom two things: What was Lindsey doing here, and what had she done to piss Preenie off so royally?

"She used to go to our school," I explained to Tweed in a hushed voice as we neared the commotion. "Left last year after her boyfriend, the debate team captain, got her pregnant."

Heft's mother suddenly came huffing into the picture and pushed Preenie aside to address Lindsey. "I should not have to ask you to leave," she sneered.

"Chad has a right to be here," Lindsey said.

Now I was truly confused. Why would Lindsey need to defend Heft's right to be present at his own funeral?

"Chad?" Preenie scoffed. "You would name your little bastard that, wouldn't you?"

"Please," Hannah added.

"My dear, we had an arrangement...a binding monetary agreement," Heft's mother said.

"I can't believe you paid this little extortionist off," Hannah said.

"I never asked for anything," Lindsey shot back.

"Moth-ther," Preenie said, as she launched into a fake cough and a nod directed at us.

I was suddenly aware that we'd inserted ourselves into what Heft's mother would've preferred remain a private matter. Razer, on the other hand, was neither confused by the spectacle nor compelled to discretion.

"That's Heft's baby?" he said, and even stepped up closer for a better look.

"This has gone far enough," Heft's mother practically hissed. I'd never realized how ugly a beautiful woman could look.

"Leave," Preenie said to Lindsey. "We *can* call security, or the police. We can have you arrested for trespassing, you know."

"You, you...people," Lindsey said, looking accusingly at us all, but settling on Heft's mother. "You can all go to hell." Appropriately, with that, Lindsey Becker stormed away.

Never to be one denied the last word, as Heft had always told me, Preenie tossed out, "Slut," at the young mother's back.

Heft's mother and Hannah turned and walked away without giving us a second look. This was a good thing, since I suddenly realized my mouth was hanging open. Preenie, however, didn't do us the courtesy of ignoring us.

"Aren't you two supposed to be pallbearers?" She said to Tweed and Razer. "Shouldn't you hustle your posteriors over there?" she said, cutting her eyes across the cemetery lawn. She paused to glance down to my stomach. "Congratulations. Nice baby bump," she smirked.

The bitch was just evil. I had several snappy things to say but all I managed was a flabbergasted sigh punctuated by pursed lips. Preenie, very satisfied with herself, turned on the balls of her little black stilettos and followed off after her mother and sister, no doubt in search of puppies to kick.

"Wow," Tweed said. "I mean, wow...."

"I guess they're grieving," Razer said. "You know, anger, that's a stage."

My dad, who'd been lagging behind with some of the older crowd, came up and asked what 'the fuss' had been about.

Watching the three Preston women go, I answered him. "The fuss was finding out I won't be naming my baby after Chad if it's a boy." It was my dad's turn to be perplexed, so I added, "And I don't need to worry about breaking the baby news to Heft's parents anymore. Because that's what I won't be doing. Ever."

Chapter Twenty

Scissors's dad wasn't home. I'd seen him drive off earlier that night in his ratty car, hood three different shades from the rest of it. And my girl, alone at home, had settled down on her bed with headphones on to pick at her chipped fingernail polish. Nothing else doing. No magazine. No girlfriend on the phone. For sure no Heft. Nada. It was during those doldrums that she got down on herself. You could put money on it. Especially just a night after the funeral like it was. I sat in the dark and watched her for a while. I even thought about going to the window and calling over to her. That'd be a first. Forget that. I decided to do one better.

I was going to knock. I always knocked wherever I went because I hate the sound of buzzers. Irritating as all get out. Always sound like alarm clocks and who the hell likes those? And to this day I can't tell our front door buzzer from the lobby buzzer. You'll be at the intercom pressing the lobby door button to let whoever in, and wondering why they keep buzzing, until finally you say hello into the intercom only to have them answer back through the front door because they're all of two feet away, standing in the hall. Happens all the time. Makes it hard to open the door without looking like you ride the short bus. Real irritating, Am I right?

So, like I said, I was going to knock, but then I realized that with her headphones on I'd practically have to pound the door down for Scissors to hear me from her room. I pressed the annoying buzzer.

She answered the door in some faded jeans that were probably brand new, with an equally faded red t-shirt a size or two too big. But other than that it was just a plain shirt. Not one of those crap shirts with logos or labels or whatever. She looked really good. She always did.

"Hey, Rocky," she said, making a little joke of my roughed-up appearance. A little unexpectedly she wrapped her arms around me and hugged me for the longest time. I was worried this meant she was going to start crying. She didn't though.

"Yeah, um, hey, sorry about the buzzer. I usually knock. Hate those things."

"Yeah, me too. No problema." She dropped the hug but still held my free hand as she looked at the pizza box I was holding with the other. "Sorry, pizza man, but we didn't order," she said with a sly grin.

"Hey, yeah, no, I know. I just thought. I don't know. You had dinner?"

"I dunno. Yeah, I guess," she said with a shrug.

I wasn't sure if that meant yes to eating or yes she'd already eaten. So I just said, "Great."

"C'mon in. But take your shoes off, will ya," she added as she left me at the front door.

I kicked off my tattered sneaks.

"No, that's cool. We do the same thing at our place," I said, lying about the shoes. Don't ask me why. Just something to say, I guess.

I followed her and she said I could sit at the kitchen bar where there were three stools. We had the same set up in me and Pops's place, I guess it was a building thing, except there was no place to sit at ours--no stools and all--and even if there had been, you weren't going to find any open counter space to do much of anything at all except maybe have a smoke or chew gum or something. It was where Pops had liked to keep his mound of newspapers and mail and whatnot.

Scissors and me, we were both acting a little goofy, embarrassed to make small talk, even more afraid of the big talk. So she got some plates and napkins and I pretended not to watch her as she stood on her tip-toes to get paper plates too.

"Need a fork?" she asked.

"Nah."

"Me neither," she said.

She came back with our plates and sat down on the bar stool beside me. She could have sat with a stool between us, but she didn't. Don't think I didn't notice. The girl was pretty cool that way.

That's when I also noticed how incredible she smelled. It wasn't like just perfume or something, either. It was like this amazing combination of everything from shampoo to fabric softener, to just, I don't know…her. I'd studied about pheromones in biology class and all, but still, pretty wild.

I guess I was acting a little dopey. She put the paper plates on top of the regular plates. I guess I gave her a strange look or something.

"My dad says it's easier to wash them this way. I'd just use the paper, but he buys the cheapie ones and they don't stand up to the job, yanno?"

"Right. No, makes sense. Smart man."

She liked that. The "smart man" comment, that is. If there's one thing I know about girls it's that no matter how much they can't stand their old man, they still love it when you say something good about the guy. Weird thing, sometimes they'll even argue with you for whatever it is you said, but still, you could tell, they ate it up that you had something positive to say about the bastard. And the ones that don't, trust me, steer clear. They're messed up.

"I really loved your part of the service by the way," she said. "It was really, really touching. The best."

I wasn't good with compliments. Even more so when it's from a girl like Scissors. I mumbled something about it being no big deal. I was glad when she decided to let it go.

She'd opened the pizza box. "Umm, okay," she said, pausing a little in disappointment at the contents.

On the counter in front of us, a little less than half of a two day old cold pie.

"Oh, yeah," I said, "Need to nuke it. It's still good. For real. Pizza Haven, best in the Heights, you know. Even better cold, ya ask me."

"Really?" she said, not like asking, but calling me out on my claim.

"Well, okay. Not *better*. But still, pretty damned good slice."

I started to reach for a slice. She had the box and was gone before I even got close.

"Let's put it in the oven. It'll be better. Microwave just makes it soggy. It'll get brown and crispy in the oven," Scissors said.

That sounded good to me. "Great. I love brown and crispy."

"It'll just take a while longer. Has to preheat and then like twenty minutes. Want to watch TV or something?"

Hanging out sounded even better than pizza. "Sure," I shrugged, "Whatever."

She fixed us some sodas and we hung out in the living room. Scissors sat at the other end of the couch from me. Can't win 'em all, eh? She turned the television on, but the volume stayed muted and she flipped through the channels while we took turns making sarcastic remarks about the shows or the actors or just whatever. We hit a little lull as we landed on the very tail-end of what I quickly realized was a truly depressing flick.

Scissors must have recognized it. She turned up the volume and sat back. The scene we'd come in on turned out to be the last. If I'd caught it before this night I'm sure I would've thought it was just a bunch of people at a party. But somehow, I guess with Heft's death still hovering over me, I immediately realized they were attending a wake. A wake not too unlike what Scissors and I'd just been through. The camera panned slowly around the room as the soundtrack had this guy singing in sort of a falsetto over the polite chatter. Normally that sort of fare wouldn't grab me, but it was really haunting. Beautiful, even. Finally the camera settled on a small group of the mourners gathered around a television watching old home movies of what only could've been the dead guy back when he was a little tyke. Grainy and faded choppy snippets of a family vacation during the fall of maybe the boy's fourth or fifth year. Playing on the swings. Bundled up with the family on a wind-swept beach. Tossing a baseball on a lawn of swirling and scattering leaves. Real hard stuff to take. The credits started up with the end of the movie within a movie, and instantly Scissors killed the volume again and flipped the channel. We both were teary-eyed and trying to hide it.

"The oven will be ready for the pizza when they get around to the weather," she said with a nod to the NY 1 twenty-four hour news channel she'd switched over to.

I agreed that we weren't going to dive into the pity pool. "Sounds good."

"My dad really likes Pops," she added quickly, trying to sound chipper.

I did the same. "Yeah, him and everybody else in the five Boroughs and the Tri-State. The old guy knows the world, you know?"

"That's cool. My dad mentioned he hasn't seen him around in a while. Was surprised he couldn't make it. Yanno, for Heft. Is he doing alright?"

"Sure. No, he's great," I said. I don't know why I lied. "So how's your dad doing?" I asked to steer us away from the whole Pops thing. So much dangerous territory to navigate.

"Good," she nodded kind of thoughtfully. "He'd be better if people didn't tag his car."

"Aww, there you go with all that again. Yeah, well, about that, see," I started, but then Scissors just busted out laughing. What a relief.

"You are so messed up, Tweed. How could you?"

"I tried to do a good job," I pleaded.

"I saw. Topnotch."

"Yeah, but then he had to go and ruin it. No respect for talent."

"None, I know. And he made me watch," she said. "The destruction of art. I felt like I was attending one of those Nazi book burnings. Heartbreaking."

"I saw you out there that day. I felt so betrayed. I thought about slicing my ear off and mailing it to you, like--"

"Van Gogh," she finished for me and we laughed. "You could save a stamp and just throw it over through my window."

"Yeah, for real," I said. I wasn't sure how to handle that subject though, and so we both just kind of sat around all stupid again for what seemed like forever.

"So what're you doing for the rest of summer? It's almost over." Scissors asked, I guess just to break our nervous lull.

"I don't know." I made a little spray painting mime. "Your dad's trunk?"

We laughed again. I loved it that she laughed so easily. It was a side I didn't know was there until just this summer. Realizing this, I wondered if maybe I wasn't the Scissors expert I'd applauded myself as being all these years gone by. It wasn't something I could kick around right at that moment though. Scissors was far too distracting to let me swim so deep.

"No, I mean, do you know where you're going after?" she said.

"What, college? Nah. I'm not a senior till next year."

"Oh. Sorry, I thought...."

"No, Razer and Heft are the old men of us three." I paused and corrected myself. "Were."

"Yeah. It's so hard to believe."

"Yeah."

Yet again she rescued us from going there. Perking up she said, "But for reals. Lucky you. I wished I had my senior year still ahead of me. If I knew then what I do now...yanno?"

"Yeah."

"No, honestly. I wouldn't mind another year. Sign me up. Make that two if they're handing them out," she said.

"So, what about you?" I asked. "How'd things go with your mom? You going back?"

"Really great. Surprisingly. But, no. No, I don't think I'll be going back anytime soon. But she told me I could if I wanted to, so I got that going for me."

"That's cool."

"And you? Where's your mom, Tweed? What's that story?"

"Sheesh.... You got me. Vegas...I think. Maybe. Not too sure, to tell the truth. That was ages ago and her and the old man, they always were kind of nomadic to begin with. Some tribes follow the caribou. My folks, they flee the bill collectors. Who knows where they are now."

"That's the suck," Scissors said.

"Not really. Their loss, you know?"

Scissors smiled a really great smile. "True dat. I like the cut of your jib, mister," she said, and gave my foot a little whack where I had it crossed over my knee. "Oven's preheated," she nodded to the forecast flashing across the television.

Fair to partly cloudy. Tell me about it.

"I'll put the pizza in," she said, leaving me on the couch.

"Cut of your jib? Who says that?" I teased.

"What can I say? I'm my Daddy's little girl."

"Don't look so little to me."

I know. I couldn't believe I'd said it either. Real player-talk.

"I know you aren't making fun of my baby bump."

I thought I'd really fouled up and stuttered trying to put together some kind of apology. But the way she looked back to me over her shoulder, with this real devilish smirk, well, I stopped feeling stupid with a quickness. I didn't make a fool of myself though. I played it cool. No more advances. At least, nothing so in the face.

The pizza turned out pretty darned good. Scissor's oven call turned out to be spot on. I never realized it before, being too lazy and all, but it would seem that pizza is one of those foods that gets better when you reheat it, like chili or lasagna. We woofed it down between some more jokes and goofing like a couple of starved hyenas. After, we fell back to the couch with some ice cream sandwiches and resumed channel surfing.

"You know, it's weird…" I said.

"I know."

"Know what?"

She shrugged. "That it's weird."

"You don't even know what I was going to say 'it' is," I said.

"Doesn't matter," she said. "You name it, and I'll tell you something weird about it."

"Oh yeah?"

"Mmm hmm," she said.

"Usually I'd call somebody out if they said something like that."

"Usually?"

"But in your case," I said, "I have a feeling that would be a mistake."

"Wise for your years, Mr. Man. So, what is it that was weird in the first place?"

"This is the first time I've seen the rest of your apartment. Normally it's the other way around. You know…living room first…bedroom to follow…."

"Yeah, ours is an out-there, bass-ackwards relationship, huh? So, the place, is it what you expected?"

I pretended to really scrutinize the surroundings for a moment. "I suspect most of the choices weren't yours. Let's just leave it at that."

"Oh, and so does Pops leave all the decorating to you then?" she laughed. "I mean, so you've spray painted TWEED through the whole house and not just your bedroom walls?"

"Hardly. No, Pops has us living in a photo gallery."

Her sarcasm dropped in an instant. "For reals? That is so cool. What kind of photography?"

"I don't know what you'd call it. Ancient retired dude retrospective, maybe. He's got the walls lined with a million pictures of other people from like the thirties through the seventies. From when he was young and whatnot."

"Other people? Who are they? Your family?"

"No. I don't know. Maybe. Just people, I guess. From his postal route, his work, different places."

"Let's go take a gander," she said, suddenly all full of excitement. She went so far as to jump up and pull me along by the hand.

"No, no. Bad idea."

"Aw…c'mon."

"Not tonight. It's too late. You know…Pops and all."

Scissors's otherwise loose t-shirt got caught up and gathered tightly around her stomach when she relented and fell back down into the couch. It was suddenly clear to me how well she'd been concealing her growing baby. But it didn't bother me. She was still the hottest girl I knew. Maybe even more so now. Her pregnancy made it clear she wasn't some little girl anymore.

"I can't believe Heft lied to us," I said. I don't know why it popped out like that, but there it was. She looked at me and I couldn't read her one bit. "About his getting that girl...what's her name? Pregnant and all that."

"Lindsey," Scissors said. "Lindsey Becker."

"Lindsey Becker. Yeah, I was supposed to be his best friend. You'd think you'd tell a best friend something like that. But no, that was the first I'd heard of her. And it was obvious Razer didn't know either." Again I couldn't read her. Then I realized I'd probably put my foot in my mouth. I felt like my words were a school of dying fish flopping around on the floor in front of us. Not knowing what else to do I threw a few more floppers out there. "So I guess his mom and dad had a pretty tight leash on him and all. Couldn't really tell anybody, I'd imagine. Not after they paid poor Lindsey off anyways. From the sound of it. Man, how tacky is that?"

"He let Paul Michaels take the fall too," she said.

"Come again?"

"The captain of the debate team. That was Lindsey's longtime steady. So it appears she wasn't exactly a one guy gal. Everybody just assumed Paul was the father. He denied it, of course. So that just made everybody think even less of him. Little did they know." She paused and then added, "Little did *I* know. I can't believe him."

I was worried she was getting too upset so I tried to make light. "I always told him his tag should have been Nimrod and not Heft. Stupid name. Never would tell us where he got it. It was like it was his big mystery-secret. Lost to the ages now."

"No it isn't," Scissors said.

"What?"

"A secret or lost," she said.

"You knew?"

"Everybody does."

I corrected her. "Yeah, well I don't. Razer don't."

"Oh. That's weird."

"So...spill it. What's it with the Heft nickname? Must have been juicy if he didn't want me and Razer to know. Something truly embarrassing."

"Not in the least," she said. "The exact opposite, really. See, the school held a contest our sophomore year to redesign the school crest. We'd had this family donate an ultra-huge mega-endowment and the school wanted something to commemorate, you know honor that. So they held a contest. Our civics teacher made it an extra credit assignment. He said that if one of his class won, then he'd raise that person's final grade by a letter."

"And so Heft won?"

"Not quite. Just listen. So Heft entered and our civics teacher said his design was inappropriate and he needed to resubmit."

"Inappropriate. Math checks out. Sounds like Heft."

"Heft got into, like, this huge argument in the middle of class and said this was just like what happened to this other high school kid from back in the fifties, Robert Heft. Robert Heft had designed the new fifty star flag for an assignment back when Hawaii and Alaska were joining the States, see, and he got a bad grade and so he'd challenged the teacher that if he could get congress to adopt his design then he should get an A. And that's what happened."

"And so our boy Chad did like that Heft guy and won the school crest competition and got himself the A?"

"Nope. He did manage to get the teacher, Mr. Potts to agree to it that if he won, he'd get an A. But then, yanno, when he did win, and by a write-in landslide of the student body vote, the faculty said no-way-Jose. Heft's design was still inappropriate and would not be the new crest. The deal was off."

"What bullshit. What utter bullshit."

"Not really."

I couldn't believe Scissors would side with the typical corrupt authority of some high school faculty.

"How do you figure?" I asked.

"Tweed, Heft's design was supposed to have what he said was this torch in the center. Yanno, for the light of knowledge and all that jazz."

"Yeah? So?"

"You obviously never saw it. It was a dong, Tweed. I mean a huge, throbbing dong."

We sat for a heartbeat of silence before we erupted in laughter.

"Classic," I said.

Scissors agreed. "Classic, no doubt. Why do you think he won by a landslide?"

"I can't believe he never told Razer and me."

"Yeah, so he became practically like a folk hero at our school. After that, everybody called him Heft. Kids still doodle the crest on the books and stuff. It's considered a violation of the school code to get caught with it."

"Nice. Sucks to whoever won."

"I wouldn't say that. I still got the bump in my final grade."

"You? You had the winning entry?"

"Second place takes the crown," she said and pumped her arms in victory.

She was smiling. She was gorgeous. Most beautiful girl I ever knew.

"That deserves some kind of congratulations," I said.

"I got my A," She said.

"Yeah, but I never had the chance to give you anything. You know, belated...."

"Really? Such as?"

I shrugged and gave a coy tilt of the head. I edged closer. She matched me ever so slightly. I couldn't say I hadn't been thinking about this moment, and not just lately, but for maybe years. Her breathing had picked up and her chest was rising more and more as if to pull me in.

My move was cut short by the jingling of keys at the front door.

Chapter Twenty-one

Me and Scissors and Razer were on the subway again for the second time in less than a week. The A train, this time though. And I wasn't decked out in a black suit anymore. Which, let the record show, had been courtesy of Heft's dad. He'd sent me rushing down to this place on Fifth Avenue when he'd found out I didn't have a 'proper' suit for the funeral. I guess I really needed a black one since I'd agreed to be a pallbearer and all. The sales guy had been ready for me. He had me fitted and good to go in half a nanosecond. The suit was delivered by messenger the next morning. Gives you an idea how the other half lives. It was pretty sharp, I had to admit. My only suit. When I thanked Heft's dad later at the wake, he just nodded and poured himself back into his scotch.

A few days after the funeral, Razer had come over to see if I wanted to tag along on his usual chess day down in Bryant Park. Get things back to normal. I'd had the idea to invite Scissors. Razer was down with that and so, it turned out, was she. Daniel, Scissors's dad, even seemed to think it sounded like a good time. Not that we were inviting him or anything. A nice enough guy and all, he hadn't even gotten miffed when he'd come home and found me and her watching television on their couch the other night.

Razer and Scissors, who my boy called Clo, I noticed, had really hit it off. As we rode down to Bryant, they were all giggles and good-times. Razer, he was talking like a mile a minute, giving her his life story and about how he'd gotten into chess and all. That wouldn't have been so bad if Scissors hadn't come across as so interested. Not that I was jealous or nothing. It was just...I don't know. Unexpected. Odd being the odd man out.

I played it kind of aloof since they were so intent on entertaining themselves. I stared out the darkened window across the aisle. Propped my feet up on the pole. Sort of people-watched the crowd moving on and off around us.

I hadn't really noticed this one woman at first. She wasn't the kind I usually paid much mind since she was probably in her mid-thirties or something and sort of frumpy under all those years on top of that. Not that I meant to be all judgmental, but, seriously, why would I be checking out some middle-aged lady? But I got caught up with her when I noticed how weird she was acting.

She was reading Dickens. *Great Expectations*, to be precise. Nothing off about that except that she wasn't really reading it. Just had it open in front of her. Yeah, instead, she was staring off into this void that was about ten inches out in front of her nose. And not only was she staring, but she had this grin plastered across her face like some unbelievably amusing shit was going down between her ears. She looked normal enough, so I assumed she must have hit on some real clever passage. Some people really get a kick out of Dickens. No harm, no foul there.

The backs of both of my feet, right at the Achilles tendons, were mad sore from where the new dress shoes I'd worn for the funeral had rubbed them raw. That, and Razer and Scissors were laughing and leg slapping like a couple of best friends forever on the monkey bars. So needless to say, except I'm gonna, I was getting in a pretty foul frame of my mind watching this woman grin. I started to imagine she was actually focusing on those two even though she wasn't looking at them. I mean, she was really getting a kick out of things.

I desperately wanted to say to her, "Hey, good book, huh?" Snap her out of her little voyeuristic reverie.

"Tweed lost it," I suddenly picked up Razer saying for what might have been the second time.

I turned my previously drifting attention back towards my boy and Scissors. "Do what now?" I asked.

Razer leaned in. "Chloe was asking about my phone. I told her you lost it."

"I didn't lose it."

"No, he's right, this one. He didn't lose it," Razer said. "He gave it away." Chloe started laughing. "He just handed it to some homeless hombre and let him run off with it. Hasn't even offered to pay me back for it."

"C'mon, man. You know that was like an accident. I was trying to save your life. You said not to let the cops get you caught up between them and Rollo."

"Uh huh, yeah, okay," Razer said.

"Dude, really. It's a phone. Get over it."

"You believe this kid? First he jumps me for no good reason, starts smacking me with rolled up coins, and then he loses my stuff. Ain't right."

"You should tell Pops on him," Scissors said. "Maybe he'd ground him." She laughed.

"For realio dealio," Razer said. "I'm tellin' Pops. He'll set you straight. I demand restitution, homes."

"Yeah, right," I said.

"You damn right, right. I am. I ain't screwing around with you. You pay me for a new phone or I'm goin' to tell Pops on your ass." Then he turned to Scissors. "You know I had to throw a chess game to Rollo, that big, dumb, dead idiot, just to string him along while this one here was giving away my stuff? You believe that?"

Scissors was really getting a kick out of all this. So, apparently, was Mrs. Dickens-reader across the aisle. Who was still acting the fool. Me? Not so much. I'd had enough.

"You want to know about Pops?" I said. "You want to know?" I guess my voice kind of got away from me. Scissors and Razer stopped cutting the fool. Instead they stared at me now like I'd grown a horn out of the middle of my head. "Pops is gone, okay. Gone!"

"Tweed?" Scissors whispered. "Pops died?"

Razer looked at me in disbelief. "What the F? When, man?"

"No. He isn't dead." I looked away from them. "He just split on me, is all."

"Split?" Scissors said.

"I don't know where. He just left. Left like two, maybe three weeks ago. Gone."

"That's messed up, yo," Razer said.

"Tell me about it."

"Tweed, are you sure? I mean, where could he go?" Scissors asked.

I shrugged.

"Have you told the police? Is anyone looking for him?" she pressed.

"Police don't know," I said.

"Why not?" she demanded. Razer just shook his head.

So I set her straight. "What if I went to the police and they can't find him? Then what? Then I'm shipped off to some foster place or something. That's why not."

Razer was steady shaking his head. "That's messed up."

"What do you know?" I said. "Besides, maybe he'll come back. Where's he going to go anyway?"

"Exactly," Razer said.

"Exactly what?"

"Where is he going to go? Nowhere. That should tell you something. Pops is an old fella. He got that dementia. Your ass should've been gone to the police already. Always just thinking about the number one." More head shaking.

"Tweed, we need to go back home. Tell the super, David. Ask around the building. Call the police. We have to look for him," Scissors insisted.

I was through talking.

"Old man could be floating in the river for all this fool cares," Razer said.

"Hey, fuck you, Pedro. You don't know me."

"No. No, I don't. And I don't want to."

"Get bent. You don't know me."

Razer turned to Scissors. "See, he always just thinking of himself. Pathetic."

"Keep it up, I'll split your other lip," I said. Pretty much a hollow threat.

I knew he was right. I hated myself. I caught this image of Pops floating under the GWB and suddenly felt nauseous. Seriously. Like I was about to get sick all over the train.

"If you guys are going to fight, I'm out of here," Scissors said, trying to cool things down.

Razer was having none of it. "I was just joking about the phone, but you, man. You. First you get Heft killed, now you turn your back on Pops. No wonder your mama and daddy left you."

He meant for that last bit to hurt bad. It did. I wanted to nail him for it. But I was feeling so ill, I was afraid I'd hurl if I even made the effort.

"Killed Heft?" Scissors said. "What are you talking about?"

Razer stood up and leaned back against the aisle pole. "You wanna know? You wanna know what really happened? What this fool did?"

Speechless, Scissors nodded.

"Romeo here went around the Heights doggin' all the CC181 tags he could find with Heft's tag. Making it look like Heft was doing it."

"Why'd you do that?" she demanded from me.

"Cause he's sweet on you, girl. Jealous of his best friend. Just something shitty to do. Tryin' to get Heft into a fight. Got him into a lot worse. The only bigger fool was that clown Rollo what stabbed Heft over all that stupid shit."

"I didn't plan…," was all I could manage.

Scissors's face went flush. Her voice quivered. "You did that? You put that thug on Heft? You got him killed?"

"It wasn't supposed to happen that way," I said.

"It wasn't--"

She slapped my face hard. Then, probably not two seconds after that, when I thought she was just going to chew me out, she just slapped me again.

Like on cue, the train pulled into the 125th Street station. She walked off without a word. Razer followed her. He paused at the door.

"You can be pissed at me if you want to, man. But, way I see it, that was the least you had comin' to you. Be seein' ya, Tweed."

The doors closed and the train lurched forward. Across the aisle, the woman with the Dickens stared at me. She'd lost her jovial demeanor. She got up and moved far down the train as though the air around me was bad. She got off at the next stop only to get on in the car ahead. Left me thinking that, just like everybody else, from Mom and Dad to Pops and Scissors and Razer, she wanted to get as far away from me as she could.

I ended up riding the train all the way to the end of the line. Far Rockaway. Where else was I going to go? I had no place to be. No place where I was wanted. Nobody wondering when I was going to walk in a door. When I got out to Far Rockaway, I thought I'd just stay put and ride the same train home. Nothing doing. That didn't work out either. The conductor announced the train was going out of service. Get the hell off.

Felt like the story of my life.

I considered for the briefest just walking off into the city and throwing it all away. Considered. Even got as far as the street. And then I got angry. I refused to be pushed aside. I headed back down onto the platform and rode another uptown train back to 190th. Back to my neighborhood. My place in the world. I got out and lost myself instead in Fort Tryon. But I wasn't really lost. This was my home away from home. It was a place where Heft haunted every corner.

Since his coming of age, intellectually speaking, around thirteen or so, while Razer and I were mad peaking on girls, Heft began instead to take a great interest in what he liked to call "The Big Picture." So as you might imagine, for the next few years, he bored the hell out of us on a pretty frequent basis. When he wasn't boring, he could be fairly entertaining. This, in a crazy dude up on his soap box claiming he could conduct the clouds kind of way. Conspiracies. The industrial war machine. The capitalist-corporate juggernaut. Big Brother. He covered them all. How many days or nights in Fort Tryon had Heft railed against the ever-looming shadow of the corporate bogeyman and the hockey-masked ax wielder, capitalism? Plenty, I can tell ya. Yep, many an hour was wasted where I tried to be the voice of reason while Heft forever balanced one foot shy of tripping off into becoming one of those geniuses with all his worldly possessions in a shopping cart.

My argument in so many of those verbal bouts of romper was that it was our nature to fuck with one another. So what was the difference if it was the guy down the street screwing with you or if it was fifteen guys sitting in some boardroom somewhere. It always was and always would be. No sense getting yourself all worked up over it. Heft would pitch back that if we didn't stay vigilant, if we didn't rise against the machines and mechanism set against us, then, well, what was the point in even being to begin with.

I walked through the park and wished Heft was there for one last argument. Now that he was gone, I had to concede that maybe he'd been on to something after all.

"Maybe I'll start conducting clouds, ya crazy lump!" I screamed up into the heavens.

Some people, a couple hand in hand, that I hadn't noticed, freaked out because they weren't sure about me. He hustled her over to his other side like some valiant knight and they all but dashed along the path to make their way far, far away from me. Fine by me. I'd always preferred having the park all to myself anyway.

Fort Tryon Park. The Tryon. A topographer's wet dream with about a trillion nooks and crannies, hills and cliffs, saddles and ravines. Great overlooks on each side. To the west, the Jersey Palisades shoot up on the far side of the gray, churning Hudson. To the east, the last of Manhattan rolls off and settles flat, melting into the plains of the Bronx. Riddled everywhere through the Tryon there's masonry work from Revolutionary war times, battlements and old stone bridges like you'd imagine kept trolls. Yeah, lots of cool places to get your head straight in the Tryon. It's a sanctuary for that kind of trip. Since I've had the pleasure to need to get a lot of shit straight in my young life, I was pretty fortunate that park was so near at hand. My therapist, the park.

At various stages during my youth I'd convinced myself in turns that I was someone--or something--else. Nothing odd. The same kind of make-believe shit all kids do. To start, in my earliest childhood adventures, I was an Indian, Apache Jones, a brave warrior with a big knife. Often, my adventures centered on perilous grizzly hunts or perhaps my vision quest. I'd seen a movie about that stuff. It'd made quite an impression. So I'd do my vision quest or grizzly hunt thing, jumping around, war whooping, and running along the walls of the Tryon that, if I'd ever slipped over the wrong side of, would have been the end of me. This pastime kept me entertained as well as did a good job of pissing people off. Apparently picnics couldn't be enjoyed if Apache Jones was on the prowl. Uptight assholes yelled at me to go someplace else, and more than a few mothers scolded for me to come down from wherever I was putting myself in harm's way. It seemed even imaginary Indians had to be hassled by the White Man. But Apache Jones couldn't be tamed. His was the wilderness and free soared his spirit. This was before the pestilence of the White Man came and ruined the show, of course. A few years and a few more movies enlightened me to blankets with chicken pox, Wounded Knee, the Trail of Tears and all that other grand, depressing shit. So enlightened, I had to let the Indian thing go.

Then I entered into my historical battle reenactment phase. I was the last soldier standing the ramparts against an onslaught of Redcoats. The battlements shook with cannon fire and my bloodied bayonet glinted in the rocket's red glare many a summer twilights, I can tell you. That, or I was doing the Alamo thing, or the Custer's Last Stand thing. And can you believe I picked all that crap up in school? They really drill that patriotic rah, rah, rah, stuff into a lad. Not that that's a bad thing. Except that, before I knew it, I'd gone from Apache Jones, Indian brave with the noble heart, to killing made up brown or red men for their treacherous ways. How odd is it that with a little bit of knowledge, I'd imagined myself one way, but then, with a little more knowledge, I'd discarded that fantasy for another, and spent my free time killing that first imaginary identity. Then, with just a bit more insight, I reverted back to the original character and did it all over. Circle of life. I guess that's what brainwashing is all about.

Things changed I guess when I grew up just enough to question what the kids in Great Britain were being taught about us treacherous colonies and our illegal tea party ways. What the kids on reservations were told of Manifest Destiny. What Mexican boys and girls learned about how their country's northern border came to be. I mean, there was no way those kids got the same story we did. Am I right? I mean, c'mon. In our book the Brits and the brown man and the red man were all the bad guys; evil black-hearted villains, one and all. And chapter after chapter, without exception, we were the good guys. We were right. We did no wrong. From the first to the last. In God we trust, am I right?

As you can imagine, not only did that kind of curiosity and critical thinking land me in hot water with my teachers--who I suspect were mad primarily because they didn't know anything more than what was being spewed out of textbooks sanctified by some goose-stepping school board--but much to my surprise, that shit didn't fly with Pops either. Who knew he was such a flag-waver?

"What're you, some kind of pinko?" he'd demanded one day when I tried to explain my troubles in school. I wasn't sure what a pinko was, but it didn't sound none too good. So I let all that go too.

Finally, around twelve or thirteen or so, when I guess I entered into a more introspective and peaceful place, I fancied I was the spirit of the park. Not nothing so gay as a leprechaun or brownie, mind you. More like Puck maybe, or some other equally mischievous little fucker. I would lace my tangled hair with leaves and crap. I'd even go barefoot, the season permitting. I'd love to bullshit you and say I really pushed it. Something real crazed like I ran naked, freaking out the norms, but I never did nothing that mental. Hey, I was just a kid, but I wasn't a lunatic. Yet. And the good thing about all that pixie shit, there weren't going to be any history lessons coming around the bend to spoil all the fun. Am I right?

...

It was pretty late when I got back to my building. I didn't head to the apartment though.

Scissors's dad, Daniel, answered their door. I didn't think it was a big deal. Life is full of surprises like they say, though.

"Chloe home?" I asked, just to be polite, because I knew she was. I'd seen her light from the street.

Daniel, her dad, he just stood there blocking the way.

"Hi there, Tweed. No, Chloe…she's not, um, home. Hey, what time is it?"

"Couldn't tell you."

"Uh huh. Well, it's late. And so Chloe's not available to come to the door. Please, try to be more considerate," he said and shut the door right in my face. Not hard. Not like slammed, but still.

That, and the guy was a horrible liar. Most nice guys are though, so I really didn't hold it against him--at first. It wasn't until I was back at home, and staring at the mess of the place, that Daniel's lie started to get me down.

For something to do I started cleaning things up. The place needed it. Weeks of pizza boxes and other deliveries and empty cans and just all kinds of crap were strewn around with the dirty laundry and whatnot. The smashed plate of spaghetti that'd shut up Heft what seemed like a million years ago now, that was everywhere. Dried up even like it was it was still a real mess. Before I knew it, I was mad domesticated, washing dishes, and wiping down countertops, the whole shebang. Hell, I even swirled the little scrub brush around the toilet bowl. Still, for all my trouble, I couldn't get away from the nagging voice in my head. I guess it had something to do with abandonment issues.

See? I'm not that fouled up. At least I knew where my problems were rooted. First Mom bails on me, then Pops ups and skips out, and now even Scissors has cut me loose, sent me packing.

Yeah, I'm not slow. I know the score. But I don't hold it against Scissors. Come to think of it, I don't even blame her.

By the time I was sweeping the living room that was my conclusion anyways. I even said out loud, "Good for her," as I scooped the last of the living room dust bunnies into the dust pan. And I meant it.

I'd somehow distracted my train of thought back onto the trivial track bound for destination brain-dead for all of a minute maybe--deciding that it must be woman's work

I was doing since they called them by the cute name dust *bunnies*, but failing to find some other similar proof--when, disaster. As I was emptying the pan in the kitchen trash, I made the mistake of disrupting the stockpile of old food delivery bags and other garbage that had been accumulating there over the past few weeks.

As the one bag was jostled I was surprised to see a maggot roll out from beneath it. At first I thought it was just a grain of rice from one of the millions of Chinese takeout boxes. Then it wiggled. I snorted a little laugh because that reminded me of how David, the building super, called maggots disco rice. A real card that one is. I picked up the bag that the thing had come out from under, thinking to move it to the top of the pile as if that'd make some big difference, I guess, I don't know. But anyways, a life lesson was uncovered. There is no such thing as *one* maggot. In this nasty pool of liquid that was beyond disgusting, a team, no, a swarm, no, a vomit, yes, a vomit of maggots writhed about. I'm not certain if vomit is the correct noun of assemblage for maggots, but if it's not, well, it should be.

And so that's how my industrious endeavor came to a screeching halt. I dropped the bag back on maggot town and spent a little while in the bathroom convincing myself that I wasn't some kind of Nancy boy for yuking. Maybe if I hadn't felt like crap to begin with. I don't know.

Back on the couch I was staring at the dead gray television. Not really even considering turning it on. I was doing my best to think that my cleaning spree would somehow magically whisk Pops back home from where the hell ever, when catastrophe collided with disaster.

I knew the millions of framed pictures, these photos, which lined every wall of our apartment except my room, by heart. I'd spent my youth pouring over them. I considered it a milestone every time I met one of them eye to eye for the first time after a growth spurt. Pops wasn't one of those who'd recorded my progress with a notch on the kitchen wall like Razer's old man liked to do. So instead, I would gauge how I was coming along by the pictures. All through my youth there would be those pictures, faces I didn't know from any other place other than there in frozen moments. Handsome men standing proud next to their new Buicks and those other big-finned monstrosities people thought were so cool. Young couples dressed for a night on the town, like the people used to, all in suits and dresses. Soldiers decked out in uniforms chest-filled with medals, some smiling, others stone-faced. Old women with their grand-babies cradled in their arms.

With each passing year I would solemnly regard the ones I'd reached, considering them conquered, and then turn my gaze up to those I'd yet to meet.

Regardless, they were all strangers. I didn't know a single face in the crowd from anyplace other than our hallway, our foyer, our living room, Pops's bedroom. And none of these arrived after me, either. I guess at some point in Pops's life he'd collected photos of people. Collected, framed, and placed them on his walls. And not one of himself as far as I could see. Not one of his family. At least, no family I knew. I suppose some might be, though. Long lost cousins and whatnot. But where I was concerned, strangers as far as I knew. I still assumed most were from his route. I guess maybe I would've considered that odd except for the fact that it'd always just been that way. Maybe old Pops had gone to a garage sale one day and bought someone else's life. Who knows? Pops never offered much of an explanation, and me, being just a dumb kid, I never asked.

Heft called me out on that once, years and years ago, on a sleep-over. When I finally convinced him it was the truth that I'd never bothered to ask, well, he called me a freak. Even after all the years I still remember that. Whatever.

So imagine my surprise when I noticed this picture of me, Mom, and old Pops, framed and tacked up on the wall right over the television. It was a photo that hadn't been there before. Don't know when Pops had put it there, but it must have been sometime right before he split out because I definitely would have noticed it before.

Not only was it new to the apartment, but it was a picture I never even remembered being in. I guess either my dad or maybe David the super took it. Probably Dad, since he wasn't in it. The three of us were standing in the snow just outside the building. Oddly enough, I was in one of those "I'm with Stupid" t-shirts without even a coat. I can't imagine why, since I was obviously cold. I had my hands all crammed down in my pockets, deep as they'd go, like I was trying to get my elbows in there. I even had this weird expression on my goofy cherry-cheeked face. Looked like I was blowing out candles or some shit. Mom stood close to Pops and he had his arm around her shoulders. She leaned into him so much it was almost sweet. Me, I was on my own. Even my t-shirt said so. The finger on it pointing to where Stupid was supposed to be, it just pointed off to nobody.

I thought I broke my hand when I smashed the picture as hard as I could. It hurt like all get out. It wasn't broke, thankfully, but I had managed to cut my knuckles all to hell and back on the glass. That didn't stop me. I got cut even worse when I grabbed the shattered mess up from the floor and started yanking the photo free from the mangled frame. I guess I was being a bit of a whack job, but I tore the thing up into like a million pieces. And, since I was being such a nut, I still had a bunch of the torn and crumpled pieces in one bloody hand and a chunk of glass in the other when I ran back and threw myself on my bed like some big baby.

I guess I bawled a little bit. So what? Things had been building up for a while. I just went and pulled my finger out of the dike. And I guess it was quite the scene if anybody had been around to witness it. It was only when I realized that Scissors could see me that I pulled myself together. Well, she *could* have seen me except for one small detail. The glow of her fish tank illuminated the blinds that were pulled down over her window. All the years gone by and that was a first. Go figure.

Kind of in a funk, I sat back on my bed and let my mind wander. It didn't go very far. Really all I thought about was Scissors. I wondered if she was on the other side of her blinds. I wondered if the blinds were her idea or that liar Daniel's. I decided it had to be his. I wondered if she was cutting herself. The more I thought about her over there alone, hurting herself with nobody to know, well that kind of took possession of me. For a half an hour or more I sat there all bummed out; it was all I thought about.

I suppose if I didn't somehow have the shard of glass from the broken picture frame already in my hand I wouldn't have cut myself. I didn't give it much thought, other than to wonder what Scissors got out of it. Thought maybe I'd see what all the rage was. I slid the edge against the top of my forearm creating a gash that didn't hurt as much as I thought it would or should. So I made another. Then a third. It's not like there was anybody there to stop me.

That's when I did something crazy that really scared the hell out of me. I was sitting there on my bed in the half-light, jagged glass in hand, and I started another cut. It was the fourth. But as I started doing it, my mind sort of drifted off and I thought about Holden Caulfield. You know, the kid from *The Catcher in the Rye*. More specifically, I started thinking about how Holden worried about where the ducks in Central Park go in the winter. It was something we'd talked about in Lit and I guess I hadn't thought about since then. That'd been ages ago.

But now here I was cutting myself and thinking about ducks. Wondering what happened to the duck I saved that day with Chloe. Wondering where he was. Wondering if he found his way back to all the other ducks he knew. The ducks that'd probably given up on him and left him there. Frickin' ducks. You believe that? Me neither.

That's what scared me. How had I gotten so out of it, so far out of touch, that I could be doing what I was doing to myself and already not even thinking about it? I mean, how whack is that? It was like I skipped a step. Or seven, or eight. Apparently I excelled at being fucked up. I was a prodigy with mad talent. What was coming next? Where do you go from there? Was I going to find myself throwing myself in front of the A train while I was pondering bagels or computer chips or just whatever wild, inane crap floated into my crazy brain? Maybe that's what I was. I was going crazy. Crazy and didn't know it. After all, I'll bet crazy people don't know they're crazy; they just are.

Pretty freaked out and all, I threw the piece of glass in my waste basket along with the bits of torn up picture and went to the bathroom to clean myself up. My little experiment doing the copycat thing of Scissors was finished.

Chapter Twenty-two

The knock at the door came about fifteen minutes after I'd gotten my hand all half-ass bandaged. It was like a cop knock. One of those, 'We know you're in there and we ain't messing around, so open the fuck up' kind of knocks. Or maybe it was just the perpetual headache knocking around in my head these days. Either way, the whole deal just sort of startled me. It was late and I was a little out of it.

There wasn't a second knock, but I knew they were still there as I padded over to the door all cautious-like. I could hear their muffled conversation. I couldn't make out the exact words. No matter. I didn't even bother with the peephole. I wished I had the second I opened the door. I thought for sure I would be dealing with the cops. I'd been having a lot of cops in my life lately. It wasn't. It was worse.

It was David, the building super. He was in plaid pajama bottoms with house slippers and a plain V-neck t-shirt. "Hey, Tweed. Pops home?" he asked kind of apologetically.

Behind him, old lady Goldstein, me and Pops's nosy neighbor, peered around his shoulder like the accusatory nut she was.

"What? Wassup, David?" I said. And then because I couldn't resist it, I added, "Hello, Mrs. Goldstein. Nice night for a snoop?"

The old bat was riled. "Where is Alfonso? Tell him to come to the door! Have him come to the door!"

"Now, c'mon, Mrs. Goldstein, you promised," David said.

"Promised nothing. Something is wrong. I know. Have Alfonso come to the door and say everything is fine and I'll go. Simple as that."

"Yeah, yeah. Okay, okay. That's what we're doing here," David said, trying to soothe her. "So how about it, Tweed? I'm really sorry, but can you fetch Pops? Just take a second."

"No."

That really lit her fuse. "David, I will call the police. I will. You can believe I am deadly serious."

David was nodding like a dashboard bobble-head going over speed bumps.

"He's not here," I said.

"Poppycock," the old lady argued. She knew she was right.

David checked his wrist where his absent watch was usually strapped. Staring at the pale stripe of tan line as if it could tell him something, he needed a moment to get his thoughts together. Meanwhile, I searched for a lie.

"What is it? He at the bar?" David asked.

Before he'd gotten the word bar out of his mouth, I was saying in unison, "Yeah, at the bar."

"At the bar?" David confirmed.

"Yeah. The bar. Most likely. For sure. At the bar."

That seemed to satisfy the super. The ancient neighbor? Not so much.

"I haven't seen him in two weeks," Goldstein said. "Two weeks."

"So?" I shot back. "That's good for Pops. He hates you spying on him twenty-four seven."

"I don't spy!"

"Hey, ho. Time out," David refereed.

"And I've heard all sorts of banging and crashing. Wild goings on," she said.

"So?" I repeated.

"And *crying*," she concluded.

The phone rang. I guess it caught me as off guard as the two visitors at my door had. Before it'd had the chance to ring a third time, I said something really stupid.

"Probably him right there."

David smiled in relief. "Excellent. See, Mrs. Goldstein? That's probably Pops right there."

"Hold on," I said and rushed over to answer it. I didn't want the machine picking it up. Who knows, might be the police had found Pops…under the GWB like Razer prophesized earlier.

As David held the door ajar, old lady Goldstein called after me. "Let David speak with him, if you please," she said.

It was a call about Pops alright. But not the way I expected. Strangely out of breath, it was Razer.

"Tweed, Bishop may have found Pops. You need to get over here right now."

"Do what, man?"

"Bishop. He met a guy. Knows about Pops. You need to get over here. My place. Right now, homes."

And then he hung up just like that.

"Well?" Mrs. Goldstein shouted.

I settled the receiver back into its cradle and had an ominous thought. Razer had trapped Rollo by having him rush over to The Castle. Was this more of the same? Was this just a setup so that Razer and his crew could jump me? Would he do that over his stupid phone? Or was it something to do with revenge for Heft? For me jumping him? Then again, what if it was legit? What if the CC181 boys really did know something about Pops?

"Well?" the old bat demanded again. "Well?"

My headache was shifting into atomic. This woman…. It was no freaking mystery how she'd managed to be on Pops's bad side since as far back as I could remember.

…

My dad was living like a skittish mouse in our apartment. He was so quiet since I'd returned from Denver that when I was in my room I couldn't be sure if he was in his room, or the living room, the kitchen, or bathroom. When we bumped into one another in the hall coming in or out of the bathroom he always made this big deal of being apologetic about it like we were strangers in some European hostel or something.

He didn't play his French horn. Or, if he did, he only fingered the keys in silence. He didn't work on any little personal projects. The television got lonely. My dad just laid low. Like a man on stakeout, or maybe ducking one, he was perpetually braced for the case to crack.

It was clear that it would be up to me to get us back to normal. At first I thought if I just acted like there was no big dealio to everything that he'd fall in line and do the same. We'd fake our way back to normal. No such luck.

I needed an excuse to corner him without cornering him. It was my recent successful jaunt to Denver to rekindle things with my mom that finally gave me my answer. I'd do what she'd done to me. I would make my dad a dinner of such epic proportions, and requiring such a herculean effort, that good ol' Danny boy would be forced to sit and make small talk until there was no small talk left. Then we'd get down to business. Brass tacks as my mom liked to say.

It was somewhere between the sweet peas mixed in mashed potatoes, my dad's favorite, and our dessert of Neapolitan sundaes with Hershey's syrup, one of mine, that he'd reached his fill of appetizer conversation. He got nice and quiet while we cleared the dishes. He was still being aloof when we plopped onto the couch with our ice cream. He reached for the television remote where it rested on the coffee table. I slid it out of his reach with a big toe and wagged my spoon at him. He sighed and sat back.

"You are your mother's daughter, you know," he said. I guess he was on to me.

So we talked. My dad explained that while my pregnancy had caught him a bit off guard, it wasn't something so shocking. Other parents he knew in the orchestra had faced similar situations. He also pointed out that he reads the paper, too. And as long as I planned to stay there with him, and not run off on my own, and as long as I still planned to go to college at some point down the road, he didn't know that my baby wouldn't be the most wonderful thing in the world.

"After all, you were," he said.

I didn't get much of a chance to bask in all that sweetness, however.

"That's why that's not what's been eating at me, Chloe."

"Do what now?" I said.

He slid his half bowl of ice cream onto the coffee table. "You know I've always tried to respect your privacy," he said. I nodded. "Chloe, while you were gone I found some things. I wasn't snooping. I was…concerned."

"Yeah…?"

"Behind your dresser. A razor blade. A bloody towel. Some pliers." He paused and then added his evidence all up. "Drug paraphernalia. I found your drug paraphernalia. I imagine I would have found the drugs, but I suppose you took that with you."

"Dad…."

"No, Chloe. I won't have it. Now I'm not sure what you're doing. Something like crack or meth or something…those pliers for holding the pipe or, I don't know and frankly I don't care. But I won't let you do this. It's not going to happen."

"Dad," I tried again.

"And this isn't just about you, either. You have a child now. Or, at least, you will in what, four or five months. You can't do this to the baby, Chloe."

He stopped and finally gave me a chance to defend myself. Like I was going to argue *for* drugs. I could tell that was what he was really expecting.

The other thing was I guess I'd assumed him and Mom had covered all this over the phone. Not being married and all maybe things didn't work that way anymore I came to realize. That or maybe they were finally treating me as a person and not their possession, respecting our relationship with one another on a whole new level.

"I'm not on drugs, Dad."

"Don't insult me, Chloe. It's bad enough, but don't think you're going to sit here and insult me. You wanted to talk. I know what all this was," he said with a wave back to the dinner table. "Well, we're talking. And you know what? As long as we're talking we are going to be honest about it."

Show don't tell, my English teachers always said. I took their advice. I pulled up the sleeve of my shirt, pointing my elbow up to the ceiling to reveal the backside of my arm to him. The cuts were old. I hadn't cut since leaving for Denver. But they were still there. Nice and visible, scars and scabs. He didn't know what to say. I lowered my arm and hiked down the waist of my jeans enough to expose the slice I'd made there a few weeks earlier.

"I'm not on drugs, Dad. I'm a cutter. I cut myself."

He couldn't hide how much this upset him. His lips quivered as he breathed and his eyes glistened until they spilled over. I didn't know if it was from relief or grief. Grelief, I supposed. For the world I wished I wouldn't have to remember his face looking that way. All too often you don't get what you want in this life.

Clickity-click.

...

"Tweed, what is it? What's going on here?" David asked.

I guess I wasn't doing a very good job of playing it cool. Old lady Goldstein somehow managed to keep it zipped for half a minute. Hard to believe. I caved.

"Pops has gone missing," I confessed.

I waited for the old woman to start shrieking about how she'd known it all along. She didn't say a peep of 'I told you so,' though. She brought one tired hand up and shielded her eyes. Just under her breath she began mouthing a prayer. David put his hand under her elbow to offer his support but she gently pushed him away.

"So alright then," David said to me, "Give us the whole story. When you seen him last? Where?"

"I don't know. Few weeks ago. He was over at the bar. He got pissed with me and never came home," I said.

"Never came home? That's pretty pissed. What'd you do?" David said.

Hard to believe, but suddenly old lady Goldstein was at my defense.

"Don't play the fool, David. The boy didn't do a thing. At least nothing to merit Alfonso disappearing. It's his condition. Clearly it's gotten worse," she said. "I should have known better. I *do* know better. Oh, how did we come to this?"

"You tell the police?" David wanted to know.

"No."

"Why not?" he barked at me.

"I don't know. I had my reasons. What do you want from me?"

Again, the old lady stepped in. "Stop it. Stop it. That doesn't matter. All that matters now is we do something immediately. Something right this very minute. David, you have to go to the bar. Start your search there. I know it's late, but time is of the essence. Surely one of those people may know something. I'll go to the precinct and file a missing persons report. Young man," she said to me, "I need to get a recent photograph of Alfonso if you have one; mine are far too many years old. Meanwhile, you stay here in case by some miracle he finds his way home."

"Photograph?" I said.

"Yes, something more recent."

"Why would you have photographs of Pops?" I asked.

David laughed. "Typical teenager."

"What's that supposed to mean?"

"This neighborhood was around a long enough time before you showed up, lil' Pops," David said.

"No time. No time," Mrs. Goldstein said. She began pushing off in different directions. "There'll be plenty of time for all of this later."

"Wait," I said, "Just wait a minute. First of all, that phone call. That was Razer. He said he might know where Pops is."

That got them both very excited. After their flurry of riding me for not speaking up sooner, I hipped them to the fact that it might just be some kind of trap for me to get whaled on.

"I would say it's worth the risk, wouldn't you?" Old lady Goldstein said.

I shrugged. "I didn't say I wasn't going."

"My station wagon is parked just down the street. We'll all go over," she said.

"It's just down Broadway, Razer's place, right?" David asked.

"Yeah."

"That's alright, Ida," David assured her, "you just hold down the fort in case Pops calls or shows. I just need to get in my jeans and sneakers. Don't you worry none. Me and Tweed will handle this."

We were on the stairs when she called out after us. "Be careful! Please be careful. I'll say a prayer!"

...

David and I were trotting down Broadway at a pretty good clip. Surprised me that he could keep up. Pretty impressive for an older dude. But that was all good because no doubt if he'd fallen behind people would've been all breaking their necks and gawking, assuming they were witnessing a police chase. Then some asshole probably would have thought himself a hero to trip me.

I stopped without warning, and pretended I was catching my breath. You know, hunkered over, hands on bent knees. Like I knew he would, the big guy kept quiet for a second doing the same. I wanted him ready for what I was worried was about to go down.

I was just about to tell him we were there when Razer popped out onto his stoop. Like some dopey shadow that followed him wherever he went these days, his CC181 lackey, Bishop, came be-bopping up from out of the building behind him.

"Taa-weeeed!" the guy yelled in this high-pitch-dragging-it-out-bullshit holler. I knew I never liked this kid.

"Sup, fellas?" I said. "So where's this guy? You said something about some guy?"

"Hey, my man, David," Razer said, ignoring me.

"Hey, the Razer. How's it going?"

"Yo," Razer's lackey boy giggled.

I bet they were huffing. I didn't have time for none of that garbage.

"Well? C'mon, man. We literally ran the whole way over here. Where's the guy? Produce."

"Relax, man," Razer said.

"Literally," CC181 boy mocked.

That was it. Finito. I turned on the smartass. "Dude, why don't you go blow yourself."

Things got touchy.

He started freaking out in what he thought was English. "What you say? What you say?" To complete his little performance, he blew out his chest. It was the whole, 'I was so very lucky Razer was between us' thing. "Man, you don't know me! I will rock you, bitch!" he said, keeping it on high.

I played it cool. "Fool, you puff up like one of those tiny-assed bantam roosters your drunk-ass uncle tosses in the cockfight ring Saturday night. Cluck, cluck, little chicken. Cluck, cluck." It was a variation of a smack-down I'd used before. The 'cluck' thing was new. Improvised as the moment had inspired me.

I do believe I'd found his button. More than ever, Razer's mouthy shadow was all riled up. Apparently though, Razer just barely holding out one limp arm between us proved to be too much of an obstacle for mouthy shadow boy Bishop to get around.

"Rock you, bitch! I will rock you!" the little CC181 carried on.

"Don't wake your grandmother, cheese sandwich," I said.

"Tweed, please, man. Stop this," David said, stepping in with a hand on my shoulder.

Razer shook his head. "Tweed, see this, Benny here, he's the guy doin' you a solid. Why you wanna act all broke and shit? You embarrass me, homes," he said.

Me? *I* was embarrassing Razer? Okay, so that kind of got me. But what the hell, I had to save some face.

"A solid? What solid?" I said. "I come running over here--*literally*--'cause you call, and he starts mouthing off? Ain't nobody doing me any favors."

"Favor is," Razer explained, as if he were talking to his little sister Lily, "this homeless dude asked Benny if he knew who Tweed was. Homeless dude is looking for the tagger what goes by Tweed because your Pops is messed up and said for him to find Tweed. Said Tweed can help him. And my boy Benny gave the dude five bucks and told him sit tight while he booked it over here to have me fetch your sorry ass."

"Yeah, ya sorry ass," Benny said. "Five dollars."

"Five…? Man, I don't know what any of you are talking about," I said.

"Apologize!" Benny demanded.

"What? Man, phewff…." I waved him off. I was still trying to save face and David's tightening grip let me know I was losing.

"You know what?" Benny said turning to Razer. "Go get the field. This punk wants my help, he's got to earn it now."

I guess I looked a little confused. Thankfully, Razer translated.

"He's challenging you to chess, homes."

"What?"

"That's right," Benny the Bishop said. "You win, I tell you what you need to know. You lose…." He did this thing with his hand, kind of flipping out his pinky. It had to be some kind of new obscene gesture I'd yet to see.

I'd never seen this guy play, but c'mon, he was in a chess club. I knew I was toast.

"Razer, dude, what're you two huffing? I don't have time for any chess," I said.

"And I'm sick of hearing that too," Razer said. Then he turned to David. "I huffed with some guys like three years ago, one lousy time. One time. And this is all I ever hear come out his mouth."

"Whatever. I'm not playing anybody chess," I said.

Razer shrugged. "You the one had to open your mouth."

"Get. The. Field," Benny repeated, referring, I knew now, to the chess board.

"Razer," I said, "you and me, we're best friends. C'mon tell your boy here…."

"He ain't no boss of me," Benny said.

"And I ain't your best friend," Razer added.

"What?" I couldn't believe Razer was calling me on this.

"Maybe like two years ago, when we was kids," he said. "But, Tweed, homes, we're friends and all, but c'mon."

Things had really gotten out of hand. I was about to really lay into Razer. I mean, what the hell, am I right? Somehow David sensed it though, and all he had to do was sigh.

There's something about the sound of disappointment coming from someone that's probably the worst thing you ever want to hear. I mean, you know, when you respect that person and the disappointment they're feeling is being created by you. I had to turn this shit around.

"Jesus. Alright. Hey, man…Benny," I said, "Listen, I'm sorry, okay? No joke. I just thought you were bustin' on me, and, I don't know. Sorry. We cool?"

Benny gave me this hard look. Of all people, I understood. Everybody wants to save face. But I'd pulled off a big turn in the right direction. Razer finally lowered his arm. Still, like *Pilgrim's Progress* it was slow going.

I needed to make one more effort. I made it a good one.

"Dude," I truly pleaded, "Benny. I can't play you chess. Alright? I can't play you because we all know you'd beat me. Okay? You'd beat me. And I can't do that because I really need to find Pops. He's all I got. He's not in such good shape. So please, you know. Okay? Hey, fuck me, all right? My Pops, man. So if you know something, anything, please."

Benny held his ground and his look for a moment more, and then he deflated.

"You know what you do, Tweed?" Benny said. "You project. That's negative, man. You project." To David he added, "He shouldn't do that. It's no good."

I don't know, maybe he thought David was my dad or something. We looked nothing alike, but who knows.

"Benny, I totally agree," David said. "Tweed, stop projecting."

I threw up my hands. Surrendered. "I'm done, man. No more projecting."

"Okay then," Benny said.

So this was Benny's story, which he relayed as we all booked it over to the GWB Port Authority because that was where he'd left this guy, the homeless dude.

Pops was supposedly holed up underneath one of these buildings looking out over the Westside Highway somewhere down around 130th Street or so. One of these like six or seven that have these open recesses up under them because of this crazy steep hill they're on. I knew where he was talking about. It was a real mess of tangled up urban shit. Catwalks. Overpasses. Fences. Some run down park space. Vacant lots. These recesses up under the buildings, like I said. Apparently that part of the whole place was like hobo-central, or some shit. Even worse, it sounded like Pops was a bit out of his gourd and maybe a bit roughed up from somebody or something. He couldn't remember who he was, or where he was from, according to this guy. Some kind of amnesia kind of thing. Which sucked for sure, but I had to admit, I was a weird kind of relieved to hear, because I'd already had Mom bail on me on purpose.

All Pops knew for sure was "Tweed." He'd told this bum that Tweed could help him. He had to find Tweed. Then, kind of like as luck would have it, this bum had seen my tag. Which wasn't all that lucky, I guess, considering I'd put it all over the whole frickin' neighborhood and beyond.

"So we was bombing--I'm Bishop, by the way--me and some of the CC181," Benny was explaining to David along the way, "and this homeless guy comes over and says, 'Hey, you guys know Tweed?' You know, because he knew Tweed was a bomber too. Seen the tag and all. And I says, 'Hells yeah, I know Tweed. Who wants to know?'"

"No shit," I said.

"No shit. And there he is," Benny the Bishop said, pointing up ahead.

In the god-awful summer heat, leaning against a bridge girder across the street from the Port Authority bus station, this black dude wearing no less than a fake fur-lined red parka and matching red sweatpants, spots Benny and starts waving us over. An older dude with kind of a nasty, scraggly gray beard. None other than Ghetto Claus from the big Rollo takedown. He was still in his same get-up except he'd added a filthy *Don't Make Me Angry* Incredible Hulk t-shirt underneath his open parka.

Chapter Twenty-three

I'd spent the last few years not really talking to my dad. Not that I'd ignored him or anything childish like that, but more, just not making any more room for him in my life than he'd already carved in my first fourteen years or so. By the time I was saying goodnight to him following our big dinner date, I couldn't say I'd made up for all that, but I was pretty certain we'd made it a long way.

As I was drifting off to sleep, I made myself a promise. I would never let us be that far apart again. And when I had my own child, I'd make sure the same was true for her.

...

"I know why he's here," David said as Ghetto Claus led the way. "This neighborhood. It's Pops's old mail route. Where he delivered the mail for so many years. Must have just found his way back because it was something familiar."

"He didn't deliver no mail here," I countered.

We'd left Bishop and Razer behind. They'd said they wanted to help more, but they had some kind of chess thing to go to. I told them no problem and paid back Bishop the money he'd fronted to our Ghetto Claus guide. It took a while to get where the dude was taking us because he refused to leave his cart behind and even if he had, I doubt we could have found a cab that would have taken him as a fare. So then, it was a good two hours before we'd closed in on the scene.

We'd gone down a steep hill through some rough, neglected park and made our way back up under some old rail lines. Some underground works that'd been sealed off but then broken into. I wasn't looking forward to what was waiting for us.

"In there," Santa said, pointing a cracked and grimy finger.

"Ho, frickin' ho," I replied. I don't think anybody understood exactly, but the gist was there.

"Let me lead," David offered. I accepted.

...

Answering my repeated calls, Pops suddenly appeared in the shadows and half-light far above me. He was on another platform of what must have been an abandoned station. There were a few other homeless types with him. I caught them here and there peering and leering like suspicious tunnel rats. A rusted ladder of iron rungs protruding from the wall rose up through the darkness between us, illuminated as it went by a string of jury-rigged bare light bulbs.

The whole place reminded me of the hold of some leaky old ship. Water dripping everywhere. The sound of it seeking lower ground all around me. Over my head, below my feet. Even running dangerously down the wire of bare lights. I imagined these tunnel rats must have dreamed of drowning every time they lay their stinky, matted heads down to sleep. It was suddenly no wonder the homeless hated to bathe.

I called his name again. Pops made for the ladder with the best quickness he could muster. It was like a tattered kite that was finally being called back to Earth. Once he got onto the ladder, each time I called his name he eased down one rung closer as if I'd wound in another loop of his string.

"Pops! Pops!" I kept calling as I rushed up to help him.

Behind me, David started shouting as well. "Mr. Molina! Alfonso Molina!"

Suddenly Pops joined our cries. "I am Alfonso Molina! Alfonso Molina!"

I knew that he was speaking to himself, not us.

"Pops!" And then I had him. "I thought I'd lost you. Never do this again. Please, promise me. Please."

"I know you," he said. "Yes, I know you." I wasn't certain he really did, but as we found the bottom and hugged, he whispered my name and added, "My grandson." And then David was beside us.

Pops was disheveled. He reeked to all get out. His head had a nasty gash that looked to be probably infected. He'd lost weight. He was alive.

"I love you, Pops," I said, still hugging him. I wanted to tell him again, but I kind of got too choked up.

"C'mon, Pops, we gonna get you home," David said.

"Home," both Pops and I agreed.

We led Pops out from the dark. The sun was warm, bright. He shielded his eyes from it and laughed long.

"I know you," Pops said again.

The homeless dude, who I learned a bit later was named Fred, and who'd protected and watched over my Pops through his ordeal, patted us all on the back.

"This is Tweed," Pops said to him. "Tweed writes his name on the wall of my home. His home. In his room."

"I know he is," Fred laughed. "I found him. I told you I'd find him. I did. You be all good to go now."

"I haven't forgotten my promise either," Pops said. "Now you will keep the ring. It is yours, just as I promised." And then Pops took his emerald ring from his finger and pressed it into Fred's palm. "It is yours, my friend. Thank you."

Fred couldn't have been more pleased. I could tell David thought it a bit much, but what the hell, guy earned it.

"I don't suppose you still have your violin case?" I said to Pops. He took a second to think hard on it. When he came up empty, I said, "Don't worry about it. I suspect that's part of what got you in trouble in the first place. I think that weasel dude took it off your hands. The hard way. Doesn't matter now. Good riddance."

"Why didn't you just call the police?" David asked Fred as we made our way back up the hill where we'd fetch a cab.

That reminded me. "Hey, yeah, man," I said to our new homeless friend, "You got my cell phone." I was referring to Razer's phone.

I thought this might be some trouble. But old Fred just reached inside his coat and handed it over. I guess he was a Santa after all.

"Damn thing rings too much no how. Wakes me up," he laughed. He turned back to David then and said, "Call the police? Shoot no. Police? Mister, this man don't know his name. The police? Shoot, I do that, this old man here," he said, gesturing to Pops, "he'd be gone in the system. Flushed. Whoosh! Never see 'em again."

"And I hadn't reported him missing because I was scared of what would happen to me if they couldn't find him," I admitted. It was all pretty messed up. Broke. "I'm sorry Pops. I really am."

"It's alright, kid," David said. "That wouldn't have worked out too well, I don't imagine. Not where Pops was. They wouldn't have found him." Pops nodded his agreement.

"Yep. Would've been flushed," Fred repeated. "The both of you!"

When we reminded Pops that we were taking him home, he started to cry. I'd be a liar if I said I didn't do more of the same. Stuff is contagious.

"The old man was saved by graffiti," David said, taking my shoulder in his hand. "Unbelievable."

...

Ida Goldstein stood in the hall where we'd left her some hours ago beside our open apartment doorway. David and I did our best to pretend we weren't helping Pops any longer now that he'd finished summiting the stairwell and reached our floor. He'd shaken his elbows from us defiantly as he pushed off down the hall. He was stopped short almost immediately when he saw the old woman there. In her hands was a framed photo I recognized as being from the hall outside our bathroom. Pops out on the stoop waving his goodbyes to somebody. At least, I'd made up my mind some years ago that it must be a goodbye. Don't ask me why.

"Alfonso?" she said.

"I know you," Pops replied. "Your name is Ida. You're my gal Ida. Hello, Ida." He greeted her by resting his hand, filthy as it was, on her arm.

"Oh, Alfonso, yes."

"He refused to go to the hospital," David offered kind of defensively. "Put up a fuss like you wouldn't believe. I thought we might just bring him home for now...."

But Ida had ignored him. She and Pops disappeared into our apartment leaving David and I like training wheels that weren't needed.

"Let's get you cleaned up," I heard the old woman say. Followed by, "And we'll get something hardy in you afterwards. How about pot roast?"

Pops must have agreed because we didn't hear any complaints.

Ida stayed pretty late that night, which was fine by me. She made us this killer chicken casserole dinner from a bird and other things she had me fetch from her place. I got a bit of a scolding when she discovered the disco rice under the kitchen garbage. So I did some sprucing up while she cooked. Pops was out; down for the count after the one two punch of his shower and two helpings of chicken. Ida even helped me get him to bed.

Pops snored away as the old woman and I goofy-smiled to one another just outside his bedroom.

Not to bring attention to it or anything like that, but I started absentmindedly flicking at a small nail protruding from the hallway wall. It was where a picture of Pops had hung. The one Ida had taken for the benefit of the police.

"Oh, yes," she said. "Just wait right here a moment."

She came back with the picture and fixed it back on the nail where it belonged.

"I bet you got you a lot of old photos hanging on your walls too, huh?" I said, just making small talk.

"No. Not really."

I wasn't sure what we were doing there with that conversation killer and all, and so I was glad when she added, "There you go," as she corrected the frame's angle with one steady finger. Then she pointed to another photo next to it. "And here we are."

"Do what now?"

"Here. This is your grandfather Alfonso," she said gently tapping the glass. "And that is yours truly. Or, that is to say, it was. Many years ago." Her finger traced over the young woman standing with him.

She wasn't lying. The photo was an oldie. Black and white. I barely recognized Pops. He didn't look that much older than I was now. Good looking guy. Stylin' and profilin'. He wore a dark gray suit and his hair was thick and slicked back without a part. He had an old-timey gray fedora hat in one hand. Pulled up under his arm, this seriously nice looking girl. Hair all up in a fancy bun like they did back in the day, and wearing what must have been some really bright lipstick. But still you could see she was something. Looked like one of the USO types you'd see singing and scatting to the troops in the old World War II flicks. The both of them mad smiling these big pearly smiles. Great photo.

I did a double-take to Ida and she grinned. "You and Pops were…." I couldn't finish. Literally speechless.

She chuckled. "For quite a few years. We were almost married, you know, your grandfather and I. But things, they sometimes don't work out quite as you imagine they will. I married a friend of your grandfather's a few years later. Alan Goldstein. A good man. But I'm afraid that upset your grandfather something terrible. I never understood this. You men. No matter now. Water under the bridge. Alan's been gone almost fifteen years now this past July."

"Wow."

Her lingering amusement gave birth to a laugh. "Yes. Wow."

We went back to the living room and talked for a good while. It turned out that the old lady from across the hall wasn't so bad after all. By the time she was saying goodnight, I actually caught myself inviting her over to have lunch the next day. I used Pops as an excuse, saying she should check in on him. She agreed. She said she'd make us Cuban sandwiches, Pops's longtime favorite. Not too shabby.

I was exhausted. I felt like I was at the end of a long, long trip. Like the day we arrived from Florida so many years ago. My mind was still running in little racing loops, getting nowhere fast except the same place over and over again. Mostly that would be thinking about Scissors. Chloe. Thinking about how she didn't want anything to do with me anymore. Thinking about how for a while there things had been different. Thinking about how close we'd been. How much I cared about her. How stupid I'd been.

I decided to do two last things before what would probably be some kind of Rip Van Winkle record-setting snoozathon.

Pops's recliner made a good bit of noise as I slid it across the room and into the foyer where it securely barricaded the front door. The old man was still mad sawing logs though when I went down the hall to check on him and finish up with the second little detail before bed. From the hallway I retrieved the old photo of Pops and Ida. I took it back to the living room. There, in the prominent spot above the television, where there'd been the photo of me, Mom, and Pops, before I'd smashed it all to hell and back, I filled the vacancy with the picture of Pops and his old girlfriend, Ida.

I'm not sure why I did that. But as I padded down the hall to find my bed, well, it sure felt right.

Chapter Twenty-four

The contraction was strong and sudden and woke me from my nap. More than woke. It yanked me from my nap, from my dream of my organs constricting. I called out for my dad, but even as I did, I knew he wasn't there. The sky behind the pulled blind of my bedroom window was dark. The clock read 8:07. My dad would be at work, playing with the orchestra. I wouldn't be able to reach him until the 9:15 intermission. He'd been planning on getting me an emergency number. Been planning. My baby wasn't due for five more weeks. Another contraction took hold. Somebody tell her that.

Like some sort of speakers had been mounted inside my head, my late grandmother began singing, "Something inside that was always denied…."

She was the sweet little old woman in Red Riding Hood, the one that turns out to be the Big Bad Wolf. Oh please get out of my head, Grandmother. She wouldn't.

Grandmother sang on, "What did we do that was wrong? We didn't know it was wrong."

I used to love to hear her sing. Not anymore.

I guess I was panicking. The baby was way early and so I started going overboard thinking the very worst. The god-awful pain didn't help. Another contraction snatched me, clawed at me. Suddenly I was a character in one of my dad's cheesy horror novels. I couldn't pull myself from the sheets. The bed was eating me alive. I was about to burst and the bed was eating me alive. I squirmed and twisted and squirmed some more, but it was like one of those dreams where your arms and legs can't work, won't work, or work, but not nearly enough. Everything was incredibly too much. My limbs transformed to leaden molasses. Useless. I was stuck down on the bed like a bug in a Venus fly trap. Venus, the goddess of love. How appropriate. I laughed and the laugh was tortured into a wail.

My head started spinning. The room joined in on the spinning thing, but only faster. I guess this would be what they call complications. I called out for my dad again. This time loud enough that maybe he could hear me from where he was way down on 42nd Street.

…

I was in the middle of a bunch of nothing really, just screwing around reading a graphic novel. I should have been studying, I suppose. But that's what I was up to when I heard Chloe scream. And I mean scream. It was the first I'd heard from my girl in a few months. Truthfully, I hadn't even been sure if she was still around since I hadn't really seen anything of her either. The light in her room was on from time to time, but the blinds were always down. So for all I knew maybe she'd packed it up and split out for Denver again. Or so I'd been thinking up until that night.

I sat up, pretty unnerved by that first outburst, and she really let go again. Blood curdling like. Horror movie like. Freaked me right the F out. I ran over to my window. Her blind was drawn, as usual, but he window was open.

"Chloe! Hey, what's wrong? What's going on? Chloe?"

For a response I heard something glass break in her room. Suddenly Pops was beside me. I guess Chloe had been as loud as I'd imagined.

"What is it? Who is creating all the racket at this hour?"

"It's only eight o'clock, Pops. Neighbor girl," I said. "Chloe."

"Little Chloe? Daniel's daughter?" He peered over me.

That was a shocker. I was surprised he knew her. But, then I remembered he and Daniel used to be pretty friendly.

"Yeah. She's pregnant."

"Pregnant? Little Chloe Tobin is pregnant? No...."

I think for Pops, Chloe must have still been around ten years old. She'd always be ten years old.

"Maybe we should call 911," I said. Across to Chloe's window I shouted, "You okay? Hey, Chloe, we're going to call--"

The blind came down. And I mean down. It didn't go up. She tore it down. She was fitting the part of the horror movie. Her hair was plastered with sweat to her face and she looked pale as the dead.

"Tweed...help," she pleaded.

"Is it the baby?" I asked stupidly. She nodded. "Yeah. Yeah. Okay. Don't move. I'll be right there."

"Wait!" she gasped.

Chloe disappeared from view for a nerve racking few seconds. I was about to sprint off when she came back and threw something before I was expecting it.

"Keys," she said as the ball of loose metal struck the wall outside my window. I missed the snag. The keys fell down into the darkness between us, clattering off to who knows where.

"Shit," she cried with a grimace. I didn't know if she was cursing the pain, the lost keys, me, or all of the above. Probably D. Then again, the best answer was E) Not enough information.

"Can you get to your front door?" I asked. "Is it locked?" Another stupid question. That's why she knew I needed the keys.

For an answer she went limp--fainted, or I don't know what--but anyways, she fell away and disappeared with a resounding thump.

"That's not good. That's not good at all," Pops said.

"No…ya think?"

He ignored me in his quest for a solution. He hit on something right off.

"We could make a bridge across with your door," he said.

"Do what?"

"We take the door off its hinges." He pointed to my bedroom door. "I know how this is done. Very easy. I used to sand and hang doors. We take it off and put it out the window and you crawl over." He mimicked the act by walking his fingers along the top of his leveled forearm. He was very pleased with himself. Maybe he had a right to be. It was surprisingly lucid thinking on his part. Except for one tiny detail.

I pulled him closer to the window sill. "Take a gander," I said. "I don't mean to break your heart, but that's at least ten, maybe twelve feet, Roebling." That being the name of the guy who designed the Brooklyn Bridge. Common public school educated city kid knowledge.

"I see, yes." Pops agreed. He was still looking from the chasm to the door and back to the chasm again trying to puzzle things out when I hightailed out of there. "Call 911!" I shouted behind me. "Call 911!"

Sliding to a stop in my stocking feet, I met Ida Goldstein under the hum and clicking and flickering of a newly failing florescent light out in the hall. I guess she'd heard Chloe even from through both their doors and the length of the hall.

"Is there a fire?" she asked, genuinely concerned. She even went so far as to head for the fire alarm on the wall with one hand ready to yank away.

"No. It's Chloe Tobin. Down the hall. She's pregnant."

"Pregnant, yes, I know."

I didn't stop running for the stairwell as I called back to her, "Something's wrong. Something bad. Call 911."

Mrs. Goldstein said something else to me, but I didn't catch it. I was hurtling down the stairs for the lobby. Halfway down I stopped for the two seconds it took to rip my socks off after they'd sent me careening into the wall. Hard. Almost dislocated my shoulder. Then it was outside, barefoot down the sidewalk to the breezeway dealio that ran between our apartments. That went about thirty or forty feet before ending in three steps down to a dull red painted metal door leading into the building's basement. On the other side was the trash room where the garbage-drop chute ended. I knew this because out in the breezeway David kept a row of trashcans that he'd fill several times a week from there. Some evenings, I guess when he was tired or pissed or the trash was particularly offensive, I'd hear him under my window cursing to himself in Spanish as he moved out the garbage.

If I'd thought about it for more than a nanosecond, I'm sure I wouldn't have even gone looking for the keys. Who knew where they'd landed. Am I right? How long was I going to waste…and there they were. A little shiny silver clump huddled together on their ring right there in the middle of the sidewalk running beneath our windows.

"Thank you! Yes!" I screamed up to the heavens.

Like a relay runner I had them and was bounding back to the lobby. That's when I realized I didn't have my own keys to get back in.

This time I cursed the heavens. "Shit!"

I hit our apartment buzzer. I did the same for Ida's. Nada. Nothing zip. But I had Chloe's keys. Duh. And then I looked at Chloe's keys. Apparently Chloe was one of those girls who saved every key that'd ever pressed her palm. David, the freaking building super, sported a less formidable collection.

I started trying keys in a frenzy beginning with the ones that looked most likely.

When that got me nowhere fast I just went ape-shit and started slapping my palms across every door buzzer button on the panel. Within seconds I was getting buzzed in while the intercom was blaring with several requests to know who it was.

"Thank you," I yelled back to whoever my savior was. Not that they would hear me without the benefit of pressing the Talk button, but, whatever. It's the thought that counts.

I was up the stairs.

Apparently the old saying about things going wrong if they can, well that was getting proven to be true. Proven in spades. On the fourth floor landing I met up with Pops and Ida. She, it turned out, had been kept pretty busy trying to keep the old guy from toddling off to who knows where.

"He's like a puppy. Insisted on following you," she said before I'd even said anything.

Pops loved that remark. "Who are you talking about, old woman. I'm right here you know."

I didn't have time for the fun and games.

"Can't you just, I don't know, keep him with you?" I said and passed them by. Ascending the last set of stairs I called down to her, "The ambulance coming?"

"What? No, I haven't had a chance...."

I stopped dead. I wheeled around. "You didn't call?"

Ida was upset. "No. How could I? Alfonso was here and, and...you ran off. And I didn't know...."

"Ah, great!"

"I'm sorry. Just give us a minute."

But I was off again.

At the Tobin's apartment door I came face to face with more of the same problem I'd had in the lobby. Keys. Five bazillion keys. Ida had Pops back up the stairwell and she was still apologizing and trying to get him to settle down. I was too focused on finding the right key to really pay all that much mind. She said something about her keys and I had no idea how that was going to help. But then, like I said, I was pretty preoccupied. And then, 'click.' Whatdaya know, I got it. The bolt heaved over and I was in.

"Chloe!" I yelled. I don't know why. I knew where she was. Where she'd been.

And that's where I found my girl. At her bedroom window, face down, balanced on the mound of her huge belly. Pooled all around her, thick, dark red blood. As much blood as I'd seen the day Heft had died. I had the oddest thought, as I stood in that long moment frozen in her doorway. I imagined she floated there on her sea of blood with only the baby inside her keeping her from sinking and disappearing beneath it forever.

I was trying to revive Chloe when Ida and Pops found their way into the room. I was only aware of them when Ida gasped. Pops went into a daze and wandered to the bed and sat. He covered his eyes and mumbled something I couldn't catch.

"She didn't do this to herself," I barked. I guess that was a little premature.

"Of course not," Ida agreed. She'd been in shock for a moment just as I had. The old gal pulled herself together quickly though. "It's the baby. Chloe's hemorrhaging. You have to get her to the hospital. No time to waste. Here. Go."

The last thing I thought I needed were more keys, but that's what she'd forced on me.

"Do what?"

"My car…the white station wagon. It's right across the street in front of the building. The hospital is only a little ways down Broadway. 168th Street."

"I know where the hospital is…."

"Well then take her! Go! We can't wait for the ambulance. She can't wait. It may be too late already…." Ida stopped there, losing her breath. Eyes brimming over. But still she goaded me on, pushing me to Chloe.

The next thing I knew I was scooping Chloe up from her sea. Carrying her through the apartment. Down the hall and stairs. Slipping twice in my bare feet as her blood continued to find its way out. Then we were out the building and to the car. Shivering like a mad man with fear and adrenaline I paused there. I prayed for the sounds of sirens. Normally the night would offer them up. Not now. Not when I needed them.

After a brief struggle with the car door I managed Chloe's limp body into the backseat. The street was still quiet. No ambulances. No strangers wandering the sidewalks for me to plead for help. Just me and my dying girl.

I clipped two cars getting out of the parking space. That came as no surprise. I'd never learned how to drive. The first was the car in front, and then when I backed off of it I rammed the one behind. It was the Tobin's ratty old heap. Go figure. As if she knew the score, Chloe moaned as we ripped away from the Tobin-mobile's now-dangling front bumper. She was alive.

"Hang in there, Chloe. I got you. I got you. We're going to the hospital. Getting you to the hospital. Going right this second. Everything is going to be fine," I said.

I blew through the stop sign at the end of the street. That was accidental. A case of first-time driver nerves. The second one I planned. And when I turned onto Broadway, just because it'd worked so well so far, I blew that red light too. That worked out fine for us, but I did hear the sounds of kind of a commotion well up in our wake. Horns and maybe some high speed comingling of metal and plastic and glass. I couldn't really get the rearview mirror thing figured out enough to be sure. I screamed out my apologies. The window was still rolled up though, so I'm pretty sure that worked out none too good.

Either Chloe had slipped away again or was too quiet to be heard over the engine and traffic. And I wasn't sure if the engine of Ida Goldstein's station wagon was simply the loudest I'd ever heard, or if the roaring in my ears was my own blood pounding its way like it never had before.

I caught three more green lights and was weaving in and out of traffic and barely avoiding jaywalker after jaywalker when I suddenly caught the red light that ruined the good run I'd had so far. First there was the cab I swiped. Actually, I think he swiped me, but, whatever. So there was that, and then there was the cop who decided he wanted me to remain at the scene of the accident. Not happening.

With the cop letting his sirens raise hell on my tail, the drive got a little safer. I would have pushed on either way. Still, the pedestrians weren't such a problem with New York's finest blaring away ten feet off my back bumper. Two more squad cars joined in as we made it down the final stretch. We had us a real life police escort.

I guess I turned too sharp, too fast, too whatever, as I cut the wheel following the New York Presbyterian Hospital entrance sign. The front right tire jumped the curb and the car jolted like we'd been whacked by a giant. We went slightly airborne before immediately crashing back down. Proving some of Mr. Newton's laws, my nose planted a big kiss on the steering wheel. That led to my sort of losing what little control of the car

I'd had. It was okay though. The city planners had seen fit to erect out-of-control-car-stoppers in the form of lampposts all along the street. When the car introduced itself to one of these posts, I did another little smack of the forehead onto the steering wheel. They really needed to make those things more nose and head-butt friendly. I was still having trouble seeing right as the cops assisted me from my madly hissing and steaming vehicle.

I did a third little face plant courtesy of the officer who wanted to speak with me about my driver's license, proof of insurance, and registration. I'm not sure at what point my nose was broken, then, or previously on the steering wheel. Maybe it was once for each.

"She's dying…hemorr…the baby…help her," I managed to sputter out as the officer offered me a session of knee-to-the-spinal column massage therapy.

I heard another cop shouting about Chloe in the back of the car. Relieved now that my girl was in better hands, I decided to take a nap.

…

I spent six days in the hospital bringing my daughter, Trinity Marie Tobin, into the world. The act nearly killed me. It wasn't a lengthy labor. I had a caesarean and that was done and over with on the first day without my ever being aware it'd happened. Trinity was premature, but otherwise healthy. Yours truly, on the flipside, was nearly done in from blood loss. I went through quite a lot of the hospital's good stuff they told me later. My poor dad said it was twenty-four hours of touch and go that aged him a year for every hour. He likes to say he's ready for his retirement now.

I awoke from my ordeal on the second day, but it was the third or fourth before I could say I was back in the land of the living and not wandering some hazy-lit, pain-filled ghost world of nebulous shapes and voices. On the fifth day my father explained everything for the umpteenth time and that was when it all finally made sense and sunk in. On the fifth day, as I was scheduled for release, my mother, who'd flown in for the emergency of her granddaughter's birth and my near-death, went home and her seat at my bedside was filled with Tweed.

When he'd arrived in my hospital doorway that last afternoon, flowers and Mylar balloons in hand, and with his grandfather and my neighbor, Mrs. Goldstein, in tow, I felt like I was really seeing Tweed for the first time. He was banged up with his newly broken nose and his eyes were bandit-wrapped in bruises like a raccoon. He had that same devilish smile, although now not so much mischievous seeming, but more like he knew something humorous about life and was waiting for the rest of the world to catch on. Or maybe it was that he was glad to finally be in on the joke, I dunno. So there was that and something even bigger. It took me a little while to put my finger on it. It came to me as we talked over the days to follow. He wasn't a boy anymore. Not quite a man entirely, but certainly on the cusp. I was happy for that; I was happy for him.

Mrs. Goldstein and Pops excused themselves to go in search of Trinity in the neonatal-preemie ward down the hall, and my father had the good sense after just two hints to tag along behind them so that Tweed and I could be alone.

Although he did stop at the door as he was leaving. "Say, Tweed," my dad said. "About Mrs. Goldstein's car…don't you worry about it, okay? I'm going to take care of all that."

"Um, sure, okay," Tweed agreed.

"And I know you have a court date for the traffic violations and all that business," he said.

"Yeah, end of the month."

"So, I was thinking….Well, if you want, I mean it's up to you, but if you want, I'd be glad to go along. Explain to the judge…try to smooth things over. Ida said the same too," my dad said.

Tweed nodded. "That's, that'd be great. I would. Thank you. Thank Ida. I'll thank her. But, you know…thanks for everything. I really appreciate it."

"Not at all. It may have been a dicey thing for you to do, driving like that, but, obviously it worked out fine and dandy, so thank you." My dad rapped on the door and smiled a big dopey grin. Then, as if he couldn't figure out quite yet just how to go already, he added, "I think I'll pop down to the gift shop, too. They have one of those little wooden skeletal dinosaur models I might get. I have a project I was thinking it'd work great with."

"You do that, Dad. Take your time. Have fun," I said. He nodded and was gone.

Tweed and I were a little awkward at first after my dad left. Tweed tried to fix me a cup of water but he couldn't find the pitcher. I finally corralled him into the chair at my bedside and he settled down. He was so cute.

"How's the beak?" I asked.

He stumbled a bit trying to explain something about his sinuses so I asked to see his best Rocky Balboa impression. He shifted around like it took some preparation, kind of ducking behind his own shoulder for a second and then reappearing with a grunt and head-bob to ask if I wouldn't mind marrying him too much. We both got pretty broke up laughing then.

Clickity-click.

"Hey, listen," he said, suddenly jumping in on the lull following our laugh, "I wanted you to know, I'm really sorry about everything. About Heft and...what I did. I didn't mean--"

I cut him off there.

"Seems like none of us were batting a thousand in the decision-making department up until late, huh?"

He shrugged. "Yeah...well...."

As sudden as only little boys could, an adorable little tyke wearing a bath towel safety-pinned around his neck as a makeshift cape, burst into the room. His sneakers yipped on the highly-waxed floor as he came to his abrupt halt and sort of yell-growled, "Arrrwool!" His attempt at a terrifying countenance melted as quickly as his appearance. He looked around the room and then to us, confusion making him blush, and muttered, "Sorry." He dashed right back out of the room.

That was good for another laugh.

"My hero," I said.

"I don't know, judging by the roar, I think he might have been playing the villain," Tweed said.

I took his hand. "Wasn't talking about little Captain Bath-towel."

Now Tweed blushed. "No, you don't have to...."

"But you are, yanno? My hero."

He got that little devil's grin again. "You say so. I'm with you from here on out. What you say goes. You're the boss, applesauce."

“You saved my life, Tweed. My baby’s life. My doctor said it was one of those matter of minutes kind of things. Could have gone either way.” Tweed didn’t say anything. I could see he wasn’t playing bashful. Like all true heroes he just wasn’t comfortable in the limelight. “You know one of the last things I remember?” I asked. He shook his head. “I threw you my keys and you missed them.”

“Yeah, real heroic. What can I say…I wasn’t expecting…my bad. Butterfingers.”

“No, not that. The thing I’m saying is, when you missed them, and as you looked back to me, I thought, ‘I think he’s going to try to jump over here. All that way…he’s going to do it.”

“Yeah? You crazy? That’d be suicide,” he said with a laugh.

We were quiet then and he held my hand and we both watched the clouds outside the window for a while.

“Tell you what,” I said finally. His head jerked around like I’d stirred him from some deep place. “If you promise to let me off the hook for being such a drama queen, I’d like to start all over. Give us another chance.”

He stared at the floor for a minute, yanno, like he really had to give it a lot of consideration.

“Tweed?”

“That all sounds good except for the one part,” he said.

“What’s that?”

“For a while there, things were going pretty good. So, I mean, we don’t have to start *completely* over, do we?”

Chapter Twenty-five

So there's this girl I thought I knew but didn't. This girl that I finally, truly met. And the funny thing is, even though I do know more about her than probably just about anybody else in the world--to include her father, and her mother, and the guy who got her all knocked up--turns out I really still don't know her at all. I guess some people are like that. But that's okay, because, hey, when you're crazy about somebody, really, would you want it any other way?

Pops got settled back in and so life at home went back to something like normal again. Ida Goldstein played a major role in that. Her and David. Yeah, and Pops agreed to Marta, our new "housekeeper." Ida, she did all the leg work on finding her for us and all that too. Marta's great. She's more Pops's caretaker than a housekeeper, but we don't let him in on that. Her English, it ain't so hot, but she genuinely cares for Pops, so it's all good. I know, I know. Who knows how long all that'll last. I sure don't. Kind of like what Decker says about him and his girl at the end of my favorite flick. Who knows how long any of us has, huh? But Pops has his good days and sometimes even his better days. So me, I'll stay optimistic until it's time not to be. And no matter what, the old guy, he's got me.

Also, with Ida and David's nudging, I decided to finish up school and do my senior year. After all, the world was fast catching up and I didn't want to get passed by. Run over.

Along with going back to school, I also made a resolution to mend my friendship with Razer. Funny thing is, up until of late, I hadn't even known I needed to. But he's a great bud. He deserves more from me in the friendship department. I'd been something of a prick to him for a while now. I've come around to see that. I'm not totally thick. I plan to make things right. After all, we've been through a lot, and here's to hoping we get to go through even more of this crazy life together. He's started City College in the meanwhile. Doing great at that when he's not down to Bryant Park still steadily putting the wumps and lumps on the chess chumps to keep his wallet lined in green.

"Yo, man, great day for a game, yes?" Razer beamed to me.

He was talking about baseball, not chess for a change, though. And it was a great day. Gor-gee-ous, in fact. From behind the steering wheel of the Tobin mobile, Daniel shook his head. "God, no. All this sunshine and this pleasant cool breeze! Horrible! Let's kill the weatherman," he moaned.

"What? You playin' me?" Razer said.

The rest of us, we laughed. Razer did too after a second.

I was in shotgun. Chloe securely between Razer and Pops in the back. In her little papoose, baby Trinity slept while somewhere ahead, unseen because of the lay of the land, but just as inevitable, Yankee Stadium was in our shared future. Danny boy's treat.

I looked back to my girl and she smiled to me. Okay, maybe not quite my girl…yet. Or who knows, maybe not yet, but never. Whatever. We'll see. But like in the comic books that kept me up at night under the blankets, back when me and Pops would both pretend I was going to sleep like I'd been told, the hero, he always has a chance. All the way up to that final page, or even down to the last frame, the hero always has a chance. If not to win then and there, then at least to drag things out in a cliff-hanger of just you wait until next month's issue. Any event, someday, victory would be his.

And as far as me being a hero or not, well we're all, each and every last one of us, the heroes of our own stories. If not the hero, then maybe even sometimes the villain. But what that all comes down to is nothing but a choice. And like all choices it's ours and ours alone to make. Nobody else's. Am I right?

Along those same lines, Heft got mad at me once and said something about how I thought the world was just all about me or something like that. That I thought I was the first person or main character or whatever in the world's narrative. I could be off, but I still think he got that one wrong. If we all aren't the main characters in our own life, in our own story, then who the heck is?

All the same, even though Heft was out of the picture now, shuffled off the ol' mortal coil and all, like Hamlet put it, and even though he'd done some wrong, I still counted him as my friend. But there's another funny thing. The people you think you know, well, more often than not, you don't. Heft really didn't do wrong by Chloe in the end. I finally came around to see that. At the same time, he didn't exactly strap on his shining armor, either though. No, in the end he'd just slipped away on my girl like water or electricity, going with the flow, taking the path of least resistance. He'd looked out for number one and that's only about as sorry-ass lame as just about any of us can be on any given day depending on the harshness of circumstances. I'd seen it before. Hell, it'd even been me once upon a time.

But things hadn't gone so bad from all that. Chloe had made up with her mom. Which was really great. For her. For her mom. Even Daniel, in a way. They'd made up so much so that Chloe's mom offered to raise baby Trinity. Go figure. I guess Beth and the old guy she was shacked up with out in Denver were ready to do that sort of thing again. The offer was a huge relief for Chloe. But just in the way that it was an option. Something she didn't feel like she seemed to have before. Would she do it? Would she take her mom up on the offer? The jury still hadn't come back on that one yet. Those being Chloe's words at least twice now on our regular park walk. With each day I supposed that was becoming less and less likely though. Which is cool. Either way, I'm there for her.

"Have I told you about the time this particular gentleman paid me fifty dollars to take a cab?" Pops said from the backseat. I guess he thought we were all riding in one. Then he added, "Of course, back then the cabs were nice."

We couldn't help but razz Daniel about the car and laugh a little more. Above us, just the right amount of cotton candy clouds speckled the day's perfect blue sky.

And there was the stadium. Along with it was that great bat standing on end in the parking lot, the one I'd always thought was in some kind of disrepair, what with the grip tape peeling off the handle. But it wasn't, I suddenly realized now that I'd gotten a closer look. The tape was actually meant to stick out like that. They'd built it that way. Funny how things so often aren't like they first appear. Turns out life is a lot about taking a second, better look. Taking care not to jump into the water without knowing its depth and dangers. Not to say you can't take chances. A good high-dive always impresses the ladies. But I digress.

When you talk about yourself nothing ever seems finished. At least, you hope not.

I could beat things to death, go on and on, pummel them up to a pulp, like the way some people never get to the point, but I won't. To wrap things up, I'll paraphrase a little fast and loose from an English essay in creative writing I'd just turned in on *What I Learned this Summer....*

When the waters start to rise, to keep the sharks off your toes, you all too often throw some platitudes together about beating back the current, or toss out what my Pops calls fretting handfuls of sass or what you consider to be pithy one-liners, all in the hopes that they'll stand against the collecting tide. You do this maybe if only to convince yourself you're still on solid ground. But, before you know it, you're lost out to sea.

Then come the days on end where good fortune and calamity are just a few among the endless swells and the troughs out on the sea of squandered hopes and lofty expectations. And those misfortunes threaten every day, along with a gazillion other perils or windfalls, without any one or any thing really taking you any place. This, all while you do your best just to dog-paddle in circles and keep your head above the waterline. Until one day, you wash up, just plain finished, I guess, either safe and lucky on the shoals of prosperity or much more likely bloated and done on the ragged jetties of 'I can go no further.' It's there that you tell yourself, "Maybe I'll make it to that distant shore in my next life." And maybe that's no lie. Maybe you will. Am I right?

Me? I say screw all that. I'm cutting out of the dull water this minute. I'm cleaving the murky doldrums. I'm leaving behind the horse latitudes. I'm kicking up foam hard. I know, I know. Maybe a simple city boy like me shouldn't hazard such rough metaphorical waters. Maybe I shouldn't be so bold. Maybe. But, just the same, you'd best keep your eyes peeled from the crow's nest, or the beachhead, or wherever it is you lubbers live. I'll be the lone figure rising fast and gaining on the horizon. My name's Joshua Peters. I'll be the one sending the postcards.

END